Accolades for Pamela Fagan Hutchins

2011 Winner of the Pamela Fagan Hutchins Novel Contest
2010 Winner of the Writers League of Texas Romance Contest
2012 Winner of the Pamela Fagan Hutchins Ghost Story Contest
2012 USA Best Book Award Winner
2013 USA Best Book Award Finalist
2014 Amazon Breakthrough Novel Award, Quarter-finalist

Going for Kona:
"Spellbinding." – Jo Bryan, Dry Creek Book Club
"Can't put it down." – Cathy Bader, Reader
"Fast-paced mystery." – Deb Krenzer, Book Reviewer
"Beautifully written." – Ginger Rees Copeland, Reader
"Full of real characters and powerful emotion." – Rhonda Erb, Editor
"Highly recommended." – Nancy Katz, Reader

The Katie & Annalise Series:
"An exciting tale that combines twisting investigative and legal subplots with a character seeking redemption…an exhilarating mystery with a touch of voodoo." – Midwest Book Review Bookwatch
"A lively romantic mystery that will likely leave readers eagerly awaiting a sequel." – Kirkus Reviews
"A riveting drama with plenty of twists and turns for an exciting read, highly recommended." – Small Press Bookwatch
"Katie is the first character I have absolutely fallen in love with since Stephanie Plum!" – Stephanie Swindell, bookstore owner
"Engaging storyline…taut suspense, with a touch of the jumbie adding a distinct flavor to the mix and the romance perfectly kept on the backburner while dealing with predatory psychopaths." – MBR Bookwatch

Going for Kona

By Pamela Fagan Hutchins

SkipJack Publishing books may be purchased for educational, business, or sales promotional use. For information, please write: Sales, SkipJack Publishing, P.O.B. 31160 Houston, TX 77231.

First U.S. Edition
Pamela Fagan Hutchins

Going for Kona/Pamela Fagan Hutchins
ISBN- 978-1-939889-18-8 (SkipJack Publishing)

Sponsors

Pamela Fagan Hutchins and SkipJack Publishing gratefully thank these generous sponsors for giving so much support to this project:

Heidi Dorey
Rhonda Doyle Erb
Susanne Fagan
Nan Loyd
Jim Misko
Mandi Godwin Wellborn

Dedication

To Eric, who inspired this story by making me mad, and then telling me to go home and write *something*.

Forward

Going for Kona is a work of fiction. Period. Any resemblance to actual persons, places, things, or events is just a lucky coincidence.

Table of Contents

Chapter One

The best-looking man in the River Oaks Barnes and Noble had his hand on my thigh, and with the weight of hundreds of eyes on us, I snaked my hand under the table, laced our fingers, and slid mine up and down the length of his, enjoying the contrast of rough against soft. My index finger bumped into the warm band on his ring finger, and I let it stay there, worrying it in semicircles, first one way and then the other.

A Barbie-doll lookalike in form-fitting hot pink strutted into the spot vacated moments before by a tittering fifty-something woman. The bleach blonde brandished a plastic glass of champagne in one hand and held out a copy of our book, *My Pace or Yours? Triathlon Training for Couples*, in the other. Without letting go of my leg, Adrian took it from her and opened it to the title page, where a yellow sticky bore her name.

"Hi, Rhonda. I'm Adrian, and this is my wife, co-author, and editor, Michele." He scribbled his signature and scooted the book over to me.

"I know that, silly." Her little-girl drawl burrowed under my skin like a chigger.

I released Adrian's fingers to sign, then held the book back out to the woman. "Hello, Rhonda. Nice to meet you."

"I loved your talk, Adrian," she said, ignoring me. I bristled. We had opened that night with a reading and Q&A. The book gets a little steamy at times, which is easier to write than to read aloud, so Adrian read those parts. "It's wonderful to see you again."

He studied her, eyes narrowed a fraction. "Thanks. Have we met?"

Maybe he didn't remember her, but I was sure I had seen her recently. She didn't exactly blend in here with Khaled Hosseini on her left and John Irving on her right. I set the book on the table and fought the urge to chew a fingernail. I was well trained by my mother, the one woman in Texas who could give Ms. Manners a run for her money, and Southern Women Do Not Bite Their Nails.

A slim man with a strained, too-cheerful smile stepped forward. He held up $3500 worth of Minolta. "Miss, around here for your photo."

Rhonda swooped around the edge of the table and leaned over Adrian with her hand on the back of his neck, gripping the slice of shoulder that showed above his round-necked shirt.

The photographer held up his hand. "Look this way, please." Adrian and I dutifully swung our faces in his direction and smiled. The flash blinded me for a few seconds, but as my vision cleared I got an eyeful of expensive cleavage. Rhonda Dale remained draped over my husband.

She dropped her voice, but I was six inches from Adrian and could hear her and smell her. I live with a teenage girl, and I'd recognize Urban Outfitters' roll-on Skank perfume anywhere. "Of course we've *met*, Adrian, and I'll never forget it."

Where hot pink was before, I now saw red. Time to assert matrimonial authority. "Rhonda?" She glanced at me, barely, and her mouth tightened. I inclined my head toward the double-door exit and smiled as big as I could.

Rhonda released Adrian's shoulder, leaving crimson fingerprints behind, and took one step back. She bit her lip. She ran her fingers through one side of her bleached hair. She shifted her weight, cocked her right hip, and reached into the white pleather bag slung over her shoulder. I tensed. This woman tripped my switch.

"You'll be wanting this, Adrian." She flipped a pink business card onto the table. If Adrian were a rock star, she'd have thrown her panties and bra instead. The card sucked less. A little, anyway. She turned and walked, hips slinging and champagne sloshing, toward the ubiquitous Barnes and Noble Café and the aroma of Starbucks coffee. I could hear her heels clicking across the floor even after she disappeared from view.

Adrian turned to me and shrugged his eyebrows.

I drew mine together in return. "What just happened here?"

"No comprendo." He drew circles with an index finger beside his temple. "La señorita está loca en la cabeza." He took a sip of his Kona coffee—cup number six of the day, no doubt—a nod to his quest for the triathlon world championships in Hawaii.

My eyebrows lifted. "Was that even Spanish?" I reached for his hand under the dark green tablecloth again and squeezed hard enough to do minor damage. I whispered sotto voce so the next customer in line couldn't hear, "If you promise not to talk in that horrible accent, you'll get a nice reward later."

He shot me a grin. "Maybe you can show me what's under that necklace, Itzpa." Sometimes he used my papa's nickname for me, which was short for Itzpapalotl, a clawed butterfly with knife-tipped wings, and an Aztec goddess of war. Usually he just called me Butterfly.

I reached up to the locket suspended from a long gold chain around my neck. Adrian had given me the brilliant enameled monarch at our second "wedding," the secret B&B family affair he threw in La Grange on our first anniversary to make up for the original quickie at city hall without our kids. When we were pronounced "still man and wife," Adrian put the locket around my neck and told me I was his butterfly. I'd stashed a picture of us taken on that perfect day in the locket and had never changed it since.

I scrutinized it. "This old thing?" I dropped it and stretched my shoulders, catlike. Or rather, like a cat would. There is no feline quality to my short frame. At best I am probably a Pomeranian; at worst, a Pekingese.

He laughed and mouthed, "Thanks a lot, baby," and held his hand out toward the customer at the front of the line.

I signed the next few books on autopilot, trying not to grind my teeth over Miss Boob Job In Hot Pink strutting her stuff for my husband. I could take the Rhonda Dales of the world in stride, mostly. I'd known ever since I was assigned to edit his column for *Multisport Magazine* that Adrian attracted groupies. His following, and the fact that we were working together, were the reasons I'd resisted him at first. He tricked me into going out with him, though—research over a cup of Kona, my ass—and I melted like a butterscotch chip into a warm, sweet cookie.

Soon after, Adrian coaxed me to "just try" triathlon, something I had never aspired to do. Never, meaning no effing way, ever. Swim, then bike, then run? I didn't think so. I'd rather curl up with a novel, when I had any free time at all as the single parent of a tween. Still, I was that butterscotch chip, and it turned out that I was made for triathlon, like I was made for Adrian. It spoke to the parts of me that like rigor and suffering. I signed up for one, and then another, until here we were at Barnes and Noble, at our book launch.

"I'm Connor Dunn," a man's voice said. Something about it made me flinch and brought me back with a bumpy reentry. A certain pitch. A heaviness of import. My gaze lifted to his face and I read the creases around his eyes like rings on a tree: forty-five-ish. Dark hair, freckled, light skin. Toned, as was to be expected at a triathlon book launch. Pressed Dockers and a collared shirt: earnestly conservative. No champagne cup.

Connor Dunn was still speaking to Adrian. "We haven't met in person, but—"

My husband interrupted him, brightening. "Sure, I know who you are." Adrian turned to me. "Allow me to introduce my wife, Michele. Michele, this is Connor Dunn."

"A name I know well from Adrian's column," he said to me. "Nice to meet you."

"Likewise."

"Has anyone ever told you that you look like Eva Longoria?"

I nodded. "Nearsighted people." Eva Longoria doesn't have the butt I got from the short, curvy Mexican women on my dad's side. My blonde, Caucasian mother has no butt, but her genes passed me by in the looks department.

Adrian shook his head. "Not a chance. You look better à la natural on your worst day."

"My husband is biased," I explained to Connor.

He laughed and nodded at Adrian. "Hey, congratulations on your Kona qualification."

"Thanks. There's nothing like aging up to give you a boost." Adrian was playing it cool, but he was over the moon about the Kona Ironman world championships. At forty-five, he had qualified by winning his first race as a forty-five to forty-nine age grouper, at the Longhorn Half Ironman in Austin last fall. "Will Angela be racing?"

"Yes. She qualified in thirty-five to forty."

"That's great." Adrian turned to me. "Connor's new bride is a tri-beast like us."

Connor broke in. "I think we saw you guys last weekend at the Goatneck ride in Cleburne. I was going to introduce myself, but things got crazy."

My skin went cold. A hit-and-run driver had killed one of the cyclists during the race.

Adrian put down his black Sharpie and sighed, sagging like a deflating balloon. "Yeah, that was horrible. Michele and I were one Brahman away from it."

Connor's voice and eyebrows went up. "Brahman?"

"Adrian hit a cow. It knocked him off his bike and left him with a flat tire." I sucked in a quick breath. "I think it slowed us down just enough that we weren't the ones hit by the car, you know?"

"Yeah, I do. It's scarier and scarier out there on the road."

"We were the first ones to get to him after he was hit." Adrian's voice grew raspy. "I ended up doing CPR on him while Michele called 911."

It was a surreal picture: Adrian and the fallen cyclist were mirror images of each other, one upright and one prone, both covered in blood. They were dressed alike and had similar blue bikes. It freaked me out, big time. I couldn't keep their images from returning to me over and over.

Adrian continued. "This guy had been riding maybe a quarter mile behind the leaders—he passed us when I hit the cow—and then this car just came out of nowhere off a little dirt road and smashed into him."

"You saw it happen?" Connor leaned in, his voice a mix of dread and morbid curiosity.

I started to speak but realized both of my hands were over my mouth. I pressed my palms together and lowered them. "We heard it."

"Oh my God," Connor breathed.

It was a sound I would know anywhere. Adrian had hit a car head-on two years ago. I still don't understand how he walked away from the wreck—his bike didn't—and I will never, ever forget the sound. A thud, a wrenching of metal, a thump, then a crack as driver and bike hit the road separately. Groans. And in Adrian's case, the squealing of brakes as the driver came to a stop. Not that time, though. Not that time. That time there was silence, except for Adrian screaming "Rider down, rider down" at the top of his lungs.

I forced myself to keep talking, to expunge the rest of the memory. "We saw the car driving away. White, a small sedan, like a Taurus or a Camry or something." I shook my head. "We couldn't get the license plate number, though, and we didn't see the driver, so we were practically no help at all to the police."

Just then, our publicist put a manicured brown hand on the table in front of Adrian. It startled me. I had forgotten we were in a bookstore, that there were other people around—worse, in line watching us, listening to us, waiting for us. Scarlett—that was both her name and her nail color—said, "Only thirty minutes to go, and you've still got a line out the door. I hate to break in, but we need to keep it moving." She'd coached us on this earlier. The line must move no matter what. A moving line means book sales.

We nodded, and she backed away with her smile pointed toward the queue, a "Nothing wrong here, folks, nothing to see" smile.

To Connor, Adrian said, "Sorry, man."

Connor pulled at his collar. "Absolutely. I understand. Um, I'm going to hang around and do some shopping. Could you spare five minutes when you're done? I have something I need to talk to you about. It's the reason I came, actually."

There. That was what I'd heard in his voice. A purpose for his presence, and a threat to our plans for the evening. A post-signing tête-à-tête wasn't on the schedule. My throat tightened. "Wound so tight, she springs when I touch her," my ex-husband Robert had said about me. Well, not tonight. I breathed in and held it. I would not be rigid. I would roll with it and everything would be okay. I exhaled.

"Sure. I'll meet you in the café when we're done."

Bam. I saw spots in front of my eyes. My internal tension meter was only about a 6 out of 10. Really, it's no big deal, I told myself. Just five or ten minutes. We probably wouldn't even be late for the eight thirty reservation at Oxheart I'd made two months before. My fingernail ended up in my mouth, but I snatched it away before I could bite it. This wasn't exactly unprecedented. Adrian was a constant challenge to my need for order on his best days, just as I was to his need for flexibility. I called these opposing traits our growth opportunities when I was feeling Zen.

"Perfect. Michele, a pleasure." Connor extended his hand to me.

I shook it, and his touch jarred my nerves. We posed for the obligatory picture and he walked off toward the biographies. Nice guy, even if he was a plan-buster and a bringer of bad memories, but something else was wrong with him. I could feel it. "Do you know what he wants to talk to you about?"

"No idea." Adrian pursed his lips for just a moment. Then his expression shifted. Big smile, maybe a little less big than before, but big enough. He greeted the next person. "Sorry about the wait. I hope you're having a good time."

***

Half an hour later, we bid goodbye to our last customer and stood up.

"Congratulations. You did it." Scarlett beamed so wide the store lights reflected off her perfect white teeth. "This was a very, very successful event. The manager is thrilled. I'll have you guys on the TV interview circuit within a week." She rubbed her cherry-tipped hands together. "You're so perfect for this, it hurts."

"Thanks, Scarlett." I nestled into the crook of Adrian's arm as he slipped it around me.

"I'll say goodnight now and go close out with the manager. You kids have a fun anniversary."

"We will. Thanks again."

As she walked away, I heard her muttering, "Gorgeous, just gorgeous," to herself.

I lifted my face toward my husband. "I'm so glad to get the first one over with. Now we can relax and have some fun. You're meeting that stalker fan guy in the café first, though, right?"

"Yes, but Connor's a friend. I've corresponded with him more than a year. He's all right."

I felt a little better about it, maybe three percent. "Five minutes?"

"Five minutes."

"I'll hit the ladies' room and meet you at the café, then, okay?"

"Sounds like a plan, and I love me a good plan."

I rolled my eyes at him in response.

He swooped me over backwards. A flashbulb lit up my peripheral vision. Scarlett's hired shooter was still at it. "Hurry back."

I put the back of my hand to my forehead and said, "Be still, my heart."

He laughed and set me back on my feet, and we walked in opposite directions.

It felt strange and wonderful to have finished our book launch together, hell, to have written the book at all, instead of just enforcing the *Chicago Manual of Style* upon it. As an editor, most of my writers treat me like the punctuation police. Adrian doesn't. Words matter to him, like they do to me. Even more, my words matter to him. Mine. I hadn't even known I had my own words. Sure, I'd known I was prone to what my mother called an overactive imagination since the day I ran home from school, gasping for air, and told her I'd seen an elephant walk through my schoolyard and reach into my classroom window. That I'd felt the wiry hairs on his trunk as he lifted me from my seat, through the air, and out the window. Yet somehow—*"It was like magic, Mom!"*— I'd still been in my seat five minutes later to take the terrifying state assessment test. I'd kept that imagination under wraps until Adrian started unfastening all my buttons. And now my name was on a book jacket, too, and more words threatened to come out of me, this time forming themselves into an idea for a fantasy novel, for goodness' sake, something I hadn't told even Adrian yet because it was so crazy.

I made my way across the store toward the ladies' room. Many of the browsing shoppers were people I recognized from our signing. I tried not to race-walk in front of them.

When I finished sprucing up—and answering questions from women in the bathroom who were more interested in my marriage than in triathlon—I broke toward the sounds of beans grinding and milk steaming. Adrian and Connor were talking with their heads together like longtime confidants—and Miss Boob Job was lurking behind them, more Mata Hari than Barbie now. When she saw me, she whirled around so fast her bag flew out from her body like a stripper from her pole. My eyes followed her retreat.

When the door closed behind her, I looked back at my husband and his new old friend. Connor was punctuating his speech with sharp nods of his head and smacking his closed fist into his open hand. Adrian snuck a glance back over his shoulder and saw me, then turned back to Connor and held up a palm. Connor looked in my direction, then back at Adrian, and nodded. They shook hands and Connor left through the same door Rhonda had, all before I could reach them.

I tilted my head. "That was some conversation."

Adrian planted a firm kiss on my lips. "I love you."

"I love you, too." I started to roll my eyes, but stopped when I caught a flash of white through the window. A small sedan was driving past the bookstore, sending me into another blood-soaked flashback of Adrian on the side of the road with the dead cyclist. I shook my head to clear the image and gripped my husband's bicep. Warm. Solid.

He picked up a cellophane-wrapped bouquet of orange and yellow tulips from the table beside him and I took them from his hands. "But it's Thursday!"

Adrian brought me tulips every Friday since one hour after our first not-a-date. It was still hard to believe that a man who looked that good would work so hard to make me feel special. Tan, muscular but lean, and blond with short curls at the nape of his neck, Adrian was delectable. Like double-fudge-brownie-sundae-with-a-cherry-on-top yummy, although he would rather be compared to a gluten-free brownie sweetened with coconut nectar, hold the fudge and double the organic fresh cherries, please. He made me forget that I'm on the wrong side of forty and haven't changed my hairstyle since my fifteen-year-old started kindergarten. Sure, I have a good face and can render a pretty paragraph, but Adrian was the looker in our twosome.

He kissed the tip of my nose. "Pretend it's Friday, then, since it's our anniversary and book launch. Thank Scarlett, though. I ran out of time today, and she saved my ass."

I laughed. "Well, I have a surprise for you, too, but I'm saving it for dinner."

"Oh, that isn't all I've got, but you'll have to wait till tomorrow for your real surprise. Tomorrow night."

"Then I'll save mine until then, too."

"Copycat." He winked.

We started walking to the parking lot, my arm through his. Adrian's strides were normally twice the length of mine, but somehow we made them match.

"So, what did Connor want to talk to you about?"

"We debated Coeur d'Alene versus Lake Placid." Those were two famous Ironman triathlons.

"That's caca."

"He heard Lake Placid was the better race for a first-timer. I set him straight."

My thoughts began to tumble like Keds in a drier. The scene replayed in my mind: Little Miss Boob Job skulking around in the café within earshot of the two men. I couldn't make sense of what I'd seen, nor could I figure out the source of the dread that was seeping through me. But it was our anniversary. I had two options. I could act the paranoid fool or I could be a grown-up. I chose option B.

"Okay."

***

My stomach bulged against my waistband, but I was not about to stop now. Why had I suffered through a sixty-five-minute swim and a two-hour run that day if not to overindulge on a special occasion? I'd eat like an Ironman contender tomorrow. Meanwhile I'd savor each bite, made even more dear because my Oxheart meal cost what I'd normally spend to eat for a week.

Tex, our Vietnamese waiter, arranged my dessert in front of me and backed away with a theatrical flourish. His voice was pure epicurean hip. "Your tapioca pudding caressed by Buddha's Hand citron, ginger-galangal ice cream, and apple mint."

Oxheart was definitely on the cool side: local ingredients and hip, rustic-leaning décor, light years away from our elderly Jewish neighborhood.

Tex lifted a bowl from his tray and held it high and away from his body like he was serving up a dead rat. "Your berries, sir." He thunked the bowl down on the table. Plain ole fruit hadn't been on the menu.

"Great, thanks." Adrian was oblivious to the waiter's pique.

Tex nodded at me, gave his head a barely perceptible shake at Adrian, and left.

I dug into my pudding. "Oh my." I held a bite in my mouth and moaned, letting the flavors seep into my tongue. Heaven. Heaven in a spoon.

Adrian stabbed a strawberry with his fork, then held it suspended in the air in front of him, forgotten. He looked at me instead, looked into me, in a serious way unlike his usual self. "Lately I've noticed more strangers recognize me. I don't like it as much as I thought I would.

You've got to promise me you'll be careful. Watch out for the crazies, don't take chances, tell me if anyone does anything weird around you. You're my world, Michele."

I couldn't recall a single time my free-spirited husband had scared me, but he scared me so much right then that I pushed my tapioca away. "Nothing's going to happen to me." He shifted upwards like he was going to interrupt, so I hurried on. "I promise, though, I'll be careful. Will you promise me the same?"

"Yes. I promise."

His definition of careful and mine don't even belong in the same dictionary, but I accepted his answer. "Is something going on?"

"No." He drew out the word. "I'm just sentimental because it's our anniversary."

I narrowed my eyes.

He held up three fingers. "Scout's honor."

A lump rose in my throat. "I wouldn't last a day without you."

"Sure you would. You're the strongest person I know. You're my little Itzpa, my Butterfly." He held up his hands bent into claw shapes. I couldn't help but laugh. "Seriously, you know it's me who'd crumble." He leaned toward me and extended his hands palms up across the table. I put mine on his, our hands and fingers barely touching. "Please, honey, whatever you do, don't leave me alone in the house with those two teenagers."

The tension slipped off of me like a silk robe to the floor. Annabelle, his seventeen-year-old daughter, and my Sam were good kids, but they were your normal handful of hormones. I tickled his palms with my fingertips. "I think Belle and Sam would love it. Party every night and sleep all day."

He snorted. "Your nose is growing, Pinocchio."

I smiled and pulled my tapioca bowl back into place. I couldn't help but think, though, that if anyone's nose had grown that night, it hadn't been mine.

Chapter Two

The next morning came much earlier than I would've liked. Thank God it was a rest day: no workouts scheduled. I eyed the damp-haired woman in the bathroom mirror whose husband was shaving beside her. Well, I didn't look as bad as I felt, and our bathroom looked marvelous, if I did say so myself. We'd just had it remodeled after four years in our cozy three-bedroom house with a shower that didn't do hot. Now it did, and we had 16x16 tile and dual showerheads to enjoy it with, as we just had. The bathroom was our only true splurge as a couple, and it felt decadent.

A muffled voice came through the bathroom door. "Who's picking me up after baseball?" Sam. It sounded like he was in the entryway, just outside the bathroom.

"Not me." Belle's voice came from near his. "I have late swim practice tonight. Buh-bye." The front door whooshed open, the alarm chimed four times, and the door thwumped shut.

Adrian and I looked at each other, then I picked up my lipstick. A brownish-neutral, my favorite color, if neutral qualifies as a color. "Can you get him today? We have a *Speedboat Quarterly* to get to press. I can drive him this morning." Besides *Multisport Magazine,* Juniper Media published magazines and collector books on a variety of sports, including speedboat racing, dressage, and even Ping-Pong. They'd gone a new direction recently, too, and published a certain book called *My Pace or Yours.*

Adrian rinsed his razor, tapped it against the edge of the sink, rinsed it again, and stuck it in a cream-colored porcelain cup by his faucet. "I can, but you need to hurry home, too. We have a little trip to make tonight." He turned toward me, his eyes still green and smoky from the hours we'd spent nose to nose, toes to toes, and everything to everything else in between, the night before. People who called his eyes hazel had never woken up naked with him and seen the eyes I saw most mornings. Definitely green.

"We do?"

A tap sounded on our bathroom door and I opened it. Steam whooshed out at Sam. The scent of Adrian's pomegranate mango body wash dissipated. "Guys? My rides today?" His dark hair hung in a flop over his forehead and in front of his left eye. It would drive me nuts if I were him, and I fought the urge to lick my finger and smooth it back like I would have only a few years ago. Annabelle's crooked-tailed Siamese cat, Precious, padded along behind him, meowing as she wended her way around his ankles.

"We do," Adrian said, finishing our conversation and pretending to ignore Sam. "For your surprise." He leaned down and in, nuzzling the crook of my neck and shoulder.

"Guy-uys," Sam said. Even though he was as tall as Adrian, he still looked like a boy and acted like one most of the time. Displays of affection elicited the gross-out response I knew Adrian was going for.

I held back a smile. "I'm taking you to work, and Belle will take you from there to baseball practice." Sam was a summer lifeguard at the Jewish Community Center.

"I'm picking you up after baseball." Adrian replaced his nose with his hand on my shoulder.

"Oh, and Adrian checked out some paintball place for your birthday yesterday." I couldn't believe my baby boy was turning sixteen in one week—or that I was waiting until the last minute to pull things together for the big day.

"Sweet!" Sam bounced on his toes like an oversized Labrador puppy. "Can I drive my friends when we go?"

"May I. Nope. You can't get your license until after you turn sixteen, and your birthday is on a Saturday. The DMV isn't open on the weekend."

"Please?"

"N.O."

"Belle got to drive when she was fifteen."

"Belle had a hardship license so she could get across town to the pool and back twice a day."

"No fair."

Adrian cut in at just the right time. "Speaking of Belle and no fair, her grandmother called. She's not coming, and Belle's bummed. We've got to cheer her up."

I winced. "Oh no. We will." Her maternal grandparents lived in New York. Their daughter Elise—Adrian's first wife—fatally crashed her Porsche when Annabelle was an infant, and Adrian inherited an obscene amount of money. Enough that he could quit his all-consuming job in audit at the then-Big-Eight firm of Price Waterhouse to care for Annabelle and follow his heart into writing. Belle's grand-parents funded a trust Belle would gain access to at twenty-one, like Elise before her. Their visits were solar-eclipse rare, but to Annabelle, the love of her grandmother Diane was the moon and the sun. My heart ached for her, but I had to get my son moving. "Are you ready to go?"

Sam's eyes fluttered, dangerously close to rolling at me. "I've been ready."

I looked up at him and put my hands on my hips. "Teeth brushed?"

"Yes."

"Today?"

"Yes."

"With a toothbrush?"

"Mommm," he complained, but I stared him down. He sighed. "Yes."

"And toothpaste?"

A fraction of a second's hesitation gave him away. "Uh—"

"Get right back upstairs and brush your teeth for one minute with water and toothpaste, put on deodorant under your arms, comb your hair with a comb, and meet me at the front door in three minutes. I'm going to check, too. Don't test me."

Behind me, Adrian chortled.

Sam opened his mouth, then closed it. He spun around and within a few seconds I heard him stomping up the stairs.

"I wish Robert would let him try medication."

Sam rarely made it from one routine task to the next without prodding, even with the checklists I posted all over the house. His father resisted ADHD meds, though, and since he split Sam's expenses with me, was entitled to his say. "I didn't need it to become an electrical engineer, so why should Sam?" he kept insisting. I'd grown up with Robert in Seguin, Texas, outside San Antonio, and in my humble opinion, a good dose of Concerta wouldn't hurt him, either.

"You're preaching to the choir."

I followed Adrian to the kitchen for the last leg of our morning routine. I glanced out the front window and through the sagging arms of our oak, heavy with a full season's growth of leaves. A white sedan was parked across the street. I peered closer. An old, nondescript Ford Taurus I hadn't seen before. It probably belonged to someone we knew or someone working for someone we knew; Meyerland looks like Little Mexico by day with all the yard workers, maids, and nannies reporting for duty. More than once, neighbors have mistaken me for the help.

I walked over to Adrian, who was slathering cashew butter on a banana as the Keurig dispensed his Kona. Light spilled in through the glass block windows over his hands. "You know how I've been seeing white Tauruses everywhere? Do you recognize that one?" I pointed out the window.

He chomped a bite of his banana—breakfast number two, after an egg white and veggie omelet before our shower—then looked outside. He sucked a slow breath in through his nose and released it the same way, still chewing. He chewed some more, then swallowed. "Yeah, we need to talk about that."

"And?"

"Well, let's just say something's a tad off about the owner."

"What do you mean?"

"I'm gonna be late, Mom." I looked behind me down the hall, and there he was, his cheeks pinker and his hair neater.

"Remind me tonight and I'll tell you all about it. You've got to get out of here."

I recognized the bum rush when I got it. Adrian had almost no concept of time except when it related to speed and distance covered.

"Mom, come *on*."

I growled softly at Adrian. I didn't like waiting, but I wasn't going to cause Sam to get fired either. "Later, then." I grabbed my voluminous zebra-print bag from the kitchen counter and turned back to my husband. I let him give me a cashew-butter kiss, but I made my voice stern. "I love you. And I'll hurry home for our surprises and to hear about this mysterious driver."

"I love you, too." He called down the hall toward Sam, "See you at five after practice. Family date tonight."

"Yeah, I remember."

"*Family* date?"

Adrian's satisfied grin bordered on smug. "Wait, did I not tell you that part?"

"You know you didn't." I stood on tiptoe to kiss his smile.

"Huh. I guess that's why they call it a surprise." He emphasized the last word, widening his eyes and leaning in at me.

I shook my head and laughed as I headed down the hall that led to the driveway. Two sets of footsteps followed behind me. When I got outside, the Taurus wasn't there.

"You take the 4Runner today." I waved my hand at Adrian's SUV, which I'd been driving for the past few weeks while we tried to figure out what was wrong with my Jetta. "Since you have to pick up our bicycles from the shop."

"Are you sure? I don't want to be responsible for El Diablo giving you an aneurysm or something."

"I'm sure." I clicked to open my Jetta. Nothing happened, as usual. I opened the door the old-fashioned way, cringing at what came next: the car alarm blaring—wonk, wonk, wonk, wonk. I threw open the door and pulled the switch for the headlights to quiet the alarm. Sam was waiting at the back end of the car to catch the trunk when it popped open when the headlights switched on. He slammed it closed and I lowered myself into the seat and pulled the door shut.

"We can take it in to the shop on Monday," Adrian shouted.

I could barely hear him through the electric windows that wouldn't roll down. I muttered, "If it makes it until then," and turned on the ignition. Adrian claimed the car was possessed, and had tried to get me to hang a rosary from the rearview mirror. But much to the horror of my deceased abuelita—my namesake on my father's side—my mother had raised me Baptist. No rosaries at La Hacienda de Hanson.

Sam stuffed his red backpack into the toe space of the passenger side and dropped into the seat with a mesh bag of baseball gear and a brown paper lunch bag. He shut the door and buckled in, then immediately changed the radio station. I liked The Bull, he liked Young Country, but both played George Strait, so I didn't fight him over it.

He cut his eyes at me. "You're not going to make me drive this thing, are you?"

What the Jetta lacked in coolness it made up for in safety, so I hedged. "We'll see." I backed out, waving at Adrian, and rolled the Jetta past the hodgepodge of remodeled and enlarged 1960s ranches toward the JCC. My day had officially begun.

***

I reached the open gate of Juniper Media's lot just before eight and right on time. Juniper officed in a long multicolored brick building on the western edge of the Heights, just north of downtown. The one-story structure was part office and part industrial, like its neighborhood, which blended into the rest of Houston. We are a city infamous for lack of zoning.

I backed the Jetta into my reserved spot and shut down the engine, thankful that my electrical issues didn't wreak havoc when I turned the car off. Sweat immediately trickled down my neck as I walked toward the office. It was ninety-plus already and wicked humid, typical for August. I dug in my purse for my phone, but something made me stop midstride, hand still in my bag. I looked back toward my car. Parked three down was an old white Taurus. My stomach tightened. I walked back to it and snapped a photo of its Texas plates with my phone. The numbers were completely obscured by a thick coat of dried mud.

On edge now, I entered the lobby, strewn with Houston sports pennants and memorabilia: red, white, and navy for the Texans; red, white, and black for the Rockets; blue and orange for the Astros; orange and white for the Dynamo. I was already on sensory overload after our late night, and the garish colors jarred me. I was irritated that Adrian wouldn't tell me about the car. I needed coffee.

A familiar voice jolted me from my thoughts and I followed it to the reception desk.

"Hello. I'm here to apply for a job." The woman was clad in a fitted hot-pink blouse, black pencil skirt, and peep-toe patent-leather heels. Once again, Rhonda Dale did not blend.

I positioned myself beside her. "We meet again."

She swung her head toward me. Her mouth opened and closed, marionette-like. "What are you doing here?"

"Me? I work here. What are *you* doing here?"

"I was just applying for a job I saw posted on Craigslist."

Marsha, our longtime receptionist, piped in. "I'm sorry, ma'am, but I don't show that we have any jobs posted right now." God bless her.

"Whoopsie."

And then it hit me why Rhonda was here. This was no coincidence.

"You do know Adrian doesn't work here, right?" He was a freelancer, as in free to write his column from home, or over the Kona they stocked just for him at Fioza's Coffee Shop, or wherever his free spirit took him.

Rhonda's dark eyebrows pulled together under her bleached bangs. "But—" She shook her head in rapid, tiny movements. "Whatever." She wheeled on the point of one heel and stalked back toward the front door.

The me that first earned my Itzpa nickname in middle school when I punched a girl twice my size for picking on a fifth grader was more controlled as an adult, but still no one to mess with. All five foot two of me. "Hey, Rhonda," I called after her, "I'll tell Adrian you came by to see him. But I wouldn't recommend you do it again."

The door swung shut behind her.

Marsha looked at me from over her half glasses with their dangling bejeweled strap, chin down. "Well, good morning to you."

I guffawed to cover my anger. "Yeah. Wow, huh?" I didn't trust myself to say more. I started toward my office.

"Oh, and congratulations, Ms. Famous Author. There's a picture of you and your husband on the cover of the Entertainment section of the *Chronicle* this morning."

I turned and walked backwards with a finger to my lips as I said, "Shhh, we're trying to keep a low profile." I resumed my walk. I heard Marsha laugh behind me. She was a peach, and I owed her one for shutting Rhonda down. I turned and added, "Don't eat before work Monday. I'm bringing you cinnamon raisin bagels from New York Deli."

She beamed.

Despite putting up the good front my mother had always required, I was still pissed. I remembered when I didn't make the volleyball team in high school, I ran home and cried my eyes out. The next morning when I got ready for school, she came into my bathroom and stared at my face in the mirror. "More concealer."

My fists balled. And then I thought, Just screw it. Screw white cars. Screw Little Miss Boob Job and Adrian's secrets with new old friends. Screw unsettling bloody memories of dead bicyclists I couldn't make myself unremember. Screw paranoia. Screw all of it. The only thing truly wrong was the noise in my head, and I could quiet that with work. This, this was what separated me from the rest of the pack, the ones at home on the couch with a remote control in one hand and a doughnut in the other: mental toughness. I was the one in control of me. *Yeah.*

I marched down the hall, ready to kick butt. The vivid covers of magazines-past kaleidoscoped through my peripheral vision on the walls. I imagined it was an encouraging crowd doing the wave for me. I wouldn't let them down.

My boss interrupted me mid mental pep talk, right as I reached my office. "Good news." He stuck his head out the doorway of the office catty-corner from mine.

I stopped. Hopefully he hadn't seen me cheering myself on with my imaginary crowd. "Yeah? I could use some."

He gestured me ahead and followed me into my office, then lowered himself into the chair in front of my desk. "You and Adrian really hit a home run last night." Brian had come for the first hour, so he saw the crowd.

"Thanks." I sat, too.

"I think your book is going to be the best thing that's happened to *Multisport* in ages. To Juniper, really. Thank you for that." I nodded and Brian steepled his fingers over the knee of his crossed leg. He cleared his throat. "You know we ran lean on money last year. I held back on raises and I didn't do bonuses."

I remembered, of course. The advent of online publications and news-by-blogger had gouged a hunk out of our print periodicals. We'd rebounded with new e-offerings like subscription downloads for e-readers, and we had high hopes for this book experiment. "I understood. I agreed with your decision."

"Yes, well, that's one of the things I appreciate about you. Not everyone did. Anyway, we seem to be out of foul trouble."

Brian, like many of my coworkers, speaks in mixed sports analogies all the time. It's an occupational hazard of working with fanatics that took some getting used to. I struggled not to roll my eyes.

He went on. "I'm bumping you by five percent this year. And you'll get a five thousand dollar bonus in your next direct deposit."

"Oh, Brian, I don't know if you should do that." I reached into my handbag and retrieved a can of the still-cold Dr. Zevia organic-stevia-sweetened soda Adrian bought me the week before. He was determined to help me kick a lifelong Diet Dr Pepper habit. It wasn't the same, but I was having fewer headaches.

"Don't tell me you're asking for your waivers, Michele." His face whitened under his thinning red hair.

"Oh, no! Not that. But I need a lot of flexibility for the next three months. I'm doing the Kona Ironman with Adrian." I took a gulp of my drink, afraid of his reaction.

Brian's saggy face puckered up like a Sharpei: his version of a smile. "Did you qualify?" His voice jumped half an octave on the last word.

I spit my Dr. Zevia across the desk, laughing. "Sorry." I ripped a paper towel from the emergency roll I kept hidden in my desk drawer—my coworkers tended to overreact to sports news the second they brought drinks to my office—and started blotting. "Dear God, no. I won a lottery spot. Truly, if I just finish, it will be a miracle."

"To hell with finishing. If you survive."

"Brian!"

"Kidding. Don't worry about it. Adrian, this race, and your book are the trifecta for us. Just see to it that I get thirty-five hundred words a week from Adrian from now until you get to Kona and thirty-five hundred a day while you're there." His request made sense. We sold more subscriptions, ads, and issues of *Multisport* from September through November than any other time of year because of Kona. "Words, I need words. And pictures. Can you be his photographer?"

"Of course. Thank you."

"You're a great investment and my most valuable player." He ran the backs of his fingers under his jowls. "I remember when you came to work for me. You were still on the ropes with that putz. Sam was in elementary school, and exercise for you was running back and forth to the car, driving him around. Now look at you. Sam's doing great, you're happy, you have Adrian and Annabelle, you've co-authored a book, and you're doing an Ironman. You're batting a thousand, kiddo."

He was right. Things were as great now as they were bad then. I had come to him with no editing experience, begging for a refuge from my life as an attorney, convinced I'd missed my path when I took a sharp left turn into law school after getting my degree in English from Trinity. Only no one could understand why I wanted to "go backwards" in my career. No one except Brian. He brought me on as an editing assistant, at a seventy-five percent drop in my pay, despite my over- and under-qualification.

"And none of it would have happened if you hadn't taken a chance on me. Thank you, Brian." It was true. He and his wife, Evelyn, had treated me like family, inviting Sam and me to the lake with them, trying to set me up with the sons of their friends, buying the overpriced cookies Sam's baseball team sold as fundraisers.

Brian nodded, crinkling his face again, then stood up. "I'll let you get back to work. It's almost game time on that one." He gestured toward a colorful pile of speedboat photographs.

"Yes, it is. Thanks for the raise and bonus, Brian." And for distracting me from the shitstorm in my head, I added to myself.

Three hours later, the graphics guy and I finished pulling together the cover for *SBRQ*. I ran my fingers across the mock-up. It was beautiful—a Hustler Rockit with red and yellow flames slicing through aquamarine water, with the beaches of Destin, Florida, in the background. It was looking like we would make our deadline before the end of the day—important to all of us on a Friday.

A text dinged in from Adrian. *"I finished errands & got good start on writing. I miss you. Lunch at Beaver's/noon?"*

Warmth flooded me. I could squeeze it in if I hurried. *"See you there!"*

***

I watched for Adrian through the window of Beaver's at twelve fifteen. They had a patio, but no one set foot on it between June and September. We only have a few weeks of bearable outdoor dining temperatures each spring and fall in Houston between the wet heat and the wet cold. I'd arrived at the restaurant earlyish and ordered two iced teas, Adrian's usual Beaver's Cobb, and some baby back ribs and jalapeño poppers for me, then changed my order to a Cobb five minutes later.

Adrian's red 4Runner pulled into the parking lot and eased along the first row of cars until it reached an empty space and parked. I loved watching Adrian from a distance, imagining myself seeing him for the first time again. The thrill was always there. He got out of the SUV and started walking along the row of cars toward the entrance, his steps in rhythm with my heartbeat. A goofy grin snuck over my lips. Then he stopped. He turned and walked to the driver's side of a white car. Surely it wasn't another Taurus? I craned my neck for a better view, but I couldn't see it well enough to be sure.

When he got there, he leaned on the roof, talking to someone inside. My smile drooped. Sweat dripped between my breasts. Was the damn AC broken in here? I grabbed the front of my shirt and pulled it in rapid poofs away from my chest. Adrian's hands gripped the frame of the door and the rolled-down window. He kept talking. I kept sweating.

Finally—*finally*—Adrian stood up and walked away. The car backed out and threw gravel up behind it as it left the lot. I stood up to see who it was but never got a good look. Damn it. Adrian turned and watched it go. I tried one last time to catch a glimpse of the driver as the car turned out of the lot, but it was too far away.

I bit my lip. I wasn't going to have a snit fit on our lunch date. Really, Adrian had done nothing wrong. He had asked me to lunch, and he was here, nearly on time. All he had done was talk to someone in the parking lot, right in front of me. Nothing suspicious there. I needed to get a grip.

He sauntered up to the table. "Hi, babe." He leaned down and kissed me on the lips, then pulled out a chair and sat.

"Hi. I ordered our usual." My voice sounded tight and thin. I swallowed. You can do better, I told myself, but it was my mother's voice I heard.

"Thanks. Perfect." He slid into our booth, then locked his fingers and stretched his arms over his head, palms up. "Well, that was a weird morning. I ran into that woman, the one from the book release party yesterday."

What a relief. "Really? Where?" I tried to sound casual.

"At the GNC store. I went by there on my way here for some Tri-flex and vitamins. She came in a couple minutes after me."

Not the Beaver's parking lot? I was confused. "Did you talk to her?"

"Briefly. And then I ran like a scared little boy. She's intense."

This didn't make sense. But then everything about Rhonda so far defied reason. "I ran into her, too."

"You're kidding."

"I wish. She came in to apply for a job at Juniper."

"What?"

"Yeah. She thought you worked there." He raised his eyebrows. I paused, then blurted out, "And there was a white Taurus there, too. Adrian, I'm seeing those damn white cars everywhere. I feel like I'm going crazy."

"Going crazy? You've been crazy. For a long time." He looked at me, but I didn't give him the arm punch I normally would. He put his hand over mine. "I'm sure it's nothing."

It wasn't, though. "So, who were you talking to in that one in the parking lot?"

"That one what?"

"The white Taurus?"

His face skwunched into a thinking look, then he nodded. "Some woman who recognized me and asked me to sign our book, but then she couldn't find it, so she left. Was she in a white Taurus?"

God, I wanted to chomp my thumbnail. "I think so. I have an idea. Since we're together now, alone, you can tell me about that car in front of our house this morning."

"Adrian? Michele? Hi!" a voice bubbled just to my right.

Scarlett.

I pasted on a smile. "Hello."

Adrian pointed to a chair. "Join us."

She wouldn't, of course. She was probably here with a client.

"Don't mind if I do. I got stood up by a client I like a lot less than you two."

Mierda, I said to myself, cussing in my head in Spanglish instead of saying *shit,* because that's all my mother ever permitted. No impolite "shit," no offensive f-bomb. "Mierda" or "chinga"—and even those better be whispered under one's breath. Well, mierda, mierda, mierda.

Forty-five minutes later and after we'd committed to a TV interview the next week, Adrian and I walked out of Beaver's, with Scarlett hanging back to pay the check with her credit card, something I'm sure she would include on an invoice to Juniper later. Adrian walked behind me with one hand resting lightly on the back of my neck. His casual touch steadied my emotions. Really, I was like a hippo lurching along a balance beam today. We reached my car and I wheeled and threw my arms around him. He kissed the top of my head, and I burrowed my face in his chest.

"We're going to have such a good night." My hair muffled his words.

I leaned back and looked at him. He looked relaxed, so I tried to match. "Yes, we will." I nodded, realizing that no matter what else was true, this was. "We will."

"Goodbye, Mrs. Hanson."

"Goodbye, Mr. Hanson."

Adrian walked to his car. I waved to him one more time and he made a smooching face and blew me a kiss. I hadn't locked the Jetta, so I didn't have to go through my electronic comedy routine. I got in the hot car, turned on the air, and drove away. As the wheels of my little car turned over the uneven pavement and old bricks of the streets of the Heights, a powerful urge to return and throw myself back into my husband's arms gripped me. I shucked it off and grabbed my stress ball from the console and started squeezing and releasing it in slow one-counts.

***

The hands on the clock read two p.m. I was making great progress on *SBRQ*. I had enough time left to beat our six o'clock press deadline and still get home for our "family surprise date," but my goal was to put the project to bed by five fifty. My parents had made sure I knew that on time is good and ahead of schedule is better. I live by it.

"How're we doing?" Brian called from his office.

"We're looking good. Carlissa sold some more ad space, so we're making room for it. Jerry is working on revisions now. We'll all be here until we put it to bed." The staff hated when a deadline fell at the end of the day on a Friday, so I knew they were all working as fast as they could.

"Excellent."

I put my head down and my red pen back to work on the hard-copy proof in front of me. It slashed across the page, a rapier in my hands. Extra space. Alignment error. Typo in title. Was it wrong that I got so much pleasure out of the blood on the page? I tried to hide it, just in case.

At about four o'clock, a wave of nausea swept over me and I was momentarily confused. Images flashed in freeze frames in my mind. Adrian bent over the fallen cyclist in Cleburne. The white car speeding away. The lifeless and bloody body on the ground. The smears of blood on Adrian's shirt that didn't come out after three washes with bleach. These are just memories, I reminded myself, but a vague sense of unease remained that I couldn't reconcile. Maybe I needed a snack. I snagged a handful of macadamia nuts from a jar in my desk drawer and texted Sam: *"Remember Adrian will pick you up after practice. Please confirm."*

I didn't get a response. Typical. Although I supposedly required Sam to keep his phone with him, he carried it about one day out of fifty, and on that day it would have no charge. Ah, nature (his father) or nurture (his stepfather)? With Sam, probably both. I hadn't heard from Adrian since lunch, either; he had a knack for leaving himself stranded without his phone, too. I hated not hearing from Adrian or being able to reach Sam, and my nerves were jangling. I had to focus, though. I had to finish *SBRQ*.

At five, my cell phone rang with an unfamiliar number. I never answered those, but I remembered that Sam didn't have his phone, and Adrian apparently didn't have his, either, so I squeezed the phone between my shoulder and ear and kept working my keyboard. One hour until we went to press.

"Hello."

"Mom, Belle left me."

"No, Sam, she had late swim practice. Remember? We decided this morning that Adrian was picking you up after practice."

"Oh, yeah."

"I tried to text you. You should carry your phone. I don't know why we even pay for it."

"I do carry it. Sometimes. And Adrian's late."

"It's only five o'clock. Give him a few more minutes."

He groaned. "Yeah, more like half an hour. I'll look like an igmo standing out here. And it's hot. Can't you come get me?"

"I'm finishing something that's going to print tonight, honey. You're going to have to be an igmo. I'll see you at home. Love you."

"Ugh. Bye."

I sent Adrian a quick message: *"Don't forget Sam."*

Forty-five minutes later the phone rang again with another unfamiliar number. I closed my eyes. I just needed five more minutes of peace to finish up so I could get out of there.

"Yes?" I pushed the speaker button and set the phone on my desk. I kept typing.

"Mom, he's still not here."

I pursed my lips and released my breath slowly. I was going to kill Adrian. "I'll come get you, but you could walk home faster than I can get there." My phone flashed with yet another number I didn't recognize, but caller ID said it was the Houston Police Department.

Sam's voice whined from my phone, but I didn't really hear him. I stared at the number on my screen, and I knew. Without even answering it, I knew. With my son standing outside at Bayland Park talking on a borrowed phone and waiting for a ride that wasn't going to come, I knew.

Chapter Three

People passed by my office door, their voices serving and volleying. I clung to my phone with both hands and stared at the screen, which kept insisting I had a call from the HPD.

"I'll call you back, Sam." I pressed the button to hang up with him and accept the new call. "Hello," I said. Or at least I thought I did. I couldn't hear my own voice over the ringing in my ears.

"Mrs. Adrian Hanson?" The voice on the other end was deep.

Yes. Yes, that's me. That is who I am. But I didn't want to say it. I wanted to hang up the phone and stop the thing that was coming for me.

"Ma'am, are you there?"

I forced the words through my frozen lips. "Yes, this is Michele Lopez Hanson."

"This is Detective Young of the Houston Police Department. I went by your home to talk to you, ma'am, and since you weren't there, I took the liberty of coming to your place of work. I'm right outside, and I wonder if there's a place we can talk?"

I closed my eyes. "What's this about, Detective?"

"Ma'am, I need to talk to you face-to-face about your husband, please. I'll explain it all then."

I told him to meet me at the reception desk. I pushed myself up and grabbed my bag. My mind's eye drew back, and I saw myself from a distance, a short woman covered in oozing concrete, squarish in a thick cement shroud. A chalky scent dried my nasal passages halfway into my skull. I tried to swallow, but couldn't. My mouth tasted like writing "I won't talk back to Mrs. Simpson" on the blackboard twenty times and cleaning erasers during recess, and I knew that whatever this detective had to tell me was my punishment, but for what, I didn't know. If I did, I would take it back a thousand times and never do it again. I could be good. I *would* be good, so, so good. I willed my right leg forward, then my left.

"Michele?" someone called out from the interior cubicles. A buzz had started and was building as I made my way past. How did they know?

Another voice joined in. "Are you all right?"

I couldn't answer the questions they were lobbing at me. I could barely even walk. My legs were lead posts. My thoughts ricocheted. Am I still moving forward? Why is it so hard to see? Why is everyone staring at me? And why do I have to go listen to this detective tell me something I already know, something that can remain untrue if he just doesn't say it?

I came to a stop at Marsha's desk, where a tall black man in khaki pants and a blue blazer was standing. He held up a badge.

Marsha whispered, "Michele, this man is here to see you."

I nodded and motioned him toward the conference room with my hand, but I didn't meet his eyes. He walked in front of me, but stepped back to let me enter first, then pulled the door shut behind him. I turned to face him.

"I'm Detective Kevin Young." His voice was even deeper in person than on the phone. He handed me his card, then pulled out a wallet. "Does this belong to your husband?"

He handed me a square of black water-repellant material. I opened the Velcro closure and pulled out Adrian's driver's license and rubbed my fingertip over his picture. I tried to answer the detective, but my mouth was stuffed with something like chunks of the old foam pads Papa used to put under our sleeping bags when we went camping. My breaths became labored. I couldn't talk with a mouth full of foam, so I nodded and stifled a gag.

His bass voice rumbled. "This wallet was found in the pocket of the victim of a hit-and-run driver about two hours ago on Endicott, near Meyerland Plaza. The man matches the picture on this license. We believe it is your husband. I'm very sorry to tell you this, but he had no vital signs when the paramedics arrived. He was declared dead at the scene."

I kept nodding. The whole room had turned gray. I could barely see the detective now. Was he waiting for me to say something? He would be waiting a long time.

He squinted hard at me. "He was on a bicycle when he was hit."

Hit and run. Bicycle. My mind started playing tricks on me and I saw Adrian in a bloody heap on the side of a country road, like the blond man we'd seen die. No. That hadn't been Adrian then. And this couldn't have happened to Adrian now. I wished the detective would just stop talking. I wanted to go home to see the tulips in the vase on my bedside table where my beautiful husband put them last night. To herd our bickering teenagers into the 4Runner for our family date. To deliver my anniversary surprise, to tell Adrian we were going to do Kona together. I wanted him. Adrian. My husband.

"Ma'am? Can you hear me?"

When I opened my eyes, all I could see was the ceiling. I shifted my gaze to the concerned face of a stranger. I sat up. My cheeks felt wet. I touched my face and my fingers found tears.

"Can I call someone to come be with you, ma'am?"

I shook my head no.

My phone rang. I groped in the purse at my feet and my hand found the hard surface of my phone. I pulled it out and looked at the screen. The call dropped and the screen changed to show six missed calls from the same number. It seemed familiar, and then I remembered. Sam. Oh no, Sam.

I opened my mouth to speak and nothing came out. Foam. I swallowed hard and tried again. "My son, he's been waiting for my husband, and now me, for a ride home from baseball."

The detective's brows furrowed a V between them. "Can you ask someone to go get him? Or can we go get him together?"

I started to shake my head again, but stopped. "My boss."

"Can the receptionist help me find him?"

I nodded.

"I'll be right back."

I nodded again, at nothing, sending tears trickling down my face in starts and stops. I sat in a chair at the conference room table and put my face down on the cold wood. I closed my eyes and tried not to be alive. It didn't work, and within just a few minutes, I heard footsteps and lifted my head from the pool I'd left on the table.

It was the detective, with Brian.

"I'm so sorry, Michele. Marsha's going to give Sam a ride home." Brian's face was as red as his hair and he had tears in the corners of his eyes. He sat down beside me and put a hand on my wrist. "Can you tell me where he is?"

"The Bayland Park baseball fields on Bissonnet. Thank you." My words echoed flat and empty inside my concrete shell.

Out of nowhere Brian's assistant appeared with a glass of ice water, a cup of hot tea, and wet and dry towels for my face. Brian stepped to the door and spoke to Marsha, who stood just outside. Her face looked red like Brian's. Then Brian returned to his seat.

"Let me just get Jerry to take over for you on *SBRQ*." Brian typed on his phone.

I had forgotten about the magazine. I nodded.

He slid the phone into his pocket. "What do you need from Michele, Detective?"

The detective turned to face me. "I'll need you to come ID the body when we're done here." Bile rose in my throat. I wanted to see Adrian, but *alive*, not in a morgue. "I need to ask you a few questions first, and then we'll need to get together and talk again in a few days. I know the timing is bad, but my job is to find the driver who hit him and figure out what happened. Someone has committed a crime, and your husband is the victim."

Brian looked at me. I said nothing. He took the lead. "What kind of crime?"

"At a minimum, vehicular manslaughter, and leaving the scene. We also need to rule out intentional foul play." He turned back to me. "Do you know of anyone who would want to hurt your husband?"

A thought tapped at my brain, but I batted it away without looking at it as nausea again boiled up in me. I managed somehow to shake my head no without vomiting.

Brian answered. "Adrian was an author—his and Michele's first book just came out—and a freelance sports writer. A successful athlete. A husband, a dad. I've known him for years, and I don't know anyone who would want to hurt him."

Detective Young scribbled some notes and exhaled audibly through his nose. "I hate to have to ask this now, but where were you this afternoon, Michele?"

This question confused me. Couldn't the man see I was at work?

Brian jumped in. "Wrong call, Detective. Michele has been here since around one thirty."

His answer helped me understand the question: "Where were you?" as in "Did you kill your husband?" I was too shell-shocked to be angry.

"Do your employees swipe in and out?"

"No, but we have security video that will show she didn't leave."

The detective nodded several times in succession. "That's good. The incident occurred shortly after four. If you could make me a copy of that video, please."

"Of course." Brian pinched the bridge of his nose. "I just don't understand what happened."

"Mr. Hanson was killed by a hit-and-run-driver on Endicott, by Meyerland Plaza."

"That's no major thoroughfare."

"Correct."

"So, I don't mean to Monday-morning quarterback, but shouldn't we be talking about a broken bone or some road burn? What am I missing?"

Detective Young glanced at me as if deciding whether to answer in my presence. I guess he thought I could handle it. "We'll have to wait for the autopsy and accident report to be sure, but it seems the vehicle was speeding, and that Mr. Hanson hit his head on the curb after impact. He didn't have on a helmet."

That got my attention. "He wasn't wearing a helmet?"

Detective Young shook his head. "No."

Oh, Adrian. It made sense. Adrian often rode his bicycle to run errands, and he tended to skip his helmet on those casual rides, which made me crazy. We had argued about it. I told him his skull wasn't any harder just because he was in sandals, but he wouldn't budge. It didn't make it hurt any less to know I was right.

The men continued to discuss it, but my brain shut down. I needed something, someone, but I couldn't pin it down. Well, Adrian for one, but I needed someone else. Who was it?

"Michele?" Brian prompted me.

I looked at him. When had the detective left? Panic shuddered through me when I realized I'd lost God knows how much time. I stared at Brian, unable to form words.

Brian reached for my hand and gripped it tightly. "I'm going to drive you to do the ID, then home. We'll take your car and Evelyn will come get me. Before we do that, we need to make a few phone calls, don't we?"

"Who do we need to call?" my voice croaked out.

"I was hoping you would tell me."

I looked at him helplessly.

"A friend?"

I shook my head. I've never been the kind of woman who surrounds herself with girlfriends, and I didn't have anyone besides Adrian I could go to with my soul ripped wide open and my heart bleeding out on the floor.

"How about family? Your parents, or Adrian's parents?"

Mom. Yes. Mom would come. Mom would come and figure out what to do. She could help me with the kids and with the call to Adrian's parents. And Papa, because he always made things better. "Yes, my parents."

"You want me to talk to them?"

I nodded again.

"We'll call on the way, then. Let's get the ID over with."

***

An hour and a half later, Brian and I walked in the front door of my house, our house, Adrian's and mine. Brian, who was Jewish, reached over his head and touched the mezuzah left by the previous owners, then kissed his fingertips. I'd seen him do it before, and he'd explained that he touched the mezuzah—which held the Shema "One God" prayer on a parchment scroll—to ask God to watch over him in his travels. Adrian and I loved the mezuzahs and had left them over our doorways, but we didn't touch them. Maybe we should have, I thought. Maybe then I wouldn't have the horrific memory of my husband's pale face and closed eyes against a stainless steel table to carry with me for the rest of my life.

Sam sat at the kitchen table with his laptop, and Annabelle stood beside his chair, one hand gripping the back. They looked at me, Sam scowling and Annabelle wide-eyed. I shot a glance at the clock. It was nearly eight. How had so much time passed?

Annabelle spoke first, her voice sharp but thin, brittle. "Where's Dad?"

Before I could answer, Brian answered her. "Hi, I'm Brian, I work with your mom. We've met a couple of times."

"We know you," Sam cut in, his lips curled in a sneer. Annabelle's nose and brow creased.

I didn't think I could hurt any worse, but then I saw Sam blinking back tears, his mouth set in a grim line.

Brian put his hand on my shoulder. "Your mom got some bad news at work today, and we've all been pitching in to help her." He stopped talking.

Time to be a big girl. I looked back and forth at the two of them, my Sam and Adrian's Annabelle: our children. I breathed in through my nose and out through my mouth, then tightened my jaw before I spoke. "Adrian, your dad, he was hit by a car this afternoon. He's gone."

Annabelle dropped her head and a strange noise started from her chest, then turned into an escalating wail. I watched her long curls fall around the sides of her face. She and I had a good relationship, but she was her daddy's girl and didn't often come to me for emotional support. But he wasn't here; he would never be here to hold her, or me, again, and I didn't know what to do for her. After a beat, instinct took over and I reached her in two giant steps. I swept her into my arms and she slumped against me as her wail turned into a sob.

Sam shouted over Annabelle. "Gone, Mom? You mean he's dead?"

I looked at him, nodded, and held out one of my arms for him, but he ignored it and shoved his books across the kitchen table. They took out a plastic Rockets tumbler on their way to the floor. The cup bounced high, then lower, and lower still, each crack against the floor splashing dark liquid against the wall and baseboard. Sam ran out of the room and I heard his feet pounding up the stairs like I'd heard them a lifetime ago that morning.

"Sam?"

"Leave me alone!"

I let him go. I guided Annabelle to the couch. Her hysteria ratcheted up and we cried together until enough of the storm had passed that we could talk.

Somehow, I got the words out in answer to her questions as I rocked and held her. What happened. What I knew. What I didn't know. I realized that I had questions about Adrian's death, lots of them. As we talked, I heard cabinet doors shut and dishes clink in the kitchen. My heart quickened involuntarily until I realized it was Brian, not Adrian, taking care of us.

I pushed a strand of Annabelle's hair behind her ear. "Honey, I need to go check on Sam, okay?"

"Yeah. I know you do." She put her head down on the side pillow of the couch. I laid a blanket over her legs. How many times had her father done just that? God, how I wished I had been the mother she needed when she was a little bitty thing, so I could be more of what she needed now. Precious jumped onto Annabelle's lap, a more than adequate substitute for me. Annabelle stroked her back.

I crept up the stairs with dread, feeling lightheaded and bone-weary. I found Sam curled up on his bed. Every article of clothing he owned was on the floor, as were a photograph of his district champion middle-school baseball team, his entire collection of J.R.R. Tolkien books, a Game Boy, and a week's worth of dirty towels.

His fists covered his eyes and tears poured out from under his clenched hands. Anger radiated from him, floated in the air around him. He reeked, not of his usual teenage boy smell, but of the rank odor of grief. It was almost palpable, and I had to force myself through it. He let me slip onto the bed and put my arms around him, but he remained wooden.

In my imagination, the words flowed out of me in a soothing river. I could almost hear myself say, "Adrian loved you, Sam. He loved having a son. He's not completely gone because he will always be in our hearts. Life includes death, and we never know when it will take any of us, but don't be scared about losing the rest of the people you love, like Belle and your dad and me, because odds are it will be a long, long time before anything happens to us."

In reality, I choked on my own sorrow and only got out, "Are you okay?"

He didn't answer.

"I'm sorry, Sam. I know you're very sad. I'm sad, too."

No response.

Everything I could tell him, everything I could think of that I should tell him, felt hollow and false. I couldn't tell him that it would be all right or that I would be fine, because I didn't believe it. And I sure couldn't tell him the one thing that he and Annabelle wanted most to hear: that this was all a big misunderstanding and that Adrian was coming home.

"Do you want to talk?"

Silence.

"Michele?" Brian used a whisper tone at half volume. It carried softly from downstairs.

I patted Sam and slipped down the stairs, feeling guilty that I was relieved to escape. "Yes?"

"It's eight thirty. Evelyn is here. I straightened up your kitchen and ran another load of laundry. Is there anything else you need?"

"No, Brian, no, you have been great to me, but my parents will be here," I glanced at the clock, "any minute."

At the front door, Brian touched the mezuzah again and kissed his fingertips. I closed the door behind him and the click of the latch falling into place seemed unnaturally loud. I stood in the entryway, listening. No sound from Annabelle, nothing from Sam. Outside was quiet as death, too, and it was all that I had left, this nothingness. The only sound at all was the beat of my heart crashing in my ears. I froze in place and felt time slow until it seemed to stop. I floated above myself, and then away to a place where everything was a dark, endless blue. A part of me remained in Houston and the rest of me slipped into that other dimension, a limbo from which I couldn't move forward. The silence kept growing until it was louder than my heartbeat, until it shrieked in my head like a banshee. I clapped my hands over my ears and that untethered part of me fell back into the here and now, ripping and tearing my insides as it tumbled back into place. I didn't know if I could take this, or if I wanted to try.

The doorbell rang. I glanced up at the clock in the dining room. Nine o'clock. Thirty minutes had just vanished from my life. I had lost time again. Still, I couldn't move, and I stared at the door. It flew open and I blinked. My parents rushed in, my tall blonde mother filling the space around me and changing its shape. I opened my mouth but nothing came out, so I yielded to her force before she said a word.

Papa rushed in. "Itzpa." He put his arms around me and tried not to let me see that he was crying, too.

Chapter Four

The alarm on my phone didn't know that Adrian had died, and it chirped at five a.m. "Adrian, Michele, get up! Time to train! It's going to be a great day!" it seemed to say. I considered smashing it to bits.

What day was it? I counted back and realized it was only Sunday, but for the life of me, I didn't know what had happened to Saturday. A kaleidoscope of gray images whirled in my head. Tears, Sam angry, sleeping, Papa's hugs, Annabelle bereft, sleeping, and my mother taking care of all of us. Yes, that was Saturday.

Precious didn't know that Adrian had died either, and I could hear her helpful meow outside the bedroom door. She took her role as morning drill sergeant to the Hanson family seriously, and she enjoyed it in a restrained manner befitting her felinity. She allowed no deviations from schedule. Her claws clicked on the tile and I could picture the agitated swish of her caramel tail as she paced back and forth.

I pushed snooze. I hadn't planned for this moment. The melatonin and Benadryl I had taken the night before were still fogging my head. My heart lay inert inside my chest, and my brain processed with the efficiency of a plate of scrambled eggs, but my body tingled and itched to get up and *do* it. It was Sunday, and it was time to train. Ah, paradox, go to hell, I thought.

Maybe it was the right thing to do, though: stay in my routine, drain my anxiety with exercise, and take care of myself. It was normalcy. It was moving on.

Maybe it was, except that it felt wrong to be alive, much less doing our things without Adrian. And really, I didn't want to move on. I wanted to stay in bed, under our sheets that smelled like my husband, and pretend he was still there with me.

The alarm blared again. Without further thought, I gave in to the habit, the obsession, in a way that Adrian would have understood and applauded. I dug in my workout drawer in the dark for a pair of bicycling shorts and a jog bra, then snuck into the living room with the water bottle I kept at my bedside.

La Mariposa, my beautiful orange and black bicycle, was waiting for me in the darkness on its training stand. When Adrian gave it to me, he'd caressed its custom paint job and said, "Let's see you fly, little butterfly."

I had pictured the little bicycle racing over a country road, wheels barely touching the ground. "It's perfect. Where did you find it?"

"My imagination."

I pushed the memory away and tucked my locket on its long chain into my sports bra. I slipped on my bicycle shoes, hopped on and cleated in, then set the timer on the Garmin 310XT training watch that I never removed. For the next two hours, I pushed with my right leg and pulled with the left. I concentrated on my form, on my cadence, on not thinking at all. The spin of the pedals and wheels soon matched the spin in my head. Whursh whursh whursh whursh whursh. Faster and faster they spun, and my mind with them, into a trance. Whursh whursh whursh whursh whursh. I didn't turn the TV on or listen to music like I normally would. I just stayed there with the sound of my own breathing and the bicycle going nowhere at eighteen miles per hour.

A thought broke through my trance state. No, not a thought, more like an image that became Adrian's face. Then a sound: Adrian's voice. The image grew vivid, the sound grew louder, and they transported me back to a moment like I'd never left it.

"Get your speed up, and then lay yourself over, one arm at a time. Don't get in a hurry about it. Like this." Adrian had laid his own body flat and steady into his aerobars. We were out near Waller on a farm road with less shoulder than I liked, and he was teaching me to use the new aerobars on La Mariposa. They would help me ride farther faster by reducing wind resistance, only they required me to stretch forward and balance my weight in the armrests over the front wheel, and they scared the crap out of me.

"I'm off balance, Adrian. I'm going to fall."

As I looked back on it, I could see myself overreacting to the subtle balance shifts. When a red Chevy Silverado zoomed past, the surprise and wind gust nearly knocked me over. I'd squealed.

"You should probably sit up when cars pass us, for now."

I snapped at him. "I can handle it."

He chuckled. "Yes, I know you can."

I had snuck a glance at him then, and I froze the memory of his face in my mind now, lingering on each laugh line and the whiskers he had missed in his hasty pre-ride shave. Oh, Adrian. Adrian.

Precious hopped up on a bookshelf and watched me like she expected a conversation. Adrian's image flickered and died. Reluctantly, I turned my attention to the cat and spoke to her in short bursts between breaths.

"You're the only one I didn't tell, aren't you, Precious? I'm sorry, you're part of the family. You have a right to know." Tears mingled with the sweat dripping off my face. "Adrian is not with us anymore. He's not just on a trip. So don't be mad at him." Precious didn't like us to break routine and stay away from the house, and she would bite our ankles for days after we returned. "I'm going to need you to snuggle Belle and Sam. Remember that dog in Peter Pan? Nana? Well, you need to be like that dog. Love them."

The cat's expression didn't change, but she didn't break eye contact either. She swished her tail once and laid it to the side of her.

"I don't think I'm going to need your help, though. I'm strong. I'll be fine." A knot in my throat strangled the last few words. "Really, I will. I will be fine. I will be fine. I will be fine. I will be fine." I kept whispering the words over and over, a fast tempo in time with the pedal strokes. But I knew it was a lie.

I smelled Chanel No. 5, and a hand touched my back. I yelped in mid chant and half-jumped off the saddle.

My mother. "Good morning."

I glanced at my watch and pressed the backlighting: 6:15. Even in the predawn light I could see her pressed turquoise velour tracksuit and bright red Clinique smile. My mom gets up at six each morning, no matter what, to conquer days bulging with causes to support and First Baptist Church events to chair. Like tightly wound mother, like tightly wound daughter. She disguises it with a veneer of Southern charm, but I am the carnival version in a funhouse mirror, garish and misshapen next to her razor thinness, perfect bearing, and cool composure. Or I was until Adrian. He had made it easier to be me. He made it *all right* to be me. I was not ready to let him go.

"Good morning, Mother."

"You're up early."

Ah, here was the tricky part. Did she mean it was good that I was up early, or bad? Was she empathetic? Approving? Critical? You could never tell with her, because no matter what she said, she delivered it with a smile. I chose the most positive interpretation.

"I couldn't stay in bed." I lifted the corners of my mouth, trying for self-deprecating although it felt like a rictus on my face. "This makes me feel," I paused and searched for the words, "less bad."

She looked at me for several beats without blinking. "You are your father's child." Her emphasis on "are" made it clear that I could choose a less positive interpretation this time. "I'm going to make coffee and breakfast, then I thought we could work on the final to-do list for Adrian's service." She turned to go, then stopped and looked back at me. "I know it's hard, but we have things to do, Michele, and you have to pick up Adrian's parents at noon." She headed toward the kitchen.

Today was a compromise date for the funeral. When we made plans Friday night, my mother insisted that we had to hold the service within the week out of propriety (her version of it, at least), but I refused to have it on a weekday. I had kept my reasons to myself, but I didn't want to give people time to find out and come. I wanted to be as alone as I could in my anguish.

A light broke the darkness at the doorway into the kitchen, and I pedaled on in the living room alone.

Adrian's parents were great people, but I hadn't spent much time with them. They had Adrian late in life and never shared his zest for adventure, preferring to stay put in their quiet little town on the Oregon coast, and between the demands of work, training, and teenagers' activities, we had only visited them twice. Something to add to my list of regrets. I called them Friday night, then booked tickets for them to come to Houston on Saturday.

The weight of their emotions, of the emotions of all the other people who loved Adrian, pressed down on me. I didn't have the strength to carry theirs and mine, too.

***

An eternity passed before I arrived with my in-laws to meet my parents and kids at Crosspoint Church. I wish I could say we attended regularly, but people really knew *of* us more than they *knew* us. Long Sunday workouts took precedence over organized religion in our lives. Still, it provided a great place for a runaway Baptist girl to celebrate Easter and Christmas.

We walked into the vestibule with me on one side of my wobbly mother-in-law and my father-in-law on her other side, each of us holding one of her arms. I could still hear the whursh whursh whursh of bicycle-like static, background music to the cacophonous anti-melody of the voices around me. How could I have thought people wouldn't find out about our rushed service and show up in droves? Adrian's death had made the news in a big way: Internet, newspaper, and television. ESPN ran a segment on it every hour all weekend, with the picture of Adrian swooping me over backwards at the book launch last Thursday night, a lifetime ago. Now people came at me from all sides, but none of them Sam, Annabelle, Papa, or my mother. The interlopers hugged me, said wonderful things, cried, and wrung my hand. Some of them clung to me as if I could somehow bring Adrian back, some of them people I barely knew.

Many I did, though. A large contingent of the lean and sinewy, people from the many triathlon, bicycling, running, and swimming groups Adrian supported had come. They stood out. So did Scarlett, who had accented her mourning black with a scarf that matched her nails. I'd tried for invisibility in my black knit dress, but it didn't work. She spotted me. I wanted to clasp my butterfly with both hands and click my heels together and let my magic locket fly me someplace quiet and private, someplace I could cry with no one watching.

Scarlett made her way over to me. "Oh, honey, I am so sorry," she said. She kissed me on the cheek and swallowed me in an embrace. "If there's anything I can do, anything."

"Thank you." I pulled back to make introductions. "Scarlett, these are Adrian's parents. Mr. and Mrs. Hanson, this is Scarlett Thomas, the publicist for the book Adrian and I wrote."

They shook hands all around. Scarlett leaned in and whispered in my ear. "This really isn't the time or place, but later, soon, we need to talk about your TV interview this week. Because they still want you. Even more now. I'll call you tomorrow morning." Before I could reply, because she had left me a bit speechless—more like aghast, really—she leaned away from me and said at normal decibels, "Hey, is that Apolo Ohno?" and pointed at a short man in dark sunglasses.

"I can't imagine why it would be," I said.

Of course, I knew it was Apolo. Adrian had written an article for *Multisport* about the speed skating and *Dancing with the Stars* champ's training for Kona. Thus began an unlikely but genuine friendship. Apolo even took us to dinner once when he was in Houston. Adrian ran with a coterie of celebrity friends, but he didn't publicize it. Apolo dipped his head at me and ducked into the sanctuary.

Scarlett stared after him. "Well, okay. And I'll call you." She kissed me again. "Nice to meet you both, Mr. and Mrs. Hanson, and I'm so sorry." She left.

"Is there a place I could sit for a moment, dear?" Mrs. Hanson was swaying a little. She shrank more every time I saw her, and she made me look big. Beside us, Mr. Hanson with his white hair and beard towered like a polar bear.

"Of course," I said. I led them to some leather club chairs flanked by tables jammed with floral arrangements. Lilies as far as the eye could see, on every flat-topped surface in the lobby. I hate lilies. I hate their sickeningly sweet smell, I hate their drooping white petals, and most of all I hate that they are the flower of death. They shouldn't be here, I thought. Adrian should.

I patted Mrs. Hanson's shoulder. "You'll be fine here until we go in."

"Thanks." She squeezed my hand.

Mr. Hanson crumpled into the chair beside her and his voice quavered. "It's a lot for us. The traveling, losing Adrian. We never thought he'd go before us."

Me either. I nodded, my lips pressed together, and made a show of studying the flowers. Through my fog I couldn't help but notice a large arrangement stuck off to the side. Not lilies. Bright flowers, gerbera daisies and tulips. It drew me in like a lost bee. I excused myself from my in-laws to look at the card and almost smiled. It was from Katie Connell, one of my roommates from Baylor Law School. She had seen the ESPN segment and left me a distraught voice mail message earlier, explaining that she couldn't make the service. But her personality certainly had. I kept scouring flowers and cards, my back to the crowd.

"There you are." Sam's voice said whining but his eyes said relief.

I lifted my arm to drape it around the waist of my much taller son. "You're here. Good." He cleaned up nicely in the shiny black suit he'd insisted we buy for last spring's baseball banquet. It looked a little short at the wrists and ankles.

"Gigi dragged us here an hour ago." He tugged at his blue striped tie. "When can I take this off?"

"After the service." I reached for his hand, pulling it away from his tie. "Where's Belle?"

Sam's eyes were on his phone, which he'd pulled out of his pants pocket. He couldn't carry it when I needed him to, but he had it out at Adrian's funeral?

"Can you put that away until we get home, please?" My voice sounded tight. I flexed my jaw several times and swallowed.

Sam glared at me and shoved it back in his pocket.

"Thank you."

"Mrs. Hanson?" I turned around to see a large shiny pompadour walking toward me on short, thick legs. I gave my head a tiny shake. It was the funeral director, and he was a normal middle-aged man, except for his hair. "We're ready to seat the family now." He touched my back and applied gentle pressure to guide me toward the inner sanctum.

My parents were already there, as were the Hansons. When had they moved? I'd lost time again. Ten minutes, according to my Garmin. I grabbed Sam's hand and headed toward my family. We stood beside Papa, who patted my cheek with a hand worn rough by years working as a large-animal veterinarian. I felt a presence and realized Annabelle had moved in beside me. I slipped my other arm around her.

What came next was a blur. Adrian wasn't there, and that summed it up for me. I kept my eyes forward, and I tried to look like I was hanging on every word of the service, but I wasn't. All I could think about was how badly I wanted out of that church, the church where the minister believed in second chances and didn't take attendance. I wanted to hug the urn of Adrian's ashes to my chest and go back to our bed whose sheets were still unwashed, to pile all his clothes on top of me, to sleep. Permanently.

Instead, I stared straight ahead, numb, and willed the time to pass quickly.

Afterwards, I stood outside the church between my stepdaughter and my son and said thank you hundreds of times by rote. I offered my cheek for kisses I didn't feel. Hand after hand gripped mine and shook, until fingers darker than mine wrapped around my palm. Detective Young.

"My condolences," he said, his voice a rumble.

"Thank you. I'm not sure I understand why. I mean, you don't know us." I grappled with my words. "Why are you here?"

He leaned down and in. "I want to learn more about your husband from the people who show up."

My skin prickled. "Do you think the person who killed him is here?"

He shrugged. "I don't know. Maybe. It's worth checking to see. Again, I'm very sorry for your loss. I'll be in touch soon."

I stared after his broad back as he squeezed past some runners. He was a big man, and he dwarfed them like he did me. The body-to-body contact brushed his jacket back and I caught a glimpse of a handgun holstered at his side. Guns and police at Adrian's funeral. Adrian at his own funeral. It was all so wrong. I found myself slipping into blue nothingness again.

When a strange electricity shot through my body, I jolted back to reality. I'd lost more time. Something had registered through my haze, though. What was it? I looked around the exterior of the church, my eyes sweeping from one end of the parking area to the other.

"What's wrong, Mom?" Sam's eyes bore into me from under his lock of hair.

I mustn't scare the children, I thought. "Nothing, sweetheart."

I tried to act like whatever normal was, but I couldn't remember how. My eyes darted around, searching, searching. And then it hit me. I sank to my knees and whispered, "Oh, Adrian."

Sam and Annabelle fell to the ground on either side of me. Their fingers pressed into the flesh of my arms and I could hear an upward lilt like the ringing of a bell at the end of their unintelligible sentences. I drifted away from their voices and didn't comprehend what they were saying. I looked at Annabelle's pale face, swung my own toward Sam. His lips moved in slow motion.

But I didn't really *see* them, because I'd just seen an old white Taurus driving out of the parking lot of the church. At first, I couldn't process why it rocked me so, but then I realized it was like the one from Beaver's, like the car I had seen everywhere in the twenty-four hours before Adrian's death, even in front of our house. I struggled to remember what Adrian said about that car. It had only been a few days since we talked about it, but I wasn't the same woman anymore, and the new version of me was teetering dangerously close to non compos mentis. Slowly it came back to me. He'd called the owner "a tad off" and said he wanted to talk to me about it. Only he never had the chance.

"What, Mom?" Sam shook me.

This time I heard him. But I didn't answer. I realized my lips had been moving, and maybe sound had leaked out, and that it was possible Detective Young was right. This car and its owner, they could be the ones, the ones that killed Adrian. It could be someone we knew.

I heard an engine rev and I looked up again, to see if I recognized the driver or could read the plates, if I recognized anything. I expected to see a platinum head of hair and a flash of hot pink, but the car had pulled away and I saw nothing. I closed my eyes, gulped a breath, opened my eyes, and looked again. No car. Just a memory of standing outside Beaver's and feeling my husband's sweaty lips on mine, tasting their saltiness, and saying goodbye for the last time.

Dios mío, I needed my mind back. To focus, to think. Had I even seen the car here? Or had I just imagined it? Either way, I had to tell Detective Young about it, and about Rhonda. I tried to get up. Maybe I could still catch him.

Papa held me in place. "Whoa, let's not get in a hurry. Are you okay?" he asked as he looked into my eyes. My vet father has a lot of practice calming scared, hurt animals, and I'd seen him do it through- out my childhood. I leaned into him.

I saw another car leave the lot, saw the large African-American man driving it. Young. "I'm sorry. I, well, I guess I got lightheaded. It's all a little much." A white lie by omission, but also true. "I need to go home."

Papa shook his silver head. His dark eyes clouded, and I could see myself in his face. My relationship with my mother wasn't always the best. With Papa? I was his Itzpa. He was my quietly solid hero, a silvery draft horse who never tipped the wagon. My mother joined him, the top of her head level with his. She peered at me anxiously, looking around her, gauging the reactions of other people to me. I knew she was right. I needed to pull it together. I couldn't act like this at my husband's funeral, for Pete's sake. The Taurus was gone. I could call Detective Young later. I stood up, and so did my family.

Annabelle's improbably yellow curls fell over my shoulder. "You're sure you're all right, Michele?"

"I am, thank you."

Before the words left my mouth, she shouted, "Grandmother!"

Grandmother?

Annabelle launched herself at a well-preserved woman in slingback emerald stilettos. A dull ache grew in the back of my head. It never crossed my mind that Diane would show up at Adrian's funeral. Her look shouted money, head to toe, and mine mumbled tears, no sleep, and practicality. Jealousy stung me, but not just because Annabelle loved her. I wanted to be put-together like that, if only for a moment. I reached for Sam's hand and saw his open mouth from the corner of my eye. I heard Papa whisper to my mother, but I couldn't make out his words.

Annabelle and her grandmother talked in soft, excited voices for a few moments. Then the woman stepped toward me with her hand out. Her perfume reached me first, Shalimar, and I took her hand. Soft, limp.

"I'm Diane Pritchett, Annabelle's grandmother."

I told myself to play nice, for Annabelle. "Michele Lopez Hanson."

"Is there a place we can talk for a few moments, about my plans for Annabelle?"

Bless her heart, this was my mother's forte. She stepped in front of me and took over. "So nice to meet you, Diane. I'm Michele's mother, Cindy Lopez. We just finished with Adrian's service. It was lovely, but difficult, of course. We're taking Michele back to the house for some rest. Are you staying somewhere near? I could contact you when Michele has had a chance to get herself back together. And Belle—"

"I'm going to go out to dinner with Grandmother." Annabelle lowered her voice. "Is that all right with you, Michele?" Her eyes cut back and forth between us, round, wet, and revealing. The push-pull made my head hurt worse, but her green eyes won.

"Of course, Belle. Let's just stay in touch by text."

She gave me a quick hug as a consolation prize and walked off with her grandmother. I watched her go, watched her clamber through a door held open by a driver into the back seat of a black Lincoln Town Car. She looked at me through the rear window and crinkled her fingers in a little wave.

I slumped. This I hadn't seen coming.

Chapter Five

Mom deposited the latest edible tribute on the kitchen counter: barbecue, according to my nose and the brown paper Goode Company Barbecue bag.

"I can't believe no one cooks their own food anymore," she said. My mother always brings homemade chicken and dumplings to the bereaved, a recipe from the Mississippi side of her family. "Shoo, cat." She swatted at Precious, who had jumped up to inspect the package. The cat didn't move. Mom rotated, surveying our kitchen with a thin raised brow. Precious surveyed my mother in much the same way, tail twitching.

An endless procession of well-meaning souls—from Juniper, the neighborhood, my old law firm, and even friends from my law school and college days—had dropped off grocery platters of cheeses, store-bought desserts, deli containers of macaroni salad and coleslaw, and even boxes of Popeye's fried chicken. The triathlon crowd knew Adrian and me better, and had opted for things like training-friendly fruit and veggie trays. Mom exaggerated, though; homemade casseroles stood two-deep on the counter as well.

People made quite a run on the food after the service, but twenty-four hours later the mouths to feed had dwindled and the food had not. By Monday afternoon, we still had enough to feed Sam's baseball team. And whatever my mother's opinion about whether fast-food fried chicken is appropriate for a grieving household, I knew the Popeye's would disappear as soon as Annabelle and Sam got home.

At the thought of Annabelle, I snuck a glance at my phone. She had spent the night with her grandmother at Hotel ZaZa in the Museum District. I couldn't afford that on an editor's salary. Whatever, though. Diane could try to buy her granddaughter's affection if she wanted. I hoped I had earned it by being there for Annabelle in the last four-plus years.

Annabelle texted from the Bella Vita suite all morning: *"Wow this place is wow wow wow.* ☺.*"* Then *"R U OK? I am sad. I want to come home,"* followed by *"Grandmother got us facials & pedicures! You won't recognize me. Ha ha,"* and the last one: *"Where's Sam? He hasn't texted me back. What r u guys doing?"*

No new messages.

My mother was still yammering on about the food. "Edward, we need more coolers and ice. Can you run to Walmart?"

Papa squeezed my shoulder. "Need anything else?"

"A kiddie pool for all these Jell-O molds. I don't think they're going to make it." I couldn't care less, but it was easier to go through the motions.

My mother tsked. Cindy Lopez does not waste food. Papa laughed louder than he needed to as he walked out of the kitchen. I wanted to clap my hands over my ears, but instead, I removed the ponytail holder from my wrist and scraped my hair up into it.

"I hope I can get you to take some of this with you, Mom."

I had foisted bursting sack lunches on Adrian's parents that morning when I drove them to the airport, but their packages were grains of sand plucked from an endless beach. I wanted to lay my face on the granite countertop and sleep. I doubted I would ever care about food again.

Mom grabbed a rag and some Clorox spray. "Don't worry. We don't have plans to leave anytime soon." She sprayed the bare spots on the counter she had just cleared and started wiping them down. I dry-swallowed the lump of a thousand useless things I wanted to say. She had stayed two weeks after Sam was born, and I'd thought I had postpartum depression until she left.

My phone rang. Annabelle? No. HPD. I went outside to take the call away from my mother's ears and censure.

I like our backyard better from inside. It's lush with elephant ears and birds of paradise around the ponds, but the neighbors have too many dogs and we get their stink and spillover flies. I slapped at a mosquito and walked across a narrow rock bridge to the deck. I turned back to the ponds. They were low on water, and the pump made a futile sucking noise.

"Detective Young?"

"Good guess. Hello, Michele. You left me a message to call you back."

As I turned the water on for the pond at the faucet behind the deck, a strange feeling bubbled up and burst in my chest. I didn't want to let go of being Adrian's wife. I didn't want to become just Michele. "Mrs. Hanson, please. Yes, thank you. I wanted to tell you that I think I saw the car that hit Adrian, at the funeral after you left." I stood up at eye level with our empty birdfeeder. I'd deal with it later.

"Really? What makes you think that?"

I had expected him to sound thrilled, and instead he sounded almost blasé. It rubbed me the wrong way, but I sat on it. Maybe he'd perk up. "In the twenty-four hours before my husband died, I kept seeing white Ford Tauruses. Maybe the same one. When I asked him about it, he said the owner was a nut job and we needed to talk about it later. And then you came to my office, and of course later never came. Well, I saw another white Taurus at the funeral."

"What's the license plate number?"

I jiggled the empty propane tank that fueled the mosquito trap. "I don't know."

"Do you know the name of the owner?"

"No. But Adrian did, I think. And there's something else. There was a woman that was kind of stalking Adrian, and I think she might drive a car like that."

"Kind of stalking?"

"Yes, she came to our book launch party and was all over him, then she showed up at the Juniper offices the next day and followed him to a GNC." I sat down at the deck table and watched a blue jay splash water on its back and shake its wings. A hummingbird darted into the feeder, and I eyed the container, expecting it to be empty, like me and everything else, but the sun shone through its bulb of red nectar. Papa.

"Why did she come to your office?"

"She said we'd advertised a job on Craigslist, but we hadn't. I think she was looking for Adrian."

"He doesn't work there, does he?"

I slapped at another mosquito and missed. "No, but some people assume he does, because Juniper publishes his writing." Detective Young didn't say anything, so I added, "Her name is Rhonda Dale."

Still the detective didn't speak.

"Don't you believe me, Detective?"

"I believe you've seen this car, and I believe you've seen a woman named Rhonda Dale. You don't have the information to identify the car, or anything to tie the car or the woman to Adrian's death, though."

"But—"

"I have new information for you. An eyewitness came forward this morning. We have a statement with a description of the incident and the vehicle. And it isn't a Taurus, or even a woman."

My mouth fell open.

"Are you still there?"

"Yes." It came out as a croak, so I tried again. "Yes."

"I planned to call you today anyway to tell you, and see if it helped you remember anything else that we could use to find the person who killed your husband."

"Okay."

"The witness said the car was a white Ford F150 pickup, a few years old, and that the driver was a man in his late teens or early twenties."

"Okay."

"The paint we found on Adrian's bicycle is consistent with a white Ford."

"What happens next?" My voice rasped like a file against a horse's hoof, a low and thin sound.

"We're investigating the lead. Do you know anyone with a car like that?"

I shuffled through my mental files. It sounded like half the vehicles on the road. "I don't know anyone who drives a white Ford F150 of any year."

"All right. We've put out a BOLO for it, a Be On The Lookout. I'll call you if I have more questions."

I pressed end, but kept the phone in my hand. Maybe I was wrong. Maybe I had nothing to worry about. Who better to figure this out than the police, right? But my gut resisted. I walked back into the house.

My mother looked up when I came in. "You need to donate this food to a Christian homeless shelter before it spoils."

My hackles went up. I didn't like being told what to do in my own kitchen, especially her implication that our help should go only to shelters run by and for Christians. I guess Mom would let the heathens eat cake? Still, it was a good idea. "I'll get Sam and Belle to do it."

I checked my phone again. No messages. I wanted Annabelle home, and to know about these "plans" of her grandmother's. Adrian and I had never talked about what would happen with our kids if either of us died. I had no idea what to do. Whatever was best for Annabelle, I supposed, but what was best for her? She was about to start her senior year and her friends and her swim team were here. She'd been with us for the last four years. She had stability here. I didn't know what she'd want if she had a choice, though—to stay with us or go with her elegant grandparents to a swank New York apartment near Central Park?

Who was I kidding?

"Get Sam and Belle to do what?" Sam ambled into the kitchen and dropped his dirty baseball glove on the island. He had taken off work for a week, but he insisted on going to practice.

I wasn't sure whether I was smelling Sam, his glove, or both of them, but it wasn't good, no matter what. "Glove to your room or in your gear bag." He rolled his eyes but grabbed the glove. "All this food—it's too much. It's going to spoil. Gigi hoped you and Belle would take it to a soup kitchen or a homeless shelter."

Sam raised his eyebrows. "Not the fried chicken, though, right?"

I answered before my mother could. "We're keeping the chicken."

"Good, because, since it *is* my sixteenth birthday week and all, I get dibs on food choices all week, don't I?" His voice dwindled off, and he looked sideways at me, catching a completely blank look on my face.

I felt almost as guilty about my lack of guile as I did about the undeniable fact that I had forgotten about my own child's birthday week. Not just any birthday, but his sixteenth birthday. His "how soon can we go get my driver's license" birthday.

To realize I was a shitty mother sucked. To have my own mother there to witness it made it worse. I rushed over to Sam, avoiding my mother's eyes, and reached up to put my hands around his wiry upper arms. "Oh, Sam, oh, I'm so sorry. It's your birthday, and I can't believe we forgot—that I forgot—about it."

Sam looked down at his very large feet in the Nike practice cleats that he wasn't supposed to wear in the house. "That's okay, Mom. I understand. It's kinda tough right now."

I missed Adrian at that moment more than ever. He excelled at this stuff. I was a triple-zero failure. Adrian loved celebrations and holidays. Life with him had big blow-up Halloween decorations, over-the-top Christmas lights, tulips on Fridays, and birthdays that lasted all week long. I made sure kids did homework and cleaned their rooms. I booked the doctor and dentist appointments. I straightened up the mess when the parties ended. Adrian brought the fun, I brought the order, and right now I couldn't deliver either.

"So it's fried chicken for dinner tonight. And we need to finalize the plans for your birthday party." I wanted to keep speaking, but I had nothing to say. I couldn't remember squat about our plans for his birthday. I remembered that in another life entirely, Adrian, Sam, and I had talked about it. I tried to bring our conversation back into my frontal lobe. A movie and pizza with friends? A guy/girl party at our house? I would never have said yes to that. Paintball wars with the guys? How the hell should I know? I was a little Hot Wheels car catapulting into the double loop, and I was jumping the tracks. Someone screamed, "I should remember this—I am the kid's mother!!!" Me. I heard me scream it.

Everyone was staring at me: my mother, Sam, and Annabelle and her grandmother, who had just that moment walked in the door. Precious bolted and Diane followed her, backing up in tiny steps as I crumbled into big, ugly, snotty sobs that would not stop.

Annabelle reached my side first. Her long hair fell against my arm as she pressed her face into my shoulder. Sam took up what was becoming his regular station on my other side and started patting me. My laboring brain tuned in just long enough for me to realize that my children were doing more to take care of me than I was for them. I was committing a motherhood felony crime, and my mother was an eyewitness. To top it all off, a woman was lurking in my house who wanted to—and could—take one of my kids away from me.

I summoned words from the depths of my worthless head. "Paintball, right? You want to go do paintball with your buddies. And then you want dinner at Jax Grill, and to go to the movies." I looked into Sam's big brown eyes, wanting so badly to see a flicker of redemption, and my sweet boy made it all right.

"Yes, that's it, Mom. I understand and you don't have to—"

I wasn't going to let him make any more excuses for me. "Perfect, then. You just need to get me your birthday-week meal selections, and we'll get this in motion."

My mother chimed in. "Your grandfather can take you and your friends to paintball, and I'd love to make you a cake. I used to bake you cakes in whatever shape you wanted when you were a little boy. Remember the Pokémon cake? And the Simba cake?"

"Yes, Gigi, but—"

"I'll make you one this year in the shape of your number on the baseball team."

"Thirty-three." He grinned.

"I can help, Gigi." The eagerness in Annabelle's voice made my heart swell.

"Thank you, Belle, I would love your help. Sam can get us a menu and after I pack up some of this food for you two to drop off at a shelter, I can go to the grocery store." My mother turned to me. "Is this all right with you, Michele?"

The tightness eased. "Absolutely. It's perfect, Mom."

The rhythm of our life restarted, and Sam grabbed a glass from the cabinet and went to the refrigerator for ice. Mother started fussing with the food again. Annabelle leaned her head in to me.

"Grandmother is here." Mierda. Yes, she certainly was. "Do you have a minute to talk to her, you know, about me and stuff?"

The knot tightened again. I had to get it together. I had to do this well. "Of course."

"She's in here," Annabelle said, and walked into the living room where her grandmother was pacing and talking on the phone. Diane wrapped it up when we entered.

I passed the table where we displayed our treasures, trailing my hand across the goofy carved black bear Adrian bought me on a trip to New Mexico. I looked around me. He was everywhere, in every tacky, quirky piece in the room. A jeweled wire armadillo. A wrought iron tandem bicycle. A tin donkey. My pre-Adrian décor, although tasteful and attractive, seemed flat in comparison to the warm things he had brought into our home. Like Annabelle.

I braced myself.

"Hello, Diane."

She put her cell phone in her pocket. "Hello, Michele. Sorry to intrude."

"No problem," I lied in a forced, light tone. "So, you guys wanted to talk to me?"

Annabelle looked at her grandmother, but Diane didn't speak. Annabelle twisted a strand of hair around her finger and spoke in a rush. "Um, Grandmother—she wants me to fly back with her to New York, and I told her I needed a little bit of time here, um, because of things, and," she stared at me during a pause that I didn't fill, then looked at her grandmother and went on, "Grandmother said I could stay two more weeks here before the school year starts if you said it was okay." Annabelle clamped her teeth onto her fingernail as soon as she finished speaking.

The air left my lungs. I stood there breathless for long moments while I gathered myself, while she chewed her nails and looked at her fingertips. If Diane wanted her, I couldn't make it hard for Annabelle. She needed her family, a piece of her mother in a grandmother package. Sam needed me, at least; he would stay with me. So I would do just one thing right today and make it easy for Annabelle if it killed me.

"Of course you can stay through the summer. You're welcome here as long as you want; honey, you're welcome here anytime, for the rest of your life." With one more glance at her grandmother, Annabelle fell into my arms. I hugged her to me as tight as I could, memorizing her small, muscular frame for the time coming soon when she wouldn't be mine anymore. She hugged me back just as tightly.

When her hug loosened, I released her. Her pupils dilated completely, and she spoke again. "Michele, I have to, I mean, I sort of want to but I don't, because all my friends are here, and you and Sam and all, but Grandmother says I have to spend my last year of high school there with her and Grandfather."

There, she'd said it. It hurt, it definitely hurt, but less than it would have a week before. Really, I was ninety percent dead, brain-dead at the least, and nearly heart-dead, too. I wished the woman I had been before last Friday was there to talk to Annabelle. If she was, she could speak to that other woman, too, the one from New York who hadn't spent her last four years driving to swim practices and sitting at swim meets, and waiting for Annabelle and her friends at a million different parties and movies and trips to the Galleria. Hugging her when she cried and laughing with her when she laughed. All I had, though, was the woman I was here today, who was losing the second of the three most important people in her life within one week and didn't know what the hell to do about it.

Diane's phone rang. She pulled it out of her pocket and looked at her display. "Excuse me, but I need to take this." Before Annabelle or I said a word, she pressed a button. "Diane Pritchett speaking." She walked briskly out of the living room and out the front door, her heels clacking against my tile, each one a staccato slap to my face.

I dropped my voice and Annabelle moved close. "I love you, Annabelle Corinne Hanson. If you want me to talk to your grandmother, to ask for a different living arrangement, I will. If not, we'll miss you a whole lot, but I understand. I really do. Sam and I will be here and you can always come back if you change your mind. But don't feel bad for one single second, if this is what *you* want to do. They're your grandparents. "

"Thank you. I'll miss you guys so much." Little tears pooled in the corner of her eyes.

I smoothed her crazy curls back from one side of her face. "You can come visit us, you can text, and email, and call, and IM, and all that other stuff I don't understand—" she smiled at that. "And I'll even get on Facebook more often."

Now she laughed. "No, you won't."

"How about I'll *try* to get on Facebook more often?" I softened my voice even further. "Seriously, Belle, your dad will be with you, too, wherever you go." I touched the left side of her collarbone—above her heart—with the tips of my fingers. "Sam and I will, too. You will always have the three of us, exactly like it has been for the last four years, in here."

Now the tears rolled onto her cheeks, and mine did, too. I pulled her back into a hug and rocked her gently, patting, patting, patting.

You, too, I told myself. You will always have Adrian and Annabelle. Even if doesn't feel like it.

Chapter Six

The next morning, I was sitting next to ebony glamazon Denise Dunmore on the set of *Good Morning Houston*, my face caked in makeup and my hair teased and sprayed, hating it more than I can say. The show was on a commercial break, and the producer had goaded the audience into doing the wave. Why had I let Scarlett bulldoze me into this? The strong Michele with the salty tongue still hadn't reappeared, and when I didn't tell Scarlett "Hell, no" clearly enough, she showed up at my house at God-awful-early o'clock in the morning and brought me there straight from a sleepless night. She looked camera-ready herself, just beyond the stage. She shot me a red-tipped thumbs-up and I pretended not to see her.

Denise leaned toward me. "We'll come back from the commercial break in one minute." I watched her as she talked to me, but I had trouble concentrating on her words. She wore a green pantsuit so bright it hurt to look at it. "Thank you so much for coming in. This can't be easy."

I nodded. Denise had interviewed Adrian when he qualified for Kona, and he really liked her. I knew her to be nothing but kind and professional. Still, I couldn't muster up a smile. It was all I could do to be there.

"Do you have any questions for me before we start?"

I shook my head. "No."

"Your locket is beautiful."

"Thank you."

"What do you keep in it?"

"Nothing."

It was a fib. I'd added a smattering of Adrian's ashes after his funeral and had a jeweler solder it shut so I could swim and train in it. I didn't plan to open it again, ever. I rubbed it between my thumb and forefinger. The chain and locket stayed warm from my body, and when

I touched it, I imagined I was touching Adrian's warm skin. I wrapped myself up in the memory of him putting it around my neck.

The producer started the countdown, and when he got to one, Denise spoke into the camera. "Welcome back to *Good Morning Houston.* I'm so honored to have our next guest with us, Houston's own Michele Lopez Hanson, co-author of *My Pace or Yours: Triathlon Training for Couples.* She co-wrote and launched *My Pace* with her husband, my friend Adrian Hanson, a writer and professional triathlete who was a guest on the show last fall when he qualified for the world championships."

The audience cheered on cue. Not a damn one of them knew either of us, I'd bet.

"Their book came out less than one week ago"—at this, the picture of Adrian swooping me over backwards at the Barnes and Noble came on the screen—"and tragically, Adrian was killed less than twenty-four hours later by a hit-and-run-driver when he was bicycling in Southwest Houston." The monitor in front of us filled with a picture I had never seen, one of me outside the church after Adrian's funeral, stone-faced and severe.

The audience gasped. I tightened my stomach muscles, girding myself.

"The police suspect a white Ford F150 was involved and ask that anyone with information about the accident contact them." A phone number filled the screen. The entire segment was supposed to last about three minutes. I prayed we were nearly through.

Denise held the book up for the camera. "Here's the book they wrote together about training for a big-time triathlon as a couple— although I have to say, since I've read it, it's as much about relationships as triathlon, and it's an inspirational read, whether you are into triathlon or any other sport, or no sport at all." The monitor displayed a close-up of the book's cover. Then Denise turned toward me. "Michele, thank you for being here."

"You're welcome." Suddenly my already undersized body started shrinking until I was a tiny, sullen woman perched on the couch with my legs sticking straight out. Denise grew larger until she was a black Athena in flowing green towering over me. I managed a small voice. "Thank you for having me."

Denise's eyes widened. I wasn't sure if it was because she noticed I'd shrunk or because of my voice. I cleared my throat. She looked back at the camera. "The story of Adrian's death has gone viral, beyond the sports circles, and these pictures of Michele and Adrian have captured the hearts and interest of millions of Americans." They ran the swoop picture again, then a photo of Adrian and me crossing the finish line at the Galveston Half Ironman, my first endurance triathlon. Scarlett had outdone herself.

I shouldn't have come. It wasn't time yet. It might never be time again. I stole a glance at Scarlett and she shot me another stupid thumbs-up. I was in hell in front of a million people—more, once the video hit YouTube—and she was shooting me a thumbs-up?

"Michele, I have some bittersweet news for you," Denise said, raising a clipping from *USA Today*. The monitor filled with the image. "Your book has reached number one in nonfiction on the *USA Today* Best-selling Books list."

The audience applauded loud and long. I reached out my hand and Denise put the news piece into it. *My Pace or Yours, Adrian and Michele Hanson* was in the number one spot. I looked up at her, silent.

"Congratulations. How do you think Adrian would feel about this?"

I sucked in air and spoke from my heart on the exhale, and my body grew bigger as I did. "He would love it. He would absolutely love sharing his sport with so many people, and also sharing how to make it something that unites couples in health and a common interest."

The audience clapped again.

Denise finally smiled *at* me. "I can only speak for me, but I imagine I speak for Houston, for Texas, and beyond, when I say we all hope you carry on in his honor. You're competing in the world championships in Kona, aren't you?"

My mouth hung open. I hadn't told anyone but Brian, not even Adrian—this news was the anniversary surprise I had planned for him. The roster was public, but I'd signed up using my middle name, Isabel. "Um, yes, I am signed up. But I hadn't decided whether I would still do it, without Adrian there."

"What do you guys think?" Denise asked the audience. "Would you like to see Michele compete in the Ironman at the world champion-ships in her husband's honor? Wouldn't that be the most amazing thing ever?"

The crowd went crazy. Of course they did. The producer had told them to. And he was just marching to the beat laid down by my publicist, Scarlett, whom I wanted to rip to shreds as soon as I stepped offstage.

Denise finished cheering with the audience. "How about it, Michele?"

I smiled as best as I could, and as mad as I was, when I spoke I said something I hadn't known was true until that very second. "The only way to get Adrian to Kona is with me, and I don't know how I could live with myself if I didn't fulfill this dream for him." With those words, I returned to being me, the normal-sized Michele, and Denise shrank back to actual size, too.

And that was it. Denise showed *My Pace* again and urged everyone to get a copy. She shook my hand, thanked me, and the camera swiveled to another stage to capture another segment. Denise smiled at me and waved as she followed the camera.

I just sat there until the production assistant shuttled over to me, smiling way too big. "Come on, Michele. You're all done, and we need to get you out of here."

I let her lead me to the door, where Scarlett pulled me into a hug.

"I know that was hard, but it's over, and you did it, and you were wonderful. Your book sales are just skyrocketing, and you've helped keep this thing going, especially now that you've committed to carrying out Adrian's dream."

I extricated myself from the vise of her arms. The meek and tearful me of the last week had finally lost it. Scarlett had pressed my rage button. "It's you, isn't it, Scarlett? You're behind all this going-viral bullshit and all these people, these people, all these people . . ."

"No, Michele, of course not, but it's all wonderful. Adrian wanted to write this book with you, he wanted people to read it and be inspired by it, and he wanted to take you to Kona with him."

That, *that* was what was bothering me. "How the hell did you know I was going to Kona?"

"What do you mean?"

I found my voice, and it was loud. "I mean, I hadn't even told Adrian yet. I hadn't told anyone. No one but my boss." My boss, who had published the book, and who had invested in it big time. He had hired Scarlett to promote us, and the book. And he had told her. I knew he had.

She frowned. "I didn't think it was a secret. I had no idea, Michele. I'm very sorry."

I ground my fists into my eyes. Sure, she was sorry, except that she wasn't. She had succeeded, and did it really matter how? I couldn't trust her, and I didn't know if I could trust Brian either. Not with my feelings, anyway.

"Where's my phone?" I'd given it to Scarlett before I went on air. I needed it back so I could call Adrian. I'd started dialing his voice mail and listening to it whenever I got upset. It was better than nothing.

Scarlett handed it to me and I saw the HPD, my favorite phone number, blowing up the screen at that moment. Scarlett grabbed me by the elbow and started walking me out. I took the call.

"What."

"Wow, Michele, so I just heard you were on TV." Detective Young.

"Yeah, so what?"

"I don't often have widows on TV selling books that have gone viral less than a week after their husbands are murdered. Congratulations on your bestseller. That worked out pretty nicely for you."

"My husband is dead, you asshole. Nothing will ever work out nicely for me again." I pressed end and threw my phone at the wall. It bounced on the floor, the OtterBox protecting it as billed. I needed breaking glass and flying parts and loud screaming, not this, not any of this. I stooped to pick up the phone.

Scarlett stopped. "Are you okay?"

"What the hell do you think?"

We walked in silence to her car and she drove toward my home. After about ten minutes, she cleared her throat delicately. "This may not be the best time to ask you this, but it can't wait. I need you to do *The Today Show* in New York on Friday."

"NO! No, no, no, no, no!" I shot each word out rapid-fire through my clenched teeth.

She winced. "I need you to think about it. Talk to Brian. It's a very big deal, and it would mean a lot to Juniper. It would have meant a lot to Adrian, I think, for that matter."

"You're in no position to tell me what anything would have meant to Adrian."

"You're right, I'm sorry. Just talk to Brian. Decide tomorrow. Please."

We arrived at my house, and I got out and slammed the car door without answering her.

***

When I stood in the security line with my boarding pass for the flight back to Houston from New York that Friday afternoon, my *Today Show* makeup and hair were starting to droop, but my Ann Taylor skirt and blouse still hid my exhaustion. All I wanted was to get home so I could throw my son a party and see Annabelle before she moved away, probably for good. Unfortunately, I still had a bicycle ride to get in before bed. I didn't know how I was going to do it. With Adrian around, it wouldn't have been hard. The man just flat-out did whatever it was he decided to do, and it was easy to ride along in his wake.

"Excuse me, are you Michele Lopez Hanson?" The woman who asked was heading in the opposite direction through the accordion of security lines. She looked close to my age, if a foot taller.

I wondered if I'd dropped something. "Yes, I am."

The woman smiled brightly and reached into a long-handled bag slung over her shoulder. She pulled out *My Pace or Yours*. "I saw you on the *Today Show*, and I picked this up on the way to the airport. You're so inspiring. Would you mind signing it for me?"

I looked around me. People were watching us now. "Um, sure. Do you have a pen?"

She handed me a blue Bic.

"What's your name?"

"Beth."

I scribbled a message and my name on the cover page and handed the book and pen back to her.

"Thank you. I'm very sorry about your husband. And good luck at Kona."

"Thank you very much." I turned my attention to my phone to stymie further conversation.

I heard a woman next to Beth ask to see the cover of the book, and they struck up a conversation about the show. "She's so beautiful. And tiny. Even prettier than she was on the air." Beth's voice. I squirmed. Then I heard the other woman's voice. "She looks like the short Mexican actress on *Desperate Housewives*."

This was odd for me, and I thought how much Adrian would have loved it, and how I would have loved it with him, but not so much now. It didn't suck, it just wasn't the same as it would have been. Nothing was, not even flying. I hate flying, and the thought of getting on the plane without Adrian to hold my hand and distract me during take-offs and landings was awful.

Never mind, I told myself. Never mind. Just get home.

At the gate, I logged into wifi with my little Asus laptop. Scarlett and Brian wanted an update on the *Today Show* and I'd put off answering their many calls, texts and emails. They'd manipulated me, and ultimately both played the "do it for Adrian" card.

The terrible reality? Adrian would have wanted the book to sell and me to do Kona with him, one way or another. I did feel obligated to carry on for him, but I knew he wouldn't want to see me so miserable. It was just hard to know for sure, because, of course, if he were here, I wouldn't be miserable, and we would have exulted in all of this together. And if he'd lived, well, then the *Today Show* probably wouldn't have invited us to come on. God, the whole thing hurt my head. All I wanted to do was sleep.

I clicked send on an email to my two puppet masters. My inbox was full—fifty-seven new messages in one day. My touchpad browsed me through them almost of its own volition. Condolences, congratulations, invitations to speak, to guest, to host, to write. An infuriating email from my ex-husband accusing me of neglecting Sam when he needed me. And then something totally different. An email from a freelance reporter asking me about a reputed affair between my husband and a woman who had contacted him, a woman named Rhonda Dale. He wanted my side of the story.

I ran to the bathroom and vomited.

***

By the time I got back to Houston, the inquiry had mushroomed from one reporter to one hundred. After sending an answer to the original reporter—Absolute horseshit!—I couldn't answer the rest. Even though I had seen Adrian's face when he met Rhonda at our launch party, even though I wanted desperately to believe he had never met her, how could this not buffet me about like a cowboy caught in a stampede?

According to the "press release" she emailed to every media outlet in the universe, Rhonda and Adrian met at the New Orleans 70.3 triathlon the year before. As much as I didn't want to admit it, it wasn't impossible. I'd come down with salmonella and had to scratch, but

Adrian went to try for a Kona qualification. He missed it by seconds and stayed over to recover, then slept in and had lunch in the Quarter before driving back to Houston. I racked my brain for anything odd about how he acted when he got home, but I came up with nothing. He nursed me through the rest of my salmonella and was as attentive and loving as ever.

Rhonda's email included lurid details of a wild night in her hotel room with her "athletic stud" and weekday trysts and weekend hookups all over Houston for the next year—including in my own house, in my own bed. She said he had her meet him when he was out with me in public places, and they'd sneak off and do it in back hallways, bathrooms, and closets, because, he told her, I was "an uptight bitch with no sense of adventure."

Two things were crystalline: Rhonda knew where we went, and she was obsessed with my husband. The rest I just had to believe were the delusions of a disturbed woman.

I hated this woman for messing with my mind, and I Googled her name every five minutes on my phone as I bicycled in my living room. My parents were staying for Sam's birthday the next day, and I tried to hide my anxiety from them, which was tricky with Papa ten feet away watching his favorite movie, *Lonesome Dove*, on Netflix with me, and Mom in and out, fussing. The kids had both taken off with friends, luckily. So I searched and searched, but nothing came up about her crazy allegations, and I let myself hope.

Then I woke Saturday morning. On my first try, I found her story—with a picture of her and Adrian from our book launch party, with me cropped out—on PerezHilton.com. From there, it went everywhere, and not a single story ran my horseshit quote. They all managed to include the same one from Rhonda, though, about how she liked to pretend she was on his bicycle and ride him across the finish line.

Honestly, if I believed Adrian was capable of sleeping with a twit like her, I never would have gone out with him in the first place. I could show her a thing or two about a sense of adventure. I wasn't going to trumpet those things to the media, though. I turned my phone to airplane mode so no one would pick up a media call.

My sole goal for the day was to keep Sam and Annabelle from seeing any of that garbage. I'd spent the past two years helping Juniper Media get savvy to the ways of online news, and I knew Internet trash gives over to something new every fifteen minutes, and that weekend stories die before Monday. Newspapers don't print this crap, either. So I just had to get us through the weekend. At least. Sam and Annabelle would be consumed with birthday distractions, and my parents I didn't need to worry about. They didn't get online much, especially when they visited us. Mom would be baking and decorating Sam's 33 cake all morning, and then we'd leave for the party.

My prevention plan started to gel. I could formulate the rest of it on my run, which I had to get in before Sam woke up. I scrambled out of bed and got ready, dodging Mom by staying out of the kitchen. Five minutes later I loped out the door and into the heat and humidity with Adrian's seventies rock playlist cranked as high as I could bear on my Shuffle.

Sixty-seven minutes later, my Garmin read 9:30 a.m. I took the fastest shower of my life, listening for sounds of life upstairs. Nothing from Sam yet. Annabelle would return from swim practice any minute. The clock on the oven read 9:59 when I made it into the kitchen. Mom's cake was on the counter, but she and Papa and their car were nowhere to be seen.

Sam wanted Belgian waffles for his birthday brunch, but that would have to wait until I disabled the wifi router in the home office. I went in and eyeballed the setup, looking for a way to stop its signal that my tech-savvy teens wouldn't be able to diagnose without serious effort. I decided my best bet was to pull the phone plug out of the socket just far enough to lose contact, but not so far that you could see it with the naked eye behind seven bajillion other cords. I crawled under the desk and grabbed the DSL cord, gently pinched the plastic tab and eased it out until it unclicked, and left it barely hanging from the socket.

"What are you doing, Mom?" My head cracked into the underside of the desk, and I crawled out, grimacing. Sam was standing six inches behind me. "Wifi is out. I was trying to fix it."

"Is it working now? I have friends coming over before the party, and we need it for League of Legends."

Caca del toro. "Let's test it."

I sat down at the desktop between our floor-to-ceiling wooden shelves of books and Sam hovered over my shoulder. The flashing red lights on the router already told the story—no wifi—but I made a show of pulling up the Firefox browser. "Nope. It's dead. I've tried everything. I'll call AT&T and report an outage."

"Ah, man." Sam kicked an Amazon box an inch across the floor with his toe. Then he stood up straighter. "I'll see if we can play at someone else's house."

"Don't you think you can live without League of Legends for one day?"

"It's my birthday." Sam's voice sounded more whiney thirteen than I-think-I'm-grown-up sixteen.

If I let him game at someone else's house, he'd have Internet access and he might see a story flash across a news page. I thought fast. "Well, it was going to be a surprise, but I'd decided to let you pick up your friends—with me in the front seat, of course—and we'd all go to the batting cage and have hot dogs and canned-cheese nachos before we head out to paintball." It was an Adrian-inspired plan that I'd regret when I got the credit card bill.

I headed into the kitchen. Sam followed me and thought about it while I mixed the waffle batter. "Okay."

I breathed an inner sigh of relief. Now, if I could just convince my parents and Annabelle to come with us, maybe I could insulate them all from my new reality.

Chapter Seven

Sunday morning at six fifteen, right on my mother's schedule, my parents finally left. As soon as they backed out of the driveway I ran for my bicycle gear and straight back to the Jetta. I was desperate to fly along the Church of the Open Road, the name Adrian had given our Sunday morning rides. That day I would ride it by myself for the first of many times to come. I couldn't just wake up one day in October, hop on a plane to Hawaii, and say, "Let's do this." I would continue training twenty-five hours a week over the next two months. I had to train, and I had to do it alone.

Adrian used to ride solo when I couldn't join him, but I never had. What would I do if I got a flat tire or a broken chain and I couldn't fix what my semi-pro bicycle mechanic husband had made a non-issue before? What if I was chased by a dog? When a pony-sized spotted mastiff stormed us on one of our Sunday rides, Adrian rode between the beast and me, let it get within two feet of him, and squirted it in the face with his water bottle. The dog spun away with a yelp, tucked its tail, and sprinted for home. I'd frozen.

I had my water bottles with me, but it didn't matter. I wasn't scared of dogs. All I wanted was to get on my bicycle. Adrian had been gone for ten days, and I pretty much didn't feel anything anymore, except hollow. Not relieved that my parents left, not proud that we pulled off a good-enough birthday for Sam, not angry about Rhonda Dale trying to snatch a humiliating fifteen minutes of fame off of Adrian and me. At least the kids hadn't found out about her. FML, as Sam would say.

Dying didn't sound as scary as it used to. Besides, no one really needed me. Sam had his birth father, Annabelle had her grandparents. Everyone had someone. I wouldn't be reckless—I didn't have the energy to kill myself—I just didn't care which direction the needle swung between life and death.

Once I got out on the roads around Waller, though, all that started to change. My body warmed up and the ride felt good. The gently rolling hills, gnarly oaks, and tall pines awakened my senses. I was sorry I hadn't thought to go out there earlier. Every breath I drew in filled my void and brought me a sense of Adrian's presence as I flew low to the ground, until it was close to joy. I could feel him out there, feel a connection to him. I could have ridden to Alaska and back.

We loved to go out there early in the morning, when the fog hovered over the ground. It began to lift, and I picked up speed as I passed a mobile home with a hand-lettered yard sign that said, "Ain't nothing here worth your life." Almost immediately beyond the trailer homes was a grand, gated entrance to a ranch with magnificent horses. I'd been horse crazy as a kid, for the horses at my dad's clinic and my own little quarter horse, Joey, and the Waller ranches were my favorite part of the route. On cooler mornings, Adrian and I watched the quarter horses run through the fields with their tails held high. Donkeys lived at almost all of the horse ranches, paired to the flightiest horses to keep them calm, but I always thought they looked like status symbols, an "I'm so cool I have my own donkey" sort of thing.

Adrian had gotten a kick out of them. "Michele, I guess that makes me your ass."

I laughed, remembering, and warmth flooded me from the inside out.

When I was deep in my memory trance and out as far in the boondocks as I could go—about twenty miles from the car—an old white Ford Taurus pulled up beside and around me. Startled, I swerved. I nearly crashed as it accelerated and drove on. I steadied La Mariposa before I tried to change direction again.

A car horn blared in front of me.

"Hey!" The rush of wind and the engine of a truck muffled my yell. A beater pickup truck was heading straight at me. The driver held his hand high in a one-fingered salute.

I heard Adrian's voice and time stopped.

"You want to know how I survived that head-on, Michele? I jumped the bike, like hopping over a big speed bump. I didn't let the car or my bicycle dictate my fall."

Was this now, was it for real? I answered, although whether it was aloud or only in my mind, I didn't know: *"I've never had a fall. I can't even squirt water at a dog!"*

"You'll get your chance. Everyone does. My money is on you."

I jerked my handlebars to the right and ditched my bicycle as it hit the ground, twisting my ankles to uncleat and going into a tuck-and-roll into a grassy patch of wildflowers. My chin strap pulled hard as my roll forced the helmet around on my head, but that was the worst of it. I ended up facedown in the grass. The truck honked again and sped away.

"Adrian?" My voice sounded tiny in the quiet.

No answer.

He had been there. I was sure of it. I rolled over and stared up at a sky the color of bluebonnets. It was strangely peaceful, lying there in my bed of green with a warm afterglow of Adrian, no one in the world knowing where I was. My heart didn't hurt as much. I could have stayed there forever. That part seemed real. The Taurus and the truck didn't.

After lying there for God knows how long, I snapped back. If I didn't get moving, the fire ants would eat me alive. I'd promised Annabelle a new outfit for her first day of school. I had to keep Sam from taking a joyride before he got his license. A heavy sigh burst out of me, and I summoned my will and began testing all my movable parts. Everything worked, I had only minor scrapes, and nothing really hurt. I wiped the dirt and grass off my hands onto the leg of my white bicycle shorts. My pulse throbbed in my temples and my insides started doing their winding-up thing. I wanted to scream the F word, but I couldn't choke it out. Chingase, I thought instead. Chinga the damn truck driver, and chinga the Taurus driver, too. My first solo ride, and I had to ditch or be pancaked because of another damn Taurus. Maybe this wasn't even the same car, maybe none of these Tauruses were the same car, and maybe Tauruses didn't even matter. None of the drivers were blond, and Detective Young's witness said the vehicle was a Ford F150.

Well, chinga him, too.

"Adrian?" I said out loud. I listened with all my senses.

Nothing. My heart plummeted back down to the pit it now lived in.

Chinga everybody. I got up and grabbed La Mariposa and rode back to my car alone.

***

That afternoon I took Annabelle and Sam to Fadi's for Mediterranean food. Sam's moods had pinballed from happy to angry to forlorn to manic, and Annabelle was jetting off to New York in a week and might never come back. I needed to get a fix on both of them, to keep them close to me, so although I didn't feel like eating, I would make a good show of it. We would recharge, then head back to work and our new normals the next day. Or at least that was how I imagined it.

Sam grabbed a tray and slammed it down on the rails. Annabelle gathered her silverware and napkin with no sign that she'd noticed, but without allowing me to make eye contact with her. My tension ratcheted up. I recognized the warnings. Adrian had tried to get me into meditation, but everything in me resisted it. He'd settled for visualization and breathing exercises. Mostly I'd shined him on. I hadn't even participated in the breathing exercises in Lamaze. But now and then I used his tricks. This was one of those nows.

I pictured the bluebonnet sky from earlier that morning, my back nestled in sun-warmed grass, my hand in Adrian's and the length of his body lined up against mine. Then I breathed in time with a slow ten-count.

"Ma'am? Any dips?" The server had an edge to his tone.

"Oh, yes, sorry. Jalapeño hummus, please."

I pushed my tray as I continued to breathe and order, mentally ticking off Adrian's favorites, as well. He would get the lentil salad, and he never passed on fruit for dessert. Two chicken kabobs, oversized orders of eggplant, broccoli, and rice. When we reached the end of the line, the server handed me three heaping plates. I looked at them. One for me, two for Adrian, just like always. Had I ordered aloud for him? Rather than explain I was losing my mind, I took the plates and some to-go boxes.

Neither Annabelle nor Sam had spoken a word to me since we entered the restaurant. They went to find a seat while I paid, and when I joined them, they didn't look up. Great. Okay, I'd try to get them talking.

"Your outfit looks fantastic on you, Belle. You made a good choice." The green peasant blouse matched her eyes and set off her amazing blonde hair, and hopefully people would look up at that, instead of down at the impressive length of thigh displayed by her new skirt.

She moved some potatoes around on her plate with the tines of her fork. "Thank you." Her voice was small and polite.

"So, do you have any plans to go out with friends in the next week?"

She wriggled a little in her chair. "Maybe."

"Really? Who?"

"You don't know him."

"Describe him, then."

Annabelle looked up, but at Sam, who was looking back at her now. "His name is Jay, he's a year older than me, and he just moved here. He started with our swim team this week." She finally turned to me, and excitement crept into her voice. "He's going to swim for the University of Texas next year. Like Dad."

My throat constricted. "He sounds interesting. Has he asked you out?"

She nodded. "Last night." She smiled, with teeth.

Last night? What did she do last night? I thought she said she was hanging out with friends. "That's great!"

Sam interrupted, his tone acid. "Does he know you're moving to New York in a week?"

She glared at him. "No, butthead, I haven't told him that yet. But I will, soon."

I forced a smile to match hers. "When can we meet him?"

Sam didn't give her a chance to answer. "I don't want to meet him."

I gasped. "Sam!"

"You don't have to be mean." Annabelle's bottom lip protruded just a little bit.

"What? You're leaving our family. What does it matter if we meet him or not?" He shoved a pita in his mouth and ripped a piece off with a twist of his head. He went on with his mouth full. "Besides, Mom, you probably don't have time to do stuff with Belle and him now since you're such a media whore."

Annabelle dropped her fork on the floor.

I dropped my jaw. "What did you say?"

He chewed, calmer now. "You heard me, and it's not like I'm the only one that feels that way, is it, Belle?" He took another bite of pita and shoveled rice in after it.

I looked down at my untouched food and ordered myself not to cry. I didn't entirely disagree, but it wasn't the whole story—only I hadn't told it to the kids, just that I had a TV show to do and when I'd be back. "Belle?"

She looked daggers at Sam, then back at her food. "Well, not really, but sort of. I mean, it would be nice if you hadn't gone to New York last week. Or if you'd come shopping with me instead of just meeting me to pay for the clothes. And Dad just died, and you're on TV about the book, and talking like nothing's wrong."

Sam interrupted again. "Using him to sell your book. Classy, Mom."

I gripped the edge of the table and leaned in. "That's enough, Sam. You are entitled to your opinion, but you're not entitled to be disrespectful." I dialed it back. "Adrian wanted this book, he wanted people to read what he wrote, and I can't help it that it came out one day before he died. I have obligations to the publisher, and—" I stopped. I sounded like Scarlett.

I tried another tack. "I know it's hard right now. Nothing makes sense—to me, either. Someday it will get easier. I'm not sure when, but it will. Until then, all we have is each other." I fought to keep a tremor out of my voice. "I loved Adrian. I will always love him. I'm so sad it's hard to get out of bed. I promise I won't do anything I think he wouldn't want. I love you guys, too, and I need to talk to you more. I'm sorry. I should have explained why I had to do the TV stuff."

"It's all over the Internet." Annabelle's voice cracked. She looked up at me and wiped away tears with a savage jerk of her forearm across her face. "That woman. What people are saying they did together. Maybe if you'd stop going on TV, they'd quit talking about him like this?"

So much for protecting them.

"Was our family all a big lie?" Sam hissed, soft at first but louder with each word. "Were we a lie?"

"What? No! Of course not." My voice escalated to a shriek. "She's lying, she's crazy!" Heads turned and I looked out the window, trying to think of what to say when I didn't even know what to think. The angle of the sun through the windows made me squint, so it took a moment for me to figure out that someone was standing at the driver's door of my Jetta. I shaded my eyes with my hand. Someone was trying all the doors on my car. I jumped to my feet, knocking my chair over backwards.

"Michele, what's wrong?"

I dashed out the door and burst onto the sidewalk.

There was no one there.

I trotted out into the strip center parking lot, my head swiveling back and forth, searching, searching. Nothing. No one. What the hell?

"Mom?" Sam yelled, which got my attention. He hates a scene.

I turned back toward the restaurant. Annabelle and Sam stood together on the sidewalk. Tall and dark. Short and pale. Perfect opposites.

God, I couldn't take it. I put my hands on either side of my forehead and squeezed my temples. The kids stared at me, their eyes wide and fearful. I had to do better.

"I thought I saw someone breaking into our car."

"Where?" Sam bowed up with testosterone.

"False alarm." I crossed the parking lot to them and pulled them both close to me, Sam towering over me by a head and Annabelle eye-to-eye. They didn't resist. Annabelle even patted my back, the way I usually patted hers. I patted them both. I lowered my voice to a stage whisper. "It's possible I'm a little overwrought." Annabelle and I giggled.

Sam's body yielded a fraction and he eased farther into our group hug. "Guys, this is starting to look weird."

"Deal with it, butthead."

"Yeah, if you want me to take you to get your driver's license to-morrow, deal with it."

"If you pass, you can take me to morning practice on Tuesday."

Sam snorted. "Four a.m.? I don't think so."

We broke apart and headed back into the restaurant. I needed to make it okay for the two of them to move on. I realized I could give Sam the 4Runner instead of saddling him with the Jetta.

"Which car do you want to take for the test? Mine or Adrian's?"

"Um, Adrian's, I guess. If that's okay with you."

What else could I do?

We packed our to-go boxes and headed back outside, Sam and Annabelle in deep conversation, me on the outside once again.

One step forward into the great alone.

Chapter Eight

I stared at the computer screen in my Juniper office Monday morning. I didn't like what I was seeing, but I had no choice. I clicked "Continue" on Southwest.com, searching for a Houston-to-LaGuardia flight. Less than two weeks had passed since I'd lost Adrian, and in just a few days Annabelle would leave, too. Diane had kindly let me handle the travel arrangements and front the funds to send my Annabelle away.

She'd sent me an email: *"Be sure to send receipts with Annabelle when she comes so I can send you a check."*

See Michele play the role of the help, I thought. I sighed and fingered my locket.

The flights scrolled down my screen. I was trying to find a flight as late in the day as possible, but early enough to get her to LaGuardia in time for dinner in the city, as instructed. It shouldn't have been so hard to choose a flight, but I was still struggling through brain fog. Finally, I clicked to purchase.

"What are you up to?" I heard from the doorway.

I had managed to avoid Brian when I came in, but my luck had apparently run out. When I didn't answer, he came in and sat down, looking at my monitor. "Oh, a vacation!"

"Plane ticket to New York for Belle."

"Is she visiting colleges up there?"

"No, she's moving in with her grandparents."

He jerked his head back. "Are you all right with that?"

"What do you think?"

"Sorry, of course you're not. So sorry."

I stood up and pulled the papers from my overflowing inbox and starting going through them. One touch and done. I threw the first paper in the trash. The second paper was a keeper, a condolence letter from one of our writers. I pulled out my file drawer and grabbed a new folder, then opened my purse to get the black Sharpie I'd been carrying to sign books. I wrote "Adrian" on the tab before slipping the letter inside.

"Do you have to let her go? Legally?"

I straightened up from my sorting job. "Yes. I'm only a stepmother. I have no legal relationship to her now that Adrian is gone."

"Maybe if you fought, she'd back off. Bluff her, you know?"

"Belle's grandparents *want* her. They're family, they're the closest link to her mother. This is important to her." I picked at a hangnail. "I just hope it lives up to her expectations."

He bit his lip. "Do you think you should get a lawyer, maybe see if she'll do a visitation agreement?"

Really, I knew Brian thought of me as family, but I was not a little girl. I let just a hint of prissiness into my voice. "It's only one year, her senior year. Then she goes off to college anyway."

He nodded and stopped talking. I resumed filing. One touch and done. One touch and done. *Leave,* I willed him. But tick, tick went the clock with Brian planted there, watching me.

"Are you going to be okay, you know, money-wise?"

I slanted my eyes up to him. "Yes." Not that it was his or anyone's business, but Adrian had left his life insurance to me, along with a sizable chunk from his former wife. And I'd sell the house when things settled down. Sam and I didn't need all that space or the reminders of what we'd lost.

"Good. I want you to take this first day back as a warm-up. We'll get you back in the game tomorrow."

I nodded. "Fine. Thank you."

He cleared his throat. "I wanted to congratulate you on your book sales. They're fantastic."

I nodded again.

"Scarlett lined up more media for you. She'll be getting in touch with you soon about it. That's work time for you. I mean, don't try to squeeze it in on top of work and your training for Kona."

I looked up and settled my gaze on him, let it linger. Because you and Scarlett cornered me into Kona, I thought, and said nothing.

"I hate to ask, but could you write the pieces Adrian was going to write about it? Obviously they'll have a different hook now."

"Obviously."

"Look, I know I pushed you to jump into the media too fast. You really came through for the team. I'll never forget it."

"Neither will I—nor will my kids, for that matter. Sam called me a media whore yesterday. Belle was a little more polite."

"Oh, God, Michele—"

I jumped to my feet. "I happen to agree with them. But, as you said yourself, I'm nothing if not a team player, the perennial MVP. I will be out there helping you chum for readers, even if it attracts sharks like Rhonda Dale." By the time I got to my last point, my voice could be heard halfway around the building.

Brian's face splotched up, then his neck. He adjusted his collar. "I'm sorry. We really had no way to anticipate a development like her."

My hand sprang up to perch on my hip. "Really, Brian? Because in the world I live in, positive news only plays for ten seconds before the bottom-feeders grab the attention for themselves. If it wasn't her, it would have been someone or something else like her, just as soon as you made me the story. Really, the question now is what will it be next, and when?"

I crumpled back into my chair and let my head drop back against the cushion. "What will hit us next?"

Brian straightened and leaned toward me. "Nothing you can't han-dle."

"How do you know?"

"Anyone who knows you knows that."

I wished I could believe him, but this was coming from the one person most vested in making sure I didn't fall apart. My anger fizzled out, though. Even friends with ulterior motives beat none, and Brian had always been my friend. I had to remember that.

He jumped to his feet and reached inside his Texans Starter jacket, a year-round staple in his wardrobe. "I almost forgot. I have a letter for you. I've had it on my desk for a few days now. There have been a lot of condolence letters, but something about this one felt odd. I'm sure it's nothing, but—" He handed me an envelope addressed to "Michelle Hanson, wife of Adrian Hanson," care of *Multisport Magazine*.

One L Michele, I thought automatically. I took the envelope from his hand and my heart started to pound. It had an ominous aura to it. I swallowed my heartbeat down into my chest, and then—phhhhh— blew it out again, barely. I looked at Brian. "Luckily, there's nothing I can't handle."

"Do you want me to stick around while you open it?"

I nodded, then stalled, looking for my red leather-handled letter opener. I found it in my junk drawer, slit open the envelope, and unfolded the letter onto my blotter. The writing was a print and cursive hybrid in black ink. It looked male to me.

> *Dear Mrs. Hanson:*
>
> *I apologize that I don't know how to send this to you, other than to the magazine, but it's appropriate in a way, since that's where I read your husband's wonderful articles about his two great passions: triathlon and you. Adrian's articles really spoke to me. I first contacted him after a column he wrote on personal bests a few years ago, and we have corresponded since then.*
>
> *I am so glad I got to meet the two of you face-to-face at your launch party. I considered him a friend and kindred spirit. I send you my deepest condolences, in what I know must be a time of incredible pain.*
>
> *I will miss Adrian and his words.*
>
> *With my deepest sympathy,*
>
> *Connor Dunn*

I closed my eyes.

"Are you okay?"

I'd forgotten Brian was standing there. "Yes, I am." I formed the words slowly, testing them to see if they were true. "It's a beautiful condolence letter from one of his readers." I glanced back down. "More than a reader, I guess. A pen pal. I met him at our launch party." I left out the part about how weird the guy acted, and that I was sure

Adrian lied to me about their conversation. I wished I hadn't even thought it.

"Adrian did bring out the A game in people."

"Yes, he did. He sure brought out the best in me."

Brian stuck his hands in his pockets and rocked up on his toes. "I'll leave you alone, then."

"Thanks."

After he left, I folded the letter and put it back in its envelope. It felt strange, but was innocuous enough. I slid it into my new Adrian folder.

My computer chirped softly and an email from Detective Young popped up in my inbox. I set Adrian's folder aside. I hadn't heard from Young in a week. He'd called Adrian's death a homicide, but from where I was sitting, he didn't seem to think it mattered much.

Sometimes this made me mad. Other times, I liked not seeing HPD light up my phone. I was all over the place. One part of me couldn't believe anyone would hurt Adrian for any reason. Another part of me saw white Tauruses and platinum blondes lurking on every street corner. Still another part didn't care how it happened or why—whoever did this stole my life away. Even if it was a complete accident, even if Adrian caused it by riding out in front of a car, what kind of person doesn't jump out and administer CPR—or at least call for help? That was criminal to me, and I wanted justice.

Yet another part of me whispered that justice wouldn't bring Adrian back, that it was a false horizon, that I'd still be lost after I got it. God, my head was a mess.

I clicked on the email.

> *Michele:*
>
> *May I come to your home this evening for a follow-up interview?*
>
> *Detective Young*

I frowned. He wasn't asking to come over for a "follow-up *report*" or "to *talk* about your husband's case." He said for a "follow-up *interview*." I lawyered his email to death, pulling the words apart and putting them back together, looking for the meaning behind them.

I had a case once where a child who needed a cutting-edge leukemia treatment was denied coverage by her insurance company, whose executives held the contracts to their chests in court like armor, brandishing their definitions and treatment codes. Their words killed an eight-year-old little girl, and I'd represented them. It was the last case I took before I moved from the law to editing, where I could exert more control over language.

Words matter, and I didn't like the ones Young was using.

Chapter Nine

The kids had almost finished cleaning up after their Taco Bell takeout when I saw Detective Young's dark city-issued sedan park in front of our house.

I hollered to the kids. "Take the trash outside." The smell of Grilled Stuft Burritos turns sour quickly. Then again, I have a bionic nose, which isn't a good thing, and was most of the reason I didn't follow Papa into veterinary medicine. I headed for the front door and swung it open before Young rang the bell. He wasn't alone.

"Michele, this is my partner, Detective Marchetti. He just got back from vacation, but he's up to speed."

"Detective." I shook Marchetti's hand. "I'm Mrs. Hanson."

He nodded. "Mrs. Hanson." Marchetti was shorter than Young by four inches but heavier by forty pounds. And sweatier. Not many people love Houston when it hits a hundred degrees and ninety-eight percent humidity, but Marchetti wasn't holding up at all. I escorted them into my dining room and went to the kitchen for a pitcher of ice water and glasses.

We settled into high-backed green chairs at the glass-topped dining room table, the detectives on one side and me on the other. A gallery of family photos watched over us like a jury. I wondered if that made me the defendant. Young and Marchetti looked at each other. Marchetti nodded.

Young arranged a yellow pad in front of him. He didn't look up. "I hope we're not keeping you from your triathlon training or your busy book-shilling television schedule."

I held in my snort. Well, I guess I knew who was going to play bad cop. Why play bad cop with me when he knew I didn't kill my husband, when I was a victim of the crime, too? Was this a new strategy with grieving widows? "Not at all. I just managed to squeeze you in."

He grunted, then said, "We need to be thorough, Michele, so I'm going to ask you some harder questions tonight, just so we can dot all the i's and cross all the t's."

I checked my tension meter: 7.5. Manageable. I just had to remember to breathe and retreat to visualization. "That will be fine, Kevin." He looked up at me, and I thought I saw him almost smile. Well, at least the asshole had a sense of humor.

He stayed seated, but it was clear he had the floor as he went back over ground we'd already covered. Did Adrian have enemies? No. Who did he consider his closest friends and associates? I listed them. He moved into more pointed questions fast.

"What kind of relationship did Adrian have with his former wife's family?"

"It was fine. They live in New York and had very little interaction with him."

He asked his next question almost before I got my answer out while Marchetti took notes. "What about the relationship between Adrian and his daughter?"

"Superb. They amazed me."

"And with your son?"

"Sam? Good. They didn't fight. They'd disagree sometimes, but it never got ugly, which is more than I can say for Sam and his father." Which reminded me that I needed to answer Robert's text from earlier in the day; he was concerned about Sam and wanted to talk. Get in line.

"Okay, let's talk about your ex-husband, then. Did he resent Adrian? Feel threatened by him in anyway?"

"Robert? No. He and Adrian got along fine when they saw each other. Their paths didn't cross much." Young's pace nudged my tension up to an eight. He never broke eye contact, looked at notes, or allowed a pause. I'd faced worse as an attorney, but this was about me.

He fired off another question. "Of course, we'll need contact info for each person we talk about. Maybe if you could just keep a list as we go, and then when we finish you can pull those together for us. So where were we? Oh, yes, with you. Did Adrian ever cheat on you?"

"No."

"You're sure?"

"Very."

"No matter what I read about this Rhonda Dale?"

I snapped at him. "Asked and answered, Detective."

"Tell me about his life insurance."

"I'm the beneficiary of $500,000, about $100,000 of which I'll use to pay for Belle's college."

"His will?"

My answers were coming out faster than his questions now. Easy, girl. "What about it?"

"Tell me about his estate."

"Well, he has half of our common possessions—house, cars, personal stuff—and a few hundred thousand in savings."

He raised his eyebrows. "That's a lot for a writer-triathlete."

"His dead wife was wealthy."

"So who gets what now?"

"Everything goes to me."

"No one else?"

"No one."

"But you gave your son Adrian's truck?"

What the hell? How did he know that? "It was mine to give."

"And, of course, I can have copies of all the documents we've talked about?"

"Of course."

"Including financial records."

"No problem."

"And we can have your phone records?"

I shifted in my seat for the first time, thinking before I answered. "Why do you need them?"

"As part of our investigation, Mrs. Hanson." At least he'd dropped the use of my first name.

"Honestly, I don't care. Whatever helps."

"Will this include the kids' phones as well?"

"You didn't ask that."

"I am now."

"Take them. I don't care."

"We'll need to copy your hard drives, too, the desktop," he pointed toward the office across the hall, "and any other computer Adrian used. Passwords, too."

I thought about it. Just copies, I wouldn't lose my data. "Okay."

"And after you and I are done, I need to talk to your kids."

"All right."

If he didn't rule out these issues, I told myself, they wouldn't be able to move on to the real ones. And to finding the suspects.

He went on. "Teenage boys are often jealous of their mothers' boy-friends."

What? "Adrian wasn't my boyfriend. He was my husband. For four years, he was my husband. He was my boyfriend for one year before that."

"Yes, I understand. And, I would like to confirm the days and times Sam worked at his lifeguarding job anyway, to satisfy my lieuten-ant."

"Do you need my permission?"

"No, but it would make it easier, and it would keep any red flags from going up."

"Is this based on anything real—anything other than gender and age profiling of my son?"

"Oh, no, of course not, although he got your husband's car, and that can be important to a boy his age."

"I want to tell you to shove it. You can't even begin to know how badly I want to." My emotions swelled and lifted until I was nearly levitating above the table. "But I want you off of my son, who did nothing, and the faster we 'dot all your i's and cross all your little t's,'" I made exaggerated quote signs with my fingers over my head, "the sooner you will be. Permission granted. Sam?" I called to my son in a voice I hoped didn't scare him.

The detectives didn't react. They probably trampled over grieving widows and mothers every day.

Sam walked in.

"Remember Detective Young from the funeral? He and Detective Marchetti need to ask you some follow-up questions. I'm going to sit here with you, so try to just relax and listen and think. Their questions might seem odd, but it's going to be all right, I promise. Just tell them the truth."

Belatedly, I realized I could have called another attorney for Sam, but I knew my son, and he didn't hurt Adrian. "And just so you two know, Detectives, I am representing my son in this interview. Sam, if I tell you not to answer something, don't. We can stop anytime, so if you need a break, or if this gets to be too much, just tell me."

Sam's eyes had turned into Os within Os, rims, orbs, irises, pupils all enlarged, framed by his impossibly long lashes. "Okay."

Young lifted one eyebrow. "Representing him?"

"As his attorney." He raised both brows now, his lips puckered. "What, your research didn't tell you I practiced law?"

His expression didn't flicker. "Noted." Young gestured at Marchetti.

Ah, so paunchy Marchetti would lead. He was a complete enigma to me. I couldn't believe they were wasting their time on Sam, and anger burbled in my gut. Temper was a luxury I couldn't afford, however. I issued myself a stern warning: You're on, Attorney Lopez. Forget the mother stuff.

Marchetti inclined his head toward Sam. "Hello, Sam. I'm Detective Marchetti. Detective Young and I are partners. We're trying to figure out who killed your mom's husband. So I have to ask you some questions, and it is really important that you answer them with the truth. The whole truth. Can you do that?"

"I guess." His voice cracked. "I mean, yes."

"Good. Let's get started in the same place we do with everyone: where you were when it happened. So, where were you from three forty-five to four fifteen p.m. on the Friday before last, when your stepfather was killed?"

Sam looked at me, clearly scared. I nodded at him. He dropped his eyes down to the table. "Umm, at baseball practice."

The detective had been scribbling notes, but he looked up to stare Sam in the eye. "Can you give me the name of someone who can verify that, son?"

He's not your son, I thought.

Sam licked his lips. "Billy Mays."

"Who is he, your coach?"

"Uh, no, he's on the team. He's my friend."

"Give me the name of your coach, if you could, please."

Marchetti's fake-friendly voice made me want to punch him.

"Coach Metcalfe. Are you going to call him?"

"Yes, we are."

"Well, he doesn't take attendance. I don't know if he'll remember whether I was there or not."

"Who would?"

"I don't know. Billy, maybe."

"Okay, son, we'll remember that when we ask Coach Metcalfe about it."

Precious jumped up on the dining room table. She catwalked the length of the table and sat by Sam, then turned her unblinking eyes on me. *"You have to make them stop,"* she seemed to say. *"I know. I will. I'll try,"* I said back to her in my mind. I was lying, though. I could do nothing. I had no power, and even the cat knew it. Marchetti wasn't crossing the line, and Sam needed to answer his basic questions. Annabelle would have to do the same.

"Do you know of anyone you think would have wanted to hurt your stepfather?"

"No."

Marchetti wiped perspiration from his lip. "Did your mother tell you that the driver who killed Adrian was a teenage boy?"

Sam's mouth made an O. "Uh—"

His mother hadn't, because she didn't know that it was true, no matter what some witness said. But this explained some of their interest in badgering Sam. "Or a young man in his early twenties," I said. "And no, I didn't tell him."

"How's your new car?"

I cut Sam off. "Don't go there, Detective." Sam looked at me, wide-eyed.

"Did you know your stepfather was cheating on your mom? I mean, you know now, don't you? From the Internet?"

I jumped to my feet, but he kept talking as I yelled over him. "That's it! We're done here."

Sam leaped up, too, and he shouted over both of us. "No, he didn't! You don't know what you're talking about!" Precious was pacing back and forth in front of him, her tail puffed and whipping behind her.

The three of us finished at the same time, Sam and I standing together, the detectives seated, watching. I swallowed, fighting to regain control. I turned to Sam and reached up to his clothes-hanger shoulder and squeezed. "Thank you, Sam. You can go now."

His eyes looked wet. He nodded and left. I heard his feet pounding the stairs to his room and wanted to run after him. I crossed my arms. "Is that how it's going to go, then? You're going to traumatize my kids?"

Young stepped back into the lead. "Annabelle's not your kid, is she?"

"She is in my eyes."

"Not in the eyes of the law. And she's next. Can you get her for us, please?"

"No, I think we're done here."

"Fine with me. We can do this tomorrow down at the station."

"Have fun by yourself at your party. I don't have to produce her."

"Oh, I'd forgotten, you're the attorney. A little conflict of interest, don't you think?"

In my mind, I went for each of their throats with hands that gripped like steel. I had the strength of ten Micheles and I lifted the two of them up against the wall, one in each hand, making them gasp for air like catfish. In real life, I smiled at them as wide as I could and said nothing.

Marchetti pulled at his waistband. Fat bastard. "I know we've just met, but I've got to say you're acting like this family has something to hide. These are standard questions."

"They were up until you goaded my son with Internet gossip like you were trying to break down your chief suspect. You broke my trust."

"With all due respect, we don't actually know whether that is gossip or not."

"Well, I do. And I think I'd already told *Kevin* that woman was stalking my husband. She's nuts. I hope you're looking at her half as hard as you looked at Sam."

Young rejoined the fray. "Even though we have a description of the car and driver, I can assure you we are running a thorough investigation. In fact, we're going to talk to your father this week."

"What?"

"If your husband cheated on you for a year and your father knew, I think he'd be pretty upset, don't you? Maybe angry enough to do something about it. Didn't he grow up in the Valley? The Mexican mafia is extremely loyal, and has a long reach."

"Oh, Jesus. You've lost your mind. My father is a respected veterinarian, a Texas A&M graduate. He's not in the Mexican mafia. My boss has more reason to kill Adrian than Papa does."

Young grabbed that with both hands. "Your boss? The guy I met at your office, the one who sent me the security video?"

I had no idea about any video, but I knew Young had met Brian. "He wouldn't. I just said that to emphasize how crazy it is to suspect my father."

Young snapped his fingers. "He's the publisher for your book, isn't he? He's the one who stands to make money from it."

"Books make far less money than you'd imagine."

Young smiled and scribbled notes on his pad. I knew Brian had nothing to do with Adrian's death, so I allowed myself a delicious moment imagining him being worked over by Young and Marchetti. A balancing of the cosmic scales. Young looked up. "Good. Good. Thank you. Now, let's get this over with here. Let us talk to Annabelle. You have my promise that Marchetti will restrain himself."

Everything had gone so wrong so quickly. I wanted this over with, and eventually they were going to talk to Annabelle. Better to bite the hollowpoint than take one from the blind side. I'd shut things down the second Marchetti went off script. If I knew Annabelle, she was hunkered down in the living room listening to every word. "Belle, can you come in here, please?"

Sure enough, Annabelle immediately rounded the corner, as quiet as the cat. I made the introductions and explanations and she sat beside me with Precious in her lap, stroking the cat behind her ears.

Marchetti pulled a napkin from my dispenser in the middle of the table. He dabbed at the back of his neck and his forehead. When he started talking, he asked the same basic questions of Annabelle that he had asked Sam, but in a gentler tone. She answered them in an earnest tremor that threatened to make my lips quiver, too.

Marchetti looked at me. "So, Annabelle, you don't know of anyone that would have wanted to hurt your dad, do you, like an old girlfriend or someone that was jealous of your mother? Anyone?"

Annabelle shook her head no. "No one. My dad was awesome." And then she started to cry, just tears at first, and then sobs, soft hiccupy sobs. I scooted my chair up against hers to slip one arm around her and guide her head to my shoulder with the other. "Is that all, gentlemen?"

"It is. Thank you. Here's my list of the documents you agreed to get for us. Please let me know if there are any developments, and we'll be in touch."

Young spoke. "Is there anything else we haven't asked you about that you want to tell us?"

I pressed my lips together hard and shook my head.

"Goodnight, then. We'll see ourselves out." He picked up his notebook and pen and stood.

Marchetti lumbered to his feet, too. "Ma'am." He lifted a pretend hat from his head.

I dipped my head in return, and they left. I patted Annabelle's back gently as the anguish came off her in waves. Mine vibrated inside me like a plucked wire.

I knew only one way to deal with this. Run. Run hard, run fast, run away from these feelings.

"Sweetie, are you going to be okay?"

Annabelle's head nodded against my shoulder. Her words came out muffled. "Can I go get ice cream with Jay?"

"Be home by ten thirty. You've got early practice."

"I will. I promise."

We got up and walked up the stairs together.

I stuck my head into Sam's dark room. "Sam?" I whispered.

No answer.

I walked in and peered at his face. There was just enough light from the hallway for me to see his eyes were closed. "Sam?"

Nothing.

"If you can hear me, I'm going to go run. Belle is getting ice cream with her new boyfriend. I'll be home in an hour or two, okay?"

He snuffled. Either he was truly asleep or a great faker. I knew I shouldn't leave him, but I couldn't do anything for him while he was sleeping, and he needed to rest. And I needed to run, to fly with my own two feet.

***

I left in a rush as dusk settled over Houston. I forgot my phone, Shuffle, and water bottle, but I didn't go back for them. I drove to Memorial Park, to the mountain bike paths. Adrian and I never ran there after dark, and I never ran there alone. Tree roots crisscrossed the paths aboveground, and I'd taken tumbles in daylight. The deep woods spooked me and were peopled with crazies and homeless people, two categories that sometimes overlapped. That night I didn't care. To hell with the bad guys and tree roots, to hell with all the promises I made to Adrian that I'd take care of myself. I needed a punishing run, I needed solitude, and I even needed the danger.

I took off much faster than my training or even my racing pace, craving the searing of breath in my lungs. I longed to hurt, to feel my heart exploding against my ribs. I hadn't eaten anything since breakfast, and I ordered my weakness and hunger to go sit in a corner of my mind. I charged up and down the steep banks of the Buffalo Bayou, pushing myself, seriously anaerobic with my muscles screaming for oxygen and my parched mouth inverting itself as I clawed my way to a thinking- and feeling-free zone. Thinking sucked. Feeling was worse. I wanted numb. I needed numb.

Only numbness eluded me, and a ferocious onslaught of sorrow caught me in the wake of my anger and fear. I crumpled to my knees with my hands on the ground, gasping with dry sobs. I stumbled to my feet again, then leaned over. My hands slid off my sweaty knees. I choked and panted, then jerked myself nearly upright and started running again, ignoring the dirt and pine needles caked in my sweat. I passed a guy on a mountain bike with a headlight on its handlebars. I saw his lips moving—"Are you all right, ma'am?"—but if he was speaking aloud, I didn't hear him, and I pretended I didn't see him, either.

My feet pounded rhythmically. "Gone," they said. "Gone, gone, gone, gone. Adrian is gone. Belle will soon be gone. Sam has Robert, he'll be gone. Everyone's gone. You are gone. You can stay gone if you want to, and no one will notice. You should stay gone. Gone. Gone." And God, how I wanted to make it so. I wanted out of my body, my feeling, my life. Why did I have to keep going? Why did I have to do the hard part? Adrian didn't have to outlive me; he got to skip all this pain. I, I, I had to feel it.

Adrian, help me, my mind screamed as rage surged through me again. I didn't know who to be angry at, and it didn't matter. I wanted my partner there to hold me, to whisper with me in the early mornings, to make love to me when we woke in the middle of the night, to help me handle all the things that were swallowing me alive.

Adrian made life a party, but he did much more than that; he managed the messy situations that drove my pulse into the stratosphere. Adrian had a way with people. He had a way with *me*. For the stuff of high emotion and no answers, I turned to Adrian. When I had trouble getting Sam into a class because I couldn't deal with the woman at the front desk in the high school registrar's office, Adrian took over. When I got in a hopeless deadlock with a belligerent American Airlines gate agent at Intercontinental, Adrian stepped in. CitiMortgage sent us the wrong bill three months in a row and the customer service representative from India who barely spoke English told me the error was mine. I turned to Adrian, and he talked his way through it with them, holding me in his lap and tickling me while he did.

I couldn't handle all of this; I couldn't fix any of it. "It's not my job." The humidity absorbed my scream. I didn't know what to do. So I cried, and I ran harder and faster and farther into the dark woods.

I never checked my Garmin. I could have been running for fifteen minutes or five hours, for all I knew. But I knew it was several miles before my terrors eased at all. Slowly, that blessed numbness I sought came over me. My earthbound feet didn't lift from the ground, but I grew lighter, and I kept going. God knows when, but awareness of my body finally returned to me. And when it did, a searing pain in my left knee that I'd never felt before had taken hold. I considered stopping. Adrian would tell me to stop.

"Listen to your body, Michele. You're your own worst enemy."

"Mind over matter."

"Yes, and your mind should be smart enough to tell your matter to stop when you're injured, or at least slow down and take care of it. You'll set your training back. Ironman training is all about staying healthy and sticking to the schedule."

"Easy for you to say when you're gone."

"I'm not gone. I love you, and I'm right here."

Maybe he was. Maybe he was here now, and that was all the more reason to ignore his advice. Because what would hurt worse? My knee if I kept going, or my heart if I stopped?

So I ran on. For a very long time.

Chapter Ten

Sam and I stood in the newly remodeled contemporary cool lobby of Hobby Airport, five feet away from Annabelle and Jay, who had discovered first love, true love, in a blindingly short period of time. Their impending separation was going down with the drama of *The Notebook.* Jay had to bend halfway over at the waist to hug Annabelle. She buried her face so far into the nape of his neck that it looked like he had a long curly beard. From the heaves of her back, I imagined he'd emerge with a soggy chest.

"You need to go, sweetie." I spoke just loudly enough to be heard over her sobs and just short of shouting. Ah, but I'd been seventeen once, too, and I didn't begrudge her a scene. In fact, current emotionality aside, Annabelle had passed her terrible teens about six months before—not that she hadn't driven Adrian and me bonkers with her rollercoaster moods for a few years prior.

Sam leaned down to my ear. "Is she going to be okay?"

I smiled, sort of. "She won't think so, but she will." Louder, I added, "Belle, time to get in the security line. It's pretty long."

Annabelle pulled her face from Jay and turned her swollen eyes toward us. She leaned into Jay, clinging to his hand. "I can't go. I just can't."

I damned Diane silently with every Spanglish curse word I knew. "Think of it as a visit. You can come back anytime you want, as often as you want." As long as your grandparents will let you, I added silently.

Belle nodded and wiped her eyes. She turned back to Jay. "I'll text you."

"I'll text you, too."

She pulled Jay over to me like her Siamese twin and hugged me with her free arm.

"Take good care of Precious for me." Diane was allergic.

"Of course. I love you, Belle."

"I love you, too, Michele."

She hugged Sam the same way. "Have a great baseball season. You're going to start, I just know it."

"Yeah. I hope they have a good swim team at your new school."

This brought out a gasping sob from Annabelle. Sam looked stricken, and I patted his shoulder.

"Okay, this is it. Goodbye, guys." She let go of Jay's hand. She walked to the security line and showed her boarding pass and driver's license, then looked back at us once more.

"Goodbye, Belle." I mouthed the words and waved.

She waved back. Then she lifted her chin, just like I'd seen her father do a thousand times, and entered the line.

***

Sam didn't say a word to me as we left the airport. I took a call from my mother as we pulled out of short-term parking. She didn't waste time on pleasantries.

"Did you know some policemen hassled your father for an hour last night?" Her voice hurt my ear, and I knew Sam could hear her.

I turned the volume down on my phone and swallowed. "I'm sorry. Is he okay?"

"It was so humiliating. They came to our house, Michele. To our house. They all but accused Edward of killing Adrian. And Sam—they kept asking if Sam had problems with Adrian. It's because of the things that woman has been saying on the Internet. Can't you make her stop?"

Explaining to my mother that the Internet is a forever concept and that the articles had stopped would do no good. She takes pride in rejecting technology. I couldn't get her to use email, much less text. "It will die soon."

I heard Papa's voice in the background. "Tell Itzpa hello for me."

She didn't. "I think your father should sue her, and the police."

That would keep Rhonda going for another two years. "Probably not a good idea."

"I'm going to call a lawyer." The word "real" was omitted, but implied.

My tension meter read 7 at my most tranquil those days. At her words, it went directly to a 9. "Yeah, good idea, Mom." Count to ten, Michele, I told myself. "Uh oh, traffic is bad and I'm on the freeway. I need to hang up now. Love you. Sorry. Bye."

I glanced at Sam and saw tears in his eyes. I'm with you, kid, I thought, I'm with you. I changed the radio station to his Young Country. If he noticed, he didn't give a sign.

***

That afternoon, I shipped Annabelle's car and all her belongings to New York. It was hot and exhausting work, and afterwards, I lay down on the bed in her empty room and cried. Gone. It was like I had dreamed a beautiful dream of Adrian and Annabelle, then woken up. I had nothing Hanson left.

"You don't want another baby, do you?" I asked Adrian a few months after we met.

"Not if you don't, and even then I wouldn't say I wanted one."

"A baby might embarrass Annabelle and Sam with their friends or trap them into years of babysitting."

"And add another eighteen years of parenting for us. We're going to have so much fun when the kids move out. It's fun now, of course, but we'll have less responsibility and more time for naked Twister in the living room."

I laughed, and we played naked Twister, or something close to it. I didn't regret the decision, but for some reason, I missed what would never be as much as I missed what I'd had. Honestly, I could barely take care of Sam or myself anymore, so why did my eyes burn when I thought of it? Somehow I ended up the squat Hispanic version of my tallish blonde mother, with one child and too much on my plate. Brittle. I was brittle and hollow.

***

The next morning at her usual five a.m., Precious walked across my head, and I leapt out of bed for my first workout, and to go find Adrian. "Good morning, love." I kissed my fingertip and pressed it to the top of his urn on my chest of drawers.

Half an hour later, I pushed my locket into the top of my swimsuit and threw my bag down at the edge of the JCC pool for a seventy-five-minute swim. Sometimes I swam those minutes tethered to the edge of the pool with a bungee cord for strength training. Not that day. That day, I planned to swim freestyle the whole time, and hopefully I'd cover nearly all of the 2.4-mile Ironman swim distance. Annabelle could swim it in sixty-five minutes, and Adrian in less than fifty-five. I wasn't born a Hanson, but I did the best I could.

I had a ninety-minute playlist on my MP3 goggles. That gave me a fifteen-minute reserve for warm-up, cool-down, and false-start time, like if I had to jump out and run to the bathroom and left my music running. I couldn't risk the music ending at seventy-three minutes in the pool. I've relied on music during workouts since I started running in law school. My roommate Katie made me a mix tape for my Walkman when she saw me suffering through one- and two-mile runs. Adrian always rolled his eyes at me when I pulled out my Shuffle or MP3 goggles.

"It's a crutch, Michele. Those things aren't allowed in a race."

"I have adrenaline in a race."

"You're stubborn, you know that?"

I smiled at the memory and jumped in the water. U2's "Beautiful Day" kicked off the workout, and Adrian must've been waiting for me, because I heard his voice immediately.

"Bono has the vocal talent of a monkey."

"Don't ruin my music with your opinions, mister."

"It's a beautiful day," Adrian sang, a deliberately off-key parody of Bono.

I smiled underwater. I squeezed my eyes shut until I could almost see him. I felt the water move beside me and a hand trailed the length of my side going the opposite direction, just like Adrian always used to do when we shared a lane. The laps went by one after another, and I rode high on the water, high on the joy of Adrian's presence, his banter, his touch. Before I wanted it to be, the swim was over and I had to get out of the water and leave Adrian behind.

I dunked my head under one more time to smooth back my hair after I removed my goggles.

"Only a hundred meters short of Ironman distance. I might make a swimmer out of you yet. Now you just have to do this offshore in October with two thousand of your closest friends thrashing around."

"You'll be with me, right?"

"Of course."

"Piece of cake, then. Goodbye, my love."

"Goodbye, my beautiful little Butterfly."

Using my upper body, I levered myself up and out of the pool with the help of a good jump onto the warm cement coping. For a split second, I was fifteen years old, laying out beside the city pool with the sun baking my skin.

"Hey, Michele," a voice called to me from across the pool. Not Adrian.

"Hi, Terrence." I waved to the black lifeguard with the high-crowned set of shoulder-length braids. I walked toward the table where I'd left my towel.

"You're limping."

"Huh?" I stopped and looked down at my legs. "Oh, yeah, I guess I am. My knee has been hurting."

"Have you seen a doctor?"

"Nah, I'll be fine."

His voice rose in pitch. "You've got to be kidding me. You work harder than anyone I know. What if you don't take care of it, and you can't do your big race? That happened to me in high school, with my shoulder. I couldn't pitch for eight months. It cost me a scholarship to the University of Houston, and now I'm going to community college part time and living with my mother."

"Luckily I won't have to live with my mother."

"No, I'm serious. You should get it checked out. And I gotta say it—if your man was here, he'd be saying it."

Were, I thought. Were here. "Yeah, I probably should."

Terrence had nailed it. Adrian would have made me a doctor's appointment and taken me in himself. I knew this, but a doctor might tell me to stop training. That I wouldn't do. Still, the doubts—and Adrian's voice—stayed with me. All this training and my need to do Kona for Adrian would be in vain. I let the thoughts keep rolling around in my mind as I drove home to wake Sam up and get ready for the day.

**

Sam scooped Cinnamon Nut Clusters into his mouth and stared at the table. He had gone into a fugue state when we left Belle at the airport.

I tried to make conversation. "I sent the last of Belle's things to her yesterday. The big bedroom is all yours now."

"That's Belle's room." His voice fell to forty below zero. His black stare sucked me into its vortex.

"Okay. I understand."

"No, you don't. You don't even care." He got up and headed for his room, leaving his half-eaten breakfast on the table.

"What's that supposed to mean? I do care."

He didn't answer.

**

Later that morning I worked on my piece for Adrian's column. Second to training, that's when I felt closest to him. Adrian had made an editorial calendar for his columns leading up to Kona. Actually, we had made it together, since planning was more my thing than his. I'd pulled ideas from him one by one and typed them into our shared

Google calendar. I smiled as I pictured him pacing our office, ready to bolt.

This week we had decided he would write on the dangers of heat, dehydration, and exhaustion. Fitting, since it was hot like a steam room in Houston. Like it would be in Kona. We wrote about this in *My Pace or Yours*, so I pulled up the Word file on my computer. Copy and paste is my friend, I thought. Especially since the words Adrian brought to my surface were sinking into the deep again. I'm not a writer. I'm just a word wrangler who lived out her author fantasy through her lover.

Stop it, I told myself. Enough. Just do this.

I wrote an intro:

Hello, readers. This is Adrian's wife, Michele Lopez Hanson, and I think by now you all know that Adrian is gone. It hurts to type that, and it hurts to think it. I am lucky, though, that Adrian left me a way to honor him, and through finishing his Kona columns, and through my own attempt at Kona, my first Ironman ever. Yes, I won a lottery spot, but you won't see my name on the list. I signed up under my middle name as Isabel Hanson so I could keep it a secret from Adrian until our anniversary, and until I knew whether I would actually be able to complete the training. He died a few hours before I would have told him we were doing Kona together.

Adrian had planned to write this week about race delirium brought on by heat, exhaustion, and dehydration. For those of you who like big fancy names, this condition is called hyponatremia. It can kill you. It's a big problem in an event like Kona, and one Adrian knew of firsthand. Adrian and I raced Buffalo Springs this past June, where the temperature got up to 100 degrees and the conditions were much like Kona. He didn't account adequately for the heat and his dehydration, and he became delirious during the run. He came close to collapsing before he was yanked under a medical tent to rehydrate, and he scratched from the race. Yeah, an experienced Kona qualifier succumbed to hyponatremia. Adrian was lucky: he recovered well. Some people don't.

I closed my eyes, remembering. It had scared the hell out of me. Of course Adrian bounced back. That was Adrian. He was invincible. I put my head down on my desk and concentrated on breathing.

The irony of life after Adrian was that as much as I didn't want to let him go, I couldn't have if I tried. Between the column, Brian, Scarlett, the book, and the Ironman tribute, I was in purgatory—with Adrian and without him. I was a wreck. I'd started to believe that if we could just stay connected, I could *do* this, I could be a good mother again—or at least an adequate one—I could survive.

I lifted my head and stared at my screen. Ay chingada. I didn't want to leave the privacy of my office, but I'd sucked down a bottle of Nuun-boosted water, and now I had to go. I clicked save and got up. I looked both ways down the hall from my office door, then made a try for the bathroom.

"Michele, do you have a minute?" Mierda. Brian.

I stopped at his door. "Yes?" He looked like a giant blueberry behind his desk in his Texans jacket.

"Are you all set with Scarlett for next week's publicity schedule?"

Scarlett was dragging me to speak or sign books or answer interview questions a few times a week. It reminded me of when Dad took me to the rodeo when I was seven and a little dappled pony balked at the entrance to the arena. His lathered flanks heaved and the whites of his eyes bulged as they locked on the crowd—not on the barrels he was supposed to run his cloverleaf around. I was that pony. "Yes. Two speeches, two radio shows, and one TV spot." And it is my hell.

"Good. Good. And the training and column are going well?"

He knew the answers to these questions. "Yes, fine."

He looked down at his desk. My eyes followed his. Just a bunch of scribbles I couldn't read upside down. "That Detective Young and his partner showed up here yesterday to talk to me."

"Oh, really?"

"Yeah, they grilled me like a suspect. Scarlett said they did it to her, too."

"We got the same treatment at our house. They told me they're just being thorough."

"I'm sure you're right."

I turned to go, but he said, "One thing, though. The fat partner had a lot of questions about Sam. Sam and Adrian. I told him Sam is a great kid, but I got the sense they have the wrong idea about him."

My back stiffened. "Yes, it appears they do. Did you get any idea of why?"

"No. And I asked."

"Thanks, Brian."

I made my escape to the bathroom.

As I waved my hands uselessly back and forth and up and down underneath the automatic water faucet, Marsha walked in.

"I can't get that thing to work half the time, either." She stopped and leaned against the dark blue wallpaper, an Astros border ringing the room at ceiling level above her head. "I just put someone into your voice mail, a guy named Connor Dunn. He said he's a friend of Adrian's."

"Thanks, Marsha."

"I've been meaning to get you alone." She reached for the glasses on her jeweled strap and put them on, then took them right back off.

Finally, the water came out. I rubbed my hands underneath the stream to rinse off the soap. "Okay."

"I remember that psycho woman, Rhonda Dale, and how she was here stalking Adrian." I waved my hands under the paper towel sensor. Nothing. "I know her stories were lies. She lied when she was here that day. Something was very off about her. I don't care what everybody else says."

"Thank you." I gave up on the towels and shook my hands to dry them.

She moved to the counter and put her purse on it. "I can testify or do an affidavit or something, you know, if you ever need it." She pulled out her makeup kit.

I walked to the door and grabbed the handle. "You are so sweet. I will remember that. Thank you so much, Marsha. Have a great afternoon."

She looked after me, lipstick in hand. "Sure, Michele. Anything you need, you know that."

On the other side of the bathroom door, I paused to slow my breathing. Marsha was trying to help me, and yet I felt like a prisoner who had just broken out of the gulag. I took a reading on the tension meter: a surprising 9. I needed to work out again. That would calm me down.

My phone vibrated. Text from Annabelle. *"Are you there? Jay is coming to NY to see meeeeeeee!!!!"*

I smiled a little bit. The phone rang in my hand. My ex-husband. Oh, joy. Stress meter at 9.5. I contemplated letting it go to voice mail, then thought better of it and took the call as I walked to my office to get my things.

"Hello, Robert."

"Sam told me he has plans and wants to reschedule." It was Sam's weekend with Robert.

"I'm sorry." I paused for him to go on. He didn't. "What would you like for me to do about it?"

"I'd like for you to support me and make him come stay with me."

I read another text from Annabelle while Robert was speaking: *"OK, you must be busy. Hug Precious for me. I miss you guys. Text me soon."*

Guilt. I jumped back into my conversation with Robert as I reached my office. "Did he say anything about his plans?" I sat down and logged off my computer.

"No. I assumed you would know."

I was spending the weekend riding and running in Huntsville. I needed Robert to keep Sam. "He's working a ton, and when he's not working he's at baseball. Must be a recent development. Yes, I'll support you." I prepared to hang up, transaction completed.

Robert kept talking. "How is his hygiene when he's with you? I can't get him to brush his teeth. Shouldn't he have outgrown that?"

I hadn't noticed one way or the other lately. He didn't get past breakfast before I left most days, so it wasn't on my radar. "I think we should revisit the idea of medication," I said.

"He needs consistency and discipline, not pills."

I closed my eyes. "I'll let you know what I find out about this weekend. Goodbye, Robert."

I sent my son a message: *"Sam, need answer ASAP about why you told your dad you can't stay with him. What plans do you have? I will be out of town. Need to work with him, and stay at his house. Sorry."*

The light to my voice mail flashed on the desk phone. I dialed in and listened, thinking it might be Connor Dunn. A hang-up. Oh, well. Next, Annabelle. I forced myself to take the time to answer her back, including lots of the expected LOLs and smiley winking emoticons about Precious and her visit from Jay. I hit send. There. Done.

I looked at my Garmin. It was 10:59, just a little short of the lunch-hour departure I'd planned for. Good enough.

Chapter Eleven

I pulled all the way up the driveway to the house. The heat beat down on me as soon as I opened the car door and I trotted inside and wolfed down an Apple Pie Quest Bar as I changed into my running clothes. On my way back through the kitchen, I snagged a banana, a spoon, and Adrian's jar of cashew butter, added a fresh water bottle and my Nuun tablets, and hit the door ten minutes after I arrived. I couldn't wait to get to the gym, put on my headphones, and find my husband.

I walked out the door and came to an abrupt halt. Detective Young's car was blocking my Jetta. He started across my lawn toward the front door.

"Hello, Detective."

He looked my way and stopped. "Hello, Michele."

"It's Mrs. Hanson."

"All right, Mrs. Hanson."

I stayed with my car between us and put my hand on its roof. Hot. Very hot. I removed it. Just then, a white Taurus drove by. I double-took. My voice sputtered. "Hey—there goes an old Taurus—like the one I've been telling you about—"

I ran down the driveway to get a better look, but it had turned the corner and I couldn't see the driver or the license plate number, but I recognized it as a Texas plate. I looked back at Young, who hadn't moved. I walked back to where he waited in the shade of our big oak, my tension nearly hitting the top of the scale.

"Sorry to bore you, Detective. What can I do for you? Is there some progress in the case?"

"Unfortunately, no. In fact, this isn't even about the case. I'm trying not to overstep, but, well, I have a teenage son, too, and I decided I would want another parent to come to me in your situation."

"What exactly is my situation, Detective? Is my son still under suspicion? I thought you had an eyewitness to a car that definitely does not belong to anyone in my household." I tried to tamp down the wall building in my chest.

"I've had to spend some time on this case, like I told you I would in the beginning, looking at people who might've had a motive to hurt your husband, even if only to rule them out. At this time, Sam is a person of interest."

"A person of interest?"

"Yes, a person we believe may have more information or involvement than we know of yet."

I rolled my neck and hoped Young felt guilty when he heard it pop. "Go on."

"Sometimes it helps to circle back and look at the people in the victim's life again. The killer is usually there somewhere, and when I come back with fresh eyes, well, sometimes I see them off to the side where I didn't before. So I came back to watch Sam and the people around him."

"Okay . . ."

"There's a Chevron station on South Post Oak. Are you familiar with it?" I nodded. "There's a guy that sometimes sells drugs behind the dumpster there in the parking lot. Our officers usually run him off; sometimes they pick him up. He's done a little time, but he keeps going back to his spot."

Again I nodded.

"Last night I watched your son and his buddies."

I interrupted. "Wait a minute. So you're *still* watching Sam? Is he under surveillance?" If Young or Marchetti named Sam a suspect, the media would crucify him.

"I'm trying to find out what happened to your husband."

"So you're not saying my son is an official suspect."

"He's not an official suspect."

"My son and some of his buddies—you were saying?"

"Yeah, well, they pulled up to the Chevron. Your son was driving your husband's old car. One kid pumped some gas. Your son went in and bought a Sobe No Fear—"

"Sounds like a killer to me."

Young pressed his thumb between his eyes for a moment. "The other kid went behind the dumpster and bought what looked like marijuana."

Mierda. I didn't know who Sam was out with or where they went last night. Come to think of it, I hadn't seen any of his friends at our place in a while. "Why didn't you bust them?"

"I don't work narcotics, Michele."

I let the Michele slide. Suddenly I'd lost all my fight. "Anything else?"

He stared at me hard, not speaking.

I sighed. "Okay, so 'anything else' wasn't the right question."

"Nope."

Suddenly the right question was obvious. "So, why exactly is Sam a person of interest? Is it because you're looking for a teenage boy close to Adrian, and stepsons are jealous of stepdads?"

"Actually, no."

"What is it, then?"

"Sam's coach said he and his friend Billy Mays skipped baseball practice on the day your husband died."

Sam lied? My mind reeled back in time to my fourteenth birthday when my mother gave me a shadow box with colorful butterflies hanging inside. My throat had closed, panicked—for them, for me, trapped between two pieces of glass, unable to breathe. "But it's not a school team, it's Summer Select—the coach doesn't even take attendance."

"So said Sam. Coach Metcalfe disagrees. To Sam's credit, the coach said Sam never skipped practice before."

I chomped down on a fingernail and severed it at the quick. "Sam didn't have a car. We don't have a white F150."

"Surely you don't mean to suggest that teenagers don't drive underage, or drive friends' cars?"

"You're reaching, Detective."

"Billy Mays' father has a white F150."

I wanted to whimper, but I stood up straight. "What are you saying?"

"Sam had opportunity, and he had motive." He held up a hand to silence me. "I've seen killings with far less motive than Sam had. And now he may have had the means."

"Did you talk to Billy and his father?"

"Mr. Mays said he had his truck with him, and Billy said he was with Sam the whole time and Sam didn't do it. We're checking out their stories."

"You have no means, and you have a witness negating opportunity." I spoke the truth, but not all of it. The truth was that Sam lied to me and to the police. That rocked me, and made me suspicious about last night. I didn't know what else to say. "Are we done here?"

"Yes, that's all."

I faked moxie I didn't have. "You'll let me know if there are real developments in my husband's case?"

"Yes, ma'am."

He got in his car and drove away. I got in my car and put my head in my hands.

After a few sweaty minutes, I started the car and turned on the AC, then texted Annabelle.

"Belle, hi sweetie. Help me on something important?"

"Hey Michele! Sure! LOL!"

"Sam is really bumming. Has he said anything to you, have you noticed?"

"Ummmm, can you NOT tell him we talked?"

"Yup. Promise."

"My friends say he is totally with the bad boys. Sam LOL But I don't believe it." Another quick text followed. *"I think he's just sad."*

Me, too. *"R U OK?"*

"I'm by myself all the time, and I miss you guys & Jay & Precious. I don't ever see Grandmother. She's really busy." A few more texts came in rapid succession. *"Grandfather always works. They're making me go to boarding school. I leave in a week."*

Annabelle never texted in long strings. If they just meant to send her away, why couldn't they let her stay here with us and go to school with her friends and Sam? *"Oh sweetie. I'm sorry. Can I help?"*

"Tell Precious I love her. The boarding school has a swim team at least. Oh yeah, & I'm thinking of going to UT instead of Stanford. Don't laugh."

"Why would I laugh??"

"Because I'm such a baby that I just want to come home."

"Does this have anything to do with a certain boy who will be swimming for UT?"

"Ha ha yeah but also because I can come home & see you guys some weekends."

I held the tears in, but they were just below the surface.

***

A few hours later, I was immersed in my bathtub up to my eyeballs. In the battle of mind over matter that day on the treadmill, matter won—specifically my injured knee—before I managed to connect with Adrian. I really needed his comfort. My anxiety was off the charts over Sam, my knee, and everything.

I dried off my hand, picked up my phone, and pressed dial on the number of the orthopedist I'd saved in my contacts. A pleasant-voiced woman answered, took my insurance information, and worked me in on Monday. Good. In the meantime, I had a fifteen-mile run and a seventy-five-mile bike ride that weekend in Huntsville. I couldn't skip those workouts. I could only hope they didn't make everything worse.

And after Sam got back from his dad's, I would send him to a therapist. Hell, maybe I'd go, too. I sent Sam a message. *"We need to talk. Text me."*

Chapter Twelve

I bumped my head on the top of my two-man tent when I got up at four thirty a.m. at Huntsville State Park. Adrian and I had always used a five-man tent, and I regretted downsizing. It had been years since I'd camped alone in a two-man as a law school student in search of spring-break solitude to study for finals, and it wasn't as roomy as I remembered. I rolled up my pad and folded the sheet I used as a cool barrier between me and any biting insects that made it into my tent.

When I crawled out of my tent amongst the towering pines, it was still dark, and only down to eighty-two degrees. I was pretty sure they built the state pen in Huntsville because it was the most miserable weather in Texas. But there I was, voluntarily running in that steam pit, even looking forward to it.

By four forty-five I had popped four ibuprofen, put on my gear, and started positive visualizations while ministering to my knee with a Hothands heat pack. Michele, running through a forest in fifty-five degrees with a soft trailing breeze and a knee that felt great. Michele, not worrying about the trouble her teenage son has gotten himself into until Sunday night, even though he managed to avoid her and ignore her messages Friday night. Michele, unreachable for calls from the media, her ex-husband, or Detective Young. Michele, safe from white Tauruses and skanky blondes.

Michele running through a sauna without a breeze, more like it. I didn't care how Adrian coached me last spring; it was hell.

"I have to train in race-like conditions," he'd said. "Kona favors those from a hot, windy climate, but with more hills than Houston. I need me some hills, like the ones in La Grange." We'd fallen in love with the bicycling in the rolling, forested hills in the countryside around La Grange when we were there for our second wedding, and every time we returned to Hill Country afterwards.

"I'll find you some hills as long as you'll buy me one of those fan-misting visors for the hot runs," I said.

"Hmm. How about I run backwards and blow on you instead?"

Michele, crazy and believing she is on a secret date with her dead husband.

I broke down my tent and stuffed my gear in the trunk of the Jetta, then drove over from the far end of the Prairie Branch campground to the Chinquapin trailhead and was ready to go by five o'clock. A few other cars were already spilling forth a trickle of hikers, mountain bikers, and runners. Two big slobbery dogs with silverfish-gray hair and blue leashes danced around a pudgy young man in brand-new Nikes whose shirt sported a price sticker on the back left shoulder.

Adrian had tried to talk me into a puppy a few weeks before his death. "Maybe we should get a dog."

"Precious would never forgive us."

I patted the dogs' silver heads on Adrian's behalf before I started stretching.

"Beautiful animals."

The newbie fondled the ears of the one nearest him. "Thanks!"

As I leaned over and stretched the heels of my hands to the ground, my butterfly locket inverted and hit me in the mouth. Like a peck from Adrian. I gave it a kiss and tucked it into my jog bra, then mentally prepared for my run. I had been trained by the best, after all. Hydration and fueling would be critical. I'd planned to run two laps of the trail, plus a detour on the Prairie Branch Loop along Raven Lake. The summer months weren't the prettiest in the park, but, still, the scenery would be lovely, with the trees crowding up against the banks of the 210-acre lake and swamp birds everywhere—cranes fishing, herons nesting, and pairs of male and female cardinals darting through the air. Continuing my stretching, I inhaled a Chocolate Chip Cookie Dough Quest Bar and tucked packets of Gu energy gel in my waist-band. I strapped on a fuel belt and slipped my bottles of Nuun in it.

Four varieties of poisonous snakes live in Huntsville State Park: rattlers, water moccasins, coral snakes, and copperheads. Four too many, and it was the perfect temperature for them. I hoped they were still sleeping. There were lots of stinging, biting things, too. In a crazy way, though, all of that just made it more awesome. Stretching done, Bon Jovi's "Living on a Prayer" pounding, and an orangesicle glow peeking over the horizon, I bounded out of the parking lot and onto the trail.

"Mongoose, mongoose."

I tingled in anticipation of hearing Adrian's voice. I sucked in the thick, humid air in the near-dark. The pines smelled amazing. A light rain the previous night added to the fresh, clean scent. Adrian and I usually did our long runs at the gator-filled Brazos Bend State Park because it's a shorter drive, but Brazos Bend has a ripe, swampy odor. When we had time, I preferred Huntsville for the smell.

I focused on the ground in front of me as I ran, hopping over mud, running around sand, placing my feet down carefully on slick pine needles and picking my way through tree roots, rocks, and pine cones. The trail markings stink and the paths wind around sharply and shoot up and down without warning. It was getting lighter fast, but it was still hard to see, and when my ankle rolled and threw me off balance, I flailed and fought the fall with gigantic steps, but ended up doing a shoulder roll off one side of the trail. I sat up and looked behind me at my erratic tracks, which started back at a medium-sized rock. I squinted. I could have sworn the damn rock shot me the bird, so I shot one back.

I surveyed my parts: bloody hands, knees, and elbows, but I'd survive. My bad-knee side took the worst of it. I twisted around and saw more blood. I lifted my shirt to see my lower back. Sure enough, trail burn. I wiped off the dirt and leaves. "Dios mío!" I yelled.

A dark-haired man stepped into my line of vision. "Wow! Talk about a Grade A tumble." At least that's what I thought he said. I pulled my earbuds out.

"Excuse me?"

"I said nice fall!" He smiled and offered me a hand up. He looked fit, but not fanatically so. Normal.

"Thanks. No, I'm fine." I waved his hand away and stood up, tottering a bit. Enrique Iglesias and Pit Bull still blared from my buds, but in a distorted way that sounded echoey and eerie in the empty forest.

The man stubbed his toe against the ground, digging up a little dirt. "I have a confession. I saw you leave the parking lot. I thought I would pass you with my blazing speed, and, stunned with admiration, you would wonder who I was. Then, later on the trail, I would stop and pretend to be doing something interesting, and we would meet . . . but it didn't work. It was all I could do to keep pace behind you. I'll have to resort to honesty and chivalry instead. Hello, I'm Blake." His hand came out again.

Ugh, I thought. No. Leave me alone. I'm out here to meet my husband in the woods, and you're keeping him away. Besides, why was he hitting on me? He looked younger than me. Thirty-five-ish, maybe older by a little, but if so, he had great genetics or a good colorist.

Blake's extended hand tested whether the daughter my Southern mother raised could turn her back on that tutelage. She couldn't. I shook his hand. "I'm Michele, and I'm not very graceful." I half-smiled in a manner I hoped said "Polite, but all business." I gestured at the trail. "Would you like to go first?"

"No, you go ahead. I'll maintain the rescue position in case you fall again. Think of me as your own personal SAG wagon."

I nodded, said, "Happy trails," and stuck my earbuds back in.

Knowing Blake was running behind me really knocked me off center. How would Adrian feel about this? Maybe it wasn't rational to believe my dead husband came back to me whenever I sweat, but I didn't care. I wanted this stranger to get out of our space. With my peace shattered, I noticed that my knee hurt—a lot. I picked my pace up, but the faster I ran, the worse it got. I couldn't self-sabotage just to get rid of this guy. I shortened my stride and decided to Gu and hydrate without breaking pace, fearful he would talk to me again if I stopped.

Bad decision. With my break in concentration, I tumbled again, even harder this time and onto my good knee. I rolled in a heap to the bottom of the hill. I closed my eyes. "Chingame," I whispered.

The Blake person reappeared at my side.

I sighed and removed the earbuds again.

"You know, I speak Spanish, and you've got a set of lungs." I stared at him. He touched his ears. "Earbuds. You probably didn't realize how loud you just yelled."

"I'm sorry. Not a very ladylike choice of expressions. My apologies."

"No apologies necessary. It didn't bother me." He crouched beside me. "You're really favoring that left side."

"I'll be favoring the right one now, too." I poked on my right knee, and while it smarted, it didn't seem injured. "I'm seeing an orthopedist tomorrow about the left knee."

"Hmm. I'll have to give you my contact information, and if the orthopedist route isn't right for you, you should call me. I'm a chiropractor and I specialize in sports medicine. We do therapy and rehab at my clinic. We could probably help you a lot." Was he soliciting a patient or hitting on me? "Or we could go run together sometime."

"Thanks."

"It was definitely the right choice to keep running behind you— and not only for the view."

Okay, he was hitting on me. "You're awfully forward."

"I operate under the theory that life is too short for subtlety, and I think you're really cute. If it makes any difference, you look really familiar to me, like maybe we've met somewhere before. You didn't happen to be married to Tony Parker once upon a time, did you? Because I sat next to him and his wife at a banquet a few years ago, and—"

"I agree. Life is too short for subtlety. My husband died three weeks ago, so this I know. And he wasn't Tony Parker, who I was never married to, by the way." Him or any other French basketball player. "I'm not ready for this." I stopped, then worried whether I'd made myself clear. My hand came up, fingers wide, pressing distance between us. "I don't want this kind of attention from a man."

He didn't flinch. "I'm sorry about your husband. That must be hard. I'm glad you told me." He stayed quiet for a long time, but he didn't move. Just when I thought I could leave, he started up again. "People that can be straight with each other can be friends. Let's have a do-over." He stuck his hand out again. "I'm Dr. Cooper. Blake to my friends."

Now I did smile, albeit a thin one. "Michele Lopez Hanson, also known as That Bitch, but only sometimes."

"I can see that." We both laughed. "Michele Lopez Hanson, tell me about this left knee."

Blake did a thorough exam of my knee there on the forest floor. After we talked about it, he made me run again so he could observe my gait instead of my behind.

"You've got IT band syndrome. Classic. You've over-trained, and you're unstable."

Yes, I was unstable, but how did he know that? Oh, I realized, he meant my knee. "Are you sure?"

"Pretty darn sure. Your orthopedist can rule out anything structural and give you a definitive answer, though. If it isn't IT band, then you need him anyway. Keep the appointment, but call me afterwards."

"Okay."

"I mean it. I've only known you an hour, and I know you aren't going to like what you hear from him," he said.

"Why?"

"Most orthopedists tell their patients with ITBS to quit running."

"I will not!"

"Hey, don't shoot the messenger. Just call me after you rule out something structural. I do think that at the point the pain becomes unbearable, you should quit for the day."

"Lucky for me, it isn't." I took off at a determined pace and increased limp. I didn't make it a quarter mile before Blake caught up with me.

"Time for some birdwatching. Doctor's orders."

I stopped, and I tried not to cry. I walked and Blake fell in beside me. "You go on ahead. I don't want to spoil your run."

He ignored me and we walked the rest of the loop together. He did most of the talking. An hour later, we made it back to the parking lot. I was antsy. As nice as Blake had been (once he quit hitting on me), I hated missing my time with Adrian. Hated it in a panicky way that made me want to turn around and run the loop in the opposite direction.

We were back in the land of cell signal, so I checked my phone. Nothing from Sam. I texted him again. *"Why aren't you answering me?"* I hit send.

Blake walked over to his car to get a business card for me and I recoiled. A white Taurus. My internal spring tightened and all the stress that had left me reentered with the ringing of Klaxon horns. I stared at the car. Maybe this guy hadn't just seen me for the first time today. Maybe he had seen me months ago. Maybe he had moved Adrian out of the way and bided his time, and now, here, today, I had fallen for his nice-guy act, when he was the one who killed my husband.

"Michele? Are you okay?" Blake was standing in front of me holding his business card.

I looked back at his car. It still had dealer tags on it. It probably didn't have a hundred miles on it yet. It wasn't the Taurus I'd seen before. It wasn't someone who hurt Adrian.

Get over it, Michele, I silently ordered myself. The terror was passing, but a weariness set in. "Oh, I'm fine, sorry, I was lost in thought. I have a teenage son trying to go delinquent on me, and now that I'm about to head home, all my worries are crashing back down on me."

"Sorry about that."

I pulled out my keys and moved to my passenger door. "No, don't be sorry. I'm sorry." I had to let some heat out of the car or I'd never be able to get in. I cringed through the sequence of opening my car, popping the trunk, and silencing the alarm, but the familiarity soothed me in a way. "I swear I'm not breaking in. It has electrical issues. My husband called it El Diablo. I'm just praying it will last me through the fall." After the Ironman, I'd trade it in for whatever I could get.

Blake laughed. "Please let me know how it goes tomorrow, either way. I think we should be friends."

"Thank you. Have a safe drive back into town." I climbed into my oven-like car, but the warmth was like an embrace. "Adrian," I whispered. I didn't turn on the air conditioner, just backed out quickly, eager to get to my next workout, to my husband.

Chapter Thirteen

Monday morning with Sam didn't go well.

I flicked on the light switch in his room at seven thirty. "We need to talk."

The pillow over his head muffled his voice. "Yeah, I know. You texted me."

"And you didn't answer."

"You weren't home. What did it matter?"

"Where were you last night?"

"Hanging out with friends."

"You didn't make it home by curfew, and you didn't let me know when you got home. Same as last Thursday night."

He sat up. "Geez, Mother, I didn't want to wake you up. I did so make it home by curfew, but you were zonked. You go to bed so freakin' early."

"Don't talk to me that way, please." I had to leave or I'd miss my orthopedist appointment. I didn't have time to confront Sam about lying or the incident at the Chevron station. "Today we are having a mother-son meeting. Meet me here at four fifteen, got it?"

"Got it."

I left him stomping around his room. He was spinning out of control, and it made me really angry that he would take advantage of me when I was so vulnerable. I slammed the side door on my way out to my car.

***

Four hours later, I left the orthopedist's office in tears and started digging through my wallet for Blake's card. I wiped my eyes so I could read the numbers and dialed his office. A receptionist with a warm voice put me on hold for a couple minutes, then Blake's voice came on the line.

"Michele? Good to hear from you! Sorry for the wait. I was just finishing up with a patient. How did it go with your orthopedist?"

I tried not to wail. "You were right."

"Come see us right now. We'll work you in."

"But I don't even know if you take my insurance."

"Don't worry about it. First visit's on me. We'll figure it out from there."

I hung up and pointed the car in the direction of his clinic in Bellaire. I called Brian at Juniper and gave him the rundown. My training condition, like it or not, affected my work, since to Brian, Kona was about book and magazine promotion, even if to me it was a tribute to Adrian and a chance to be with him for fourteen-plus hours on the course.

"Focus on your doctors' visits. Take all the time you need."

"I will. I'll probably need rehab visits a few times a week. I'll make sure to schedule around the stuff Scarlett has lined up for me."

"Sounds good." He stopped talking, but in a way that sounded like thinking, even over the phone. I waited. "I know you've got it in your head that this is all about me and Juniper and money, but it's not. I care about you, Michele. So does Scarlett. She brought in the most fantastic pictures of you and Adrian this morning from your book launch, and she couldn't stop talking about how much she respects you and wants the best for you."

My eyes itched and my head hurt. Something Brian said was jostling my last remaining brain cell, but I didn't have enough juice to follow it through. And although I still wasn't sure whether to trust Scarlett, I didn't doubt Brian's sincerity. How could I explain that admitting people care about me weakens me, makes me too soft? I couldn't. So I didn't try, just channeled my doppelganger's skills and acted my aching heart out. "I know. Thank you, Brian."

His voice brightened, and I knew I had hit the mark. "Hey, while I have you on the phone, your ex wants you to call him back. Marsha said he sounded a little upset."

We said our goodbyes and I ended the connection. Robert. Never a good sign to hear from him. I scrolled through my missed calls at a red light. Whoops. Several from Robert and one voice mail. No, two voice mails, and the missed calls dated back to Friday night. Worse than whoops. I pulled into a parking space at the clinic and decided to listen to the messages the next chance I got.

I rode the mirrored elevator up to Blake's fourth-floor clinic. The waiting room had a spa Zen to it, with tan-cushioned bamboo furniture and Berber carpet. Signed photos of Rockets and Texans graced the who's who gallery, along with a few professional triathletes, including one Adrian stayed friendly with after writing an article about him years ago. An athletic-looking woman checked me in and a toned man in scrubs escorted me to a treatment room.

"Dr. Cooper will be with you in about five minutes," he said. "Can I get you anything while you wait? We have green tea and ice water." Not only did everyone look fit, but they smiled.

"No, I'm fine. Thanks."

The small exam room had the same vibe as the lobby. Neutral walls, a shade darker than almond. Bamboo. Natural fibers. A chocolate leather chaise lounge. A miniature rock fountain on a side table and piped-in flute instrumental, an earthy-sounding piece. A potpourri of smells. I caught lavender and sandalwood oil, but I couldn't place the others. Chichi, but Adrian would love it. Except for the flirty doctor part. Not that Adrian was ever the jealous type. I think he secretly enjoyed it when other men admired his woman, but I never even noticed anyone else. Adrian filled my heart. Maybe his absence from my physical realm would make him more prone to jealousy now . . .

I rolled my eyes. It was ridiculous to think my dead husband could be jealous. Wasn't it? Maybe my next doctor's visit should be to a shrink. I pulled my voice mail display up on my phone. Time to get this over with. I played Robert's first one from Saturday afternoon.

His voice had an edge. "I thought you promised to make sure Sam didn't back out on me? Next time would someone have the courtesy to call me and let me know he's not coming?" The second call came in that morning, to talk about next time and being able to count on us.

Sam hadn't showed up at his father's? He defied us both and went AWOL Saturday night, even knowing we would catch him? He wasn't home when I returned on Sunday afternoon. He was taciturn at breakfast and didn't mention his father, even though he surely had a phone full of messages, too. Oh, yeah, and he was a "person of interest" in the death of his stepfather, and had told the police and me some big fat lies. Ay chingada. I grabbed my purse from the exam table and jerked the door open to leave—and ran pell-mell into the smiling Dr. Blake Cooper.

"Whoa, Michele. What's the matter?"

"I'm sorry, but I got an emergency call about my son. I have to go."

"No problem, call us tomorrow and we'll get you back in. I hope everything's okay?"

"Nothing is okay. I've messed everything up—" I stood on the deep end, ready to jump, then stepped back. "No, no, it's fine, I just—oh, I just have to go."

And I fled.

Chapter Fourteen

I ignored the speed limits and raced home. The 4Runner wasn't there, so I left my Jetta running in the driveway and ran into the house, yelling for Sam. My voice had a crazy ring to it. I gulped. Tension meter at 10. Oh, how I needed Adrian. After more than thirty-five years of competence, I fell in love with the perfect guy and ended up helpless without him. Wasn't love supposed to make me stronger?

The house was silent.

Sam kept his work and practice schedules on the kitchen bulletin board beside my training calendar. I scanned it. He should be on shift at the pool right now. I ran back out to my car and threw it in gear, calling Robert on the way and blocking the irritation from my voice. I would be mad in his position, too.

When he picked up, I got right into it. "I'm sorry I missed your calls and messages. Yes, we have a problem, and it's bigger than Sam and me changing the schedule. He promised me he would go to your place before I left Saturday morning, and he didn't tell me that he hadn't done it after I came back." I turned on Rutherglenn and cut the corner so close I hit the curb. I held on and prayed I didn't pop the tire.

"You're kidding. Where was he?"

I suspected I knew the answer to that: Sam hadn't expected to get away with it. He wanted to get in trouble. He was trying to get some attention from his negligent mother, but I didn't need to share that with my ex. "I'm headed to the pool now to find out. And I'd like to schedule him with a therapist. Losing Belle and Adrian has really done a number on him. I would appreciate your support."

"You know I don't believe in all that hocus pocus."

I didn't really give a rat's ass what Robert believed in. I let the silence stretch out. I'd sit on that phone without speaking as long as I had to, but I wouldn't back down, any more than Papa had when it came to me. I remembered my mother hissing at Papa when she thought I couldn't hear. "I don't want you and Isabel filling her head with all that Aztec sacrilege."

Finally, Robert spoke. "If you think it would help, I will back you. As a last resort."

Last resort? That would be a fight for another time. I jerked my Jetta into the JCC parking lot. "Fine. I'll let you know more when I know myself." I ended the call before he could say anything else.

The lot was jammed with cars and SUVs, and I had to squeeze into an illegal space at the farthest edge. The blacktop shimmered with fingers of heat that reached up and wrapped around my throat, and I gasped. My tension meter redlined. By the time I reached the pool, sweat was pouring down my back and my shirt was stuck to my body.

Sam sat upon the lifeguard stand overlooking the shallow end. When he glanced my way, his jaw dropped and he cut his eyes toward the other lifeguards under a tent nearby. I needed him to hear me, and my emotions were dangerously close to out of control, so I slowed down and breathed in as deeply as I could, stretching my lungs with the heavy, humid air and imagining the oxygen making its way into all the farthest recesses of my mind and body, working magic on me, pushing my stress out through my skin.

Visualize, Michele. Be what you seek.

Tension meter: 9.75.

Imagine Adrian beside you, loving you, supporting you, making it all right.

Tension meter: 9.5.

Sam works here, and his boss and friends will be able to see and hear us.

I walked purposefully toward him but wiped the raw-meat-eater look off my face.

Tension meter: 9.

I made a canopy over my eyes with my hand and looked up at him. "Sam, I need to talk to you."

He sneered through gritted teeth. "I'm *working*, Mother."

My heart ached looking at him. Even when he was angry, his youth and beauty burned my eyes. His skin had turned mocha-colored over the summer. Sun streaks shot through his dark flop of hair. Had I noticed before now? I didn't think so. "How soon until you can take a break? I'll wait."

He looked away. "Crikey, Mom. You're embarrassing me."

I put my hand on my hip. "Then find a way to take a break or see if they can let you go for the day, because I'm not leaving until we talk. I'd like for your sake that our chat occur somewhere else, but if not, then right here will do."

He glared at me but hand-motioned for his boss to come over. The boss was a kid himself. Braces crisscrossed his teeth and acne splotched his cheeks. I moved three steps away. He and Sam whispered, then he walked over to the guard canopy and tapped a short brunette on the shoulder. She grabbed her neon-orange rescue float and whistle and strode briskly but carefully to Sam's stand like she imagined people were eyeing her. She and Sam exchanged places and he walked over to me.

"Are you on break or done for the day?"

He stared into the distance. "Done," he said, packing a lot of screw-you into the word.

"All right, then. Let's take a drive—my car."

As we walked in silence, I rehearsed what I needed to say and prayed I could find a better mother than the one I had been in the last few weeks. And I fumed. Fumed at Sam, myself, and fate. Fumed at Adrian. Why hadn't he been looking where he was going? Couldn't he, with all his athleticism, have hopped out of the car's way? Why didn't he wear his damn helmet? Didn't he know I couldn't live without him? If he knew, if he cared, he would never have been that careless. He would never have let this happen. Damn him.

Sam chuffed. "What?"

"Nothing." I turned my key in the door, then jumped in and turned on the lights as the horn honked. Sam slammed the trunk and got in his side. I backed out of my no-parking spot and a minute later turned east on South Braeswood.

"Where are we going?"

I turned on my signal, checked the rearview mirror, and moved into the left lane. "We're just going to drive, Sam."

His right knee bounced up and down. "Are you going to give me a clue what this is about?"

"This is about a lot of things. One thing it's about is that you didn't spend the night at your dad's this weekend. Another is that last week, someone saw a passenger from your car buy drugs behind the Chevron and get back in the 4Runner with you. Another is you lied to me and the police about where you were when Adrian died. And another is that you have been rude and disrespectful to me for quite some time now. Which one would you like to start with?"

I glanced over and saw him tighten his lips. Deep furrows appeared between his eyebrows. The knee sped up.

I turned left on South Rice without using my blinker. "Your dad and I can only assume you wanted us to know about Saturday, since you didn't do anything to try to fool him. You just no-showed. So where were you?"

His knee was still bouncing. He tossed his head to flip his bangs off his face. "I stayed home."

"By yourself?"

Long pause. "No, a couple of guys came over."

I didn't press, because his answer felt like progress. "You don't have permission to have friends over when I'm not there, but we can talk about that later. You promised to be at your father's house, and you didn't tell him you weren't coming. I'm glad you're telling me now, but why didn't you tell one of us this from the beginning?"

He kept his eyes straight ahead. His whole body jiggled from his bouncing knee. Mumble mumble mumble.

"What's that?"

"I'll ask next time."

Yes, this definitely felt like progress, no matter how small. I inhaled long and exhaled longer. "Detective Young came to see me. The police know you lied to them."

Sam shifted his eyes to me then back to the front so fast I almost didn't see him do it. "I—" He stopped and looked down. The left knee started keeping pace with the right one.

I stopped at the red light at Beechnut, then turned on my signal and followed it to the right. Within seconds we were nearing Meyerland Plaza and passing Endicott, and my heart leaned so I turned right without thinking. "Do you realize how much trouble you could be in, lying to the police? Luckily, Billy and his father gave you an alibi. But then, I'll bet Billy already told you that, didn't he?"

"Yeah. I knew he would, though, because I didn't do anything wrong."

I laughed with no mirth. "You skipped practice and you lied. Lying to the police is a crime, Sam, and it made them put you at the top of their suspect list when they should have been looking for the real killer. What the hell has gotten into you?"

He snorted and looked at the passenger window. "You caught me. I lied. I skipped baseball practice. I'm a terrible person."

I pulled to a stop at the four-way crossing at Endicott and Jackwood. "Watch it, Sam." I accelerated through the intersection and rolled past the spot where Adrian died. Nothing marked it. Just an asphalt street and a concrete curb next to a mostly empty parking lot. My heart hollowed out, collapsed in on itself. Time slowed down while it refused to beat. I was fighting with my son on sacred ground. I couldn't bear it. I cried out, and my heart started beating again.

Sam's voice exploded. "What?"

"I don't know. I just hurt, Sam."

"You think I don't? You're driving me past where he died. What are you trying to say? Why are you doing this to me?" His cries were as loud as mine now. "I didn't kill Adrian, Mom. I just lied, all right? I wouldn't ever have hurt him—or anybody." He ended on a sob and threw his hands up to cover his face.

I softened my voice. "No, I don't think you would ever hurt any-one." I put my hand on his shoulder. We rolled to a stop at another intersection. He said nothing, so I pressed the gas and drove on. "Tell me about the drugs."

He threw his hands up in the air. "I don't know what you're talking about. I swear."

"Detective Young saw you at the Chevron station with two boys. He saw one of them buy drugs and bring them back to your car."

"If anybody bought drugs, they didn't tell me."

I stopped at North Braeswood, turned on my belated blinker, and turned right. I cocked my head and looked at my son. Highly improba-ble, but possible. And I couldn't prove it either way. It might be enough that he knew I was watching him now. I would let it go. "My first priority is your health and safety, Sam, and—"

He interrupted. "That's funny."

"Excuse me?" The light at South Rice was green, so I turned left on Chimney Rock.

"That's funny, Mom, because I don't think I'm anywhere in the top five on your priority list, and I'm sure not *the* top priority. Your priorities seem to be you, you, you, you, and you, one through five." His voice got louder. "Your training, your book, your publicity, your sadness, your job, your everything. What about me? Don't you think I'm sad, too?" He turned to me and screamed so loud his face turned beet red under his summer tan. "Do you even know that I'm still here? They're gone but I'm still here." And then he started crying. Horrible sounds, deep wrenching sobs that gouged at my heart.

I reached out to touch him, but he pushed my hand away.

He turned from me and his sobs slowed down just a little. "Don't try just because I said this stuff. It's fake. Leave me alone." He stared out the window. "I want to go home. I want everything to be the same as it used to be. I don't understand why all of you are gone, not just them, but you, too. It's worse, because I think you should still be here, but you're not. You're not."

I looked up and realized I had just run a red light, but God looks out for little children and for stupid women who don't know how to do their lives anymore without hurting themselves and everyone left that they love. This pain hurt in a new way, as bad as losing Adrian, as bad as putting Annabelle on a plane. I *was* gone. I knew that. I was failing Sam. I had to find a way to make it better, but I didn't know if I had it in me to be completely present, because I wanted to be gone. I wanted to leave this world and stay in the halfway part with Adrian. I sat there, paralyzed, as the Jetta rolled forward. I said the only things I could think of, the true things, as best I could.

"I'm sorry, Sam. I love you. It's going to be okay someday, and I know it isn't yet. I'm doing a bad job for you, but I'm not sure how to make it better. I think we could see a grief counselor, someone who's done—"

"NO!" he exploded. "You want to push me off on someone else to do your job, so you can say 'I'm a good mother because Sam talked to a counselor about his feelings,' and then you show me that you don't even care about being alive for me? No fucking way, Mom."

He was right, and I wasn't sure if I could fix it.

Chapter Fifteen

The next morning I slept in, unable to start my engines, but I had to get moving. I had an eight thirty appointment at Dr. Cooper's office. I grabbed my phone and noticed the flashing light on my way out the door.

Annabelle. *"Michele, r u there? I need to talk to you."*

I'd have to answer her later. I hustled into the clinic, where the receptionist funneled me into an examination room. I sat on the leather exam table and settled in to wait, but Blake came in almost immediately. He wore green scrubs the color of my husband's eyes.

"Play it again, Sam," he said.

It took me a moment to understand he wasn't referring to my Sam. "I sure hope not. Look, I'm sorry. I'm usually pretty reliable. I know I owe you for the missed appointment."

He held up his hand in the "stop" gesture. "How can you pay for an appointment you didn't have? We worked you in. And I told you, the first visit's on me. I hope everything is okay with your son?"

I pulled the blinds closed over my eyes. "Yes, all fine. Thank you."

Like he had at the park, Blake let me hide. His restraint or professionalism or whatever it was put me more at ease. "Give me the verdict from the orthopedist." He sat down and leaned forward with his hands on his knees.

"IT band syndrome, don't run, I'm not a good enough athlete to waste my time on therapy and rehab."

He sighed. "I'm sometimes pleasantly surprised when surgeons encourage their patients toward a natural healing approach, but not often. Well, we'll get aggressive with it. You should reduce your training, but we want to have you running at a hundred percent ASAP."

Before I could ask what he meant by "reduce," the door opened and one of his female coworkers entered. Athletic-looking and fit, of course, in blue scrubs. And tall.

"Michele, this is Dr. Greene. I've asked her to take care of you. Dr. Greene, Michele."

We shook hands and she plopped a heating pad onto my left knee and thigh. The warmth rushed through me with a sense of peace. Dr. Greene got down to business. My kind of woman. "Tell me about yourself, Michele."

I started to tell her about my knee pain, but she interrupted.

"Tell me about your lifestyle, your sport, your workouts, that kind of thing."

I obliged.

She listened like I was telling her the secrets of the universe. "When did your knee start hurting?"

"Well, my husband qualified for an age-group spot at Kona, and—"

She sat up straight. "Oh, wow, what's his age group, what's his name? I may know him, that's so cool."

Blake moved to cut in, but I pretended it didn't faze me. "He died in a hit-and-run accident a few weeks ago, but you're right, it is cool, and his name is Adrian Hanson. He qualified in forty-five to forty-nine." I sucked in a deep cleansing breath.

"I am sorry, I shouldn't have—"

"Please, don't apologize. You didn't do a thing wrong, and I'm very proud of him." I felt short of breath, even lightheaded. This was different from talking about him on TV. Intimate. Harder. "I bought a lottery spot to do it with him. I'm carrying on without him, following his training plan, but I haven't ever done a full-length Ironman. I've ramped up the training hard and fast for this. The pain started about two weeks ago, and it's gotten worse and worse."

Blake cut in. "Geez, Michele, it just hit me why I thought we'd met before. I've seen you on TV. You guys wrote a book together, right?"

Dr. Greene was nodding, too. "Yes, I've got the book. *My Pace or Yours.*" She smiled. "I follow triathlon, and he's the local hero, so I have known of him for a while. So you're Michele Lopez Hanson. I'm really delighted to meet you."

I fought the urge to fold in on myself. I stayed in the moment. "Thank you." I even smiled at her and I didn't turn to stone.

Dr. Greene fixed her blue eyes on me and got down to business. "Any old injuries or accidents, surgeries, lengthy periods of incapacity?"

"Hmmm, well, I sprained my right ankle in my late twenties. Other than that, nothing big."

She probed my knee with strong fingers, then moved up the outside of my thigh to my hip. Everywhere she touched, it felt like she was prodding it with a hot poker. A wake of red marks trailed behind her hands. "The IT band runs from the knee to the hip. You're feeling pain when it rubs back and forth around the knee during running, but the problem is in a much bigger area. And you definitely have a problem. Lots of scarring. You must have a high pain threshold." She looked like that pleased her.

"I guess so."

She looked at Blake. "Dr. Cooper, I think I've got what I need to start with Michele."

***

An hour later, we were back in the exam room, insurance checked and finances settled. From the meager charges they'd outlined, Blake had to be giving me a huge discount, but I didn't argue. The sharp smell of Icy Hot filled the room, but underneath it I could still catch whiffs of lavender and sandalwood. I allowed myself to feel hope while Blake went over my treatment plan: heat before workouts and treatments, Dr. Greene performing Active Release Therapy and Graston on me three times a week, daily physical rehab to build stability, and ice after treatments and workouts.

Dr. Greene bounced a pen against her thigh. "Your leg is going to hurt now. Can you keep from using it for twenty-four hours?"

Quick mental word game: if "use" meant run, then I could not use it, but I had a two-hour cycling workout that afternoon. "No problem." I crossed my fingers, too, just in case.

Maybe she could read my mind. "If you haven't tried it, aqua jogging can be a great substitute for running." She reached in a drawer and pulled out a piece of paper. "Here's instructions on how to do it correctly, so you can get the full benefit."

I took it from her, intrigued. "So if I follow your plan, I can do Kona in October?"

"You can do whatever your body and mind tell you. Your rational self will know the answer to that. It's likely you can. Depends on your pain threshold and your overall conditioning."

"Well, if those are the only criteria, then I'll be fine."

Blake stood up. "I have to ask. Worst-case scenario, can you defer until next year?"

"No."

"You'd lose your spot?"

"No."

He stared at me. Kept staring at me. Stared at me longer.

I broke. "I don't actually know. But I'm doing the race this year. For Adrian."

"That's valid." He deepened his voice. "Dr. Greene, have your athlete ready for Kona."

She saluted. "Yes, sir."

Chapter Sixteen

I braced myself as I walked into the house through the side door. I wasn't sure if Sam was speaking to me yet. I should have grounded him, but if Sam should be grounded, what about me? We'd both messed up, only there was no punishment I could give myself worse than the purgatory I was already in, so I cut us both a break. I got a surprise when I walked into the kitchen to find Sam at the island making sandwiches.

"Hi, Mom." His voice sounded relaxed, or, as he would call it, "chill."

"Hi, honey."

He pushed a plate at me. "That's yours if you want it."

Wonder Bread, Miracle Whip, processed ham, and American cheese. I grabbed it. "Absolutely, thanks. Did you have a good day?" I bit into the mushy bread and sweet and salty exploded in my mouth, bringing back a thousand school lunches and giggling friends. I had forgotten how good crap tasted. Adrian would forgive me.

Sam talked with his mouth full. "Yeah. Some friends want me to go bowling tonight. If you want to hang out there while we bowl, you can. They have wifi."

I didn't deserve this boy. I really didn't. I tried to play it low key, though, so I wouldn't spook him. "Sounds good, thanks."

And so, twenty-four hours after I thought he'd never speak to me again, we went bowling together. Or, rather, I watched my son laugh and bowl and be a kid—from a safe distance in the smoky grill. He didn't bring his friends to meet me, and I didn't force it. They looked normal enough, minus an earring and a pack of cigarettes or two. Normal enough to keep my fears at a dull roar.

I scrolled through the day's texts, emails, and voice mails, looking for icebergs.

Annabelle. I hadn't answered her yet, and she'd said she needed to talk to me. I tried to ignore the prickles of guilt as I typed. *"Hey Belle, you need to talk to me?"*

No reply.

"I'm here if you need me. Sorry I couldn't talk earlier."

Nothing.

I guess it was too much to expect that both kids could be doing well at the same time.

***

Side-by-side the next morning, Sam slurped his cereal and I ate my egg-white omelet. The decrease in tension emboldened me. "You know, you haven't had any of your buddies over for a while. I've missed having smelly boys around. What about asking Billy over?"

"I haven't been hanging out with him lately."

"Bring your other friends, then."

His spoon clinked against his teeth and he slurped up milk and cereal. I drew a quick breath. I couldn't let myself spoil the moment.

"Yeah, I'll try to get them to come over. They're not, like, *into* hanging out at parents' houses."

"What kind of things do they like to do?"

"Uh, go hang out and stuff."

"Well, I need you to bring them by so I can at least meet them. I don't know their names or anything about them. I zoned out for a while, but you know the rules."

"Yeah." He grinned. He ducked his face to hide it, but it was there.

"I need to go over my training calendar with you, too. That way you will know when I'll be around and where I'll be when I'm not."

"I already look at it, you know." He watched me carefully, his head tilted like a sparrow.

My lips formed a "hmm" expression. No, I didn't know. "You do?"

"Yeah."

"How come?"

He scooped up some cereal, and I braced for it. Clink. Slurp. "I just, uh, well, I make sure you put your X's in. If you do, then I know you're still going to Kona."

"There's a lot of X's these days."

He put his spoon down. "Yeah, but—"

"What?"

"You haven't X'ed your runs."

Sam was out-parenting me. I licked my lips and swallowed. "I hurt my knee, and I have to take a few weeks off from running. I start aqua jogging today in the indoor pool. Me and the little old ladies' water aerobics class."

"Oh, I didn't know. Are you going to be able to do Kona?"

"Yes, I've got a great doctor, and I'm doing therapy and rehab."

"Cool." He picked up his spoon.

I decided to capitalize on our détente. I needed information about his sister. "Sam, Belle hasn't texted me back. Do you know if something is wrong? Like, is she mad at me?"

"I don't think so. I don't know."

"Okay. Well, let me know if you hear something."

An odd exchange, not merely because we were talking to each other at seven forty-five a.m. instead of staring at our food, but because Sam was a teenager, and I had not known he took any real interest in my life except as it impacted him. I didn't know what to make of it, but it stuck with me all day. So when I got home that afternoon, I went all out and made Sam his favorite food, a disgustingly wonderful tater tot casserole my Mississippi-born maternal grandmother used to make for me after school sometimes, when she'd moved to Seguin after my grandfather died. That spicy browned hamburger meat still smells like love to me.

I set the table for two. As I was getting out the silverware, I heard Sam enter the house, and from the sound of the voices, at least one other kid, too. The boys burst into the kitchen like a shock wave.

Sam was out of breath. "Whoa, Mom, something happened, and you're gonna *kill* me."

I looked from my son to the two boys with him. They seemed a little stonerish. Hair collar-length and messy, skater t-shirts, dirty blue jeans (in August?). One of them had a silver chain hanging down from his belt loop then back up to something in his pocket, and the other I'd seen bowling the night before. They fit the description of the boys Detective Young had seen. Nothing like clean-cut Billy Mays and the other boys Sam had always hung out with. The old crowd sure wasn't perfect, but I knew their parents. I didn't know the first thing about these two. I was glad they were there, though, finally.

"Slow down, Sam. Does this involve a bloody stump?"

"No." He pushed his hair back and I noticed how long the swoop had grown. He looked coltish and wild, a mustang boy with a mane across his forehead.

"Introduce me to your friends first, and then I can kill you."

"Oh, okay, um, this is Ted, and, um, Andrew, and, um." His vague points in their direction didn't help me differentiate the two.

"I'm Mrs. Hanson, Sam's mom."

They answered in harmony. "Hey."

"Nice to meet you." I turned back to Sam. "Go on."

He spoke at a gallop. "I picked up Ted and Andrew after practice. I, uh, went in Ted's house for a few minutes. When I backed out of the driveway, I, well, Mom, I just messed up, okay?"

I put my hand on his elbow. "Slow down. Just tell me what happened."

"I backed into a lady's car."

I gave his elbow a squeeze. "It will be okay, Sam. Is everyone all right?"

A chorus of yeahs and uh huhs came from the boys.

"The lady wasn't hurt. She had an old car, and she said she couldn't even see a dent. There was one, though, and it was, like, huge. And Adrian's, uh, I mean my car, it has a big one, too."

"Did you exchange insurance information? Did the police come?"

"Nah, she said she wasn't even going to fix it, and that she didn't want me to get in trouble. She just left."

"She had a huge dent in her car but she didn't call the police, and she didn't want your insurance information? That doesn't sound right. Did she ask for your name and number?"

"Nope. We just drove off when she did, Mom."

"Well, you have twenty-four hours to call the police, so let's do it tonight. She might change her mind and call it in herself. Then you'd be in big trouble for leaving the scene of an accident."

The blonder of the two boys spoke and my head swiveled toward him. "Dude, she was weird. And that old Ford was smashed. I don't know what she was thinking."

"Which one are you, Andrew or Ted?"

He grinned. "I'm Andrew. He's Ted. You can tell us apart because he's fat. Tubby Ted."

"I'm not fat." He wasn't, but he did have a little belly. Enough to remember their names, anyway.

"Got it. Okay, boys, what kind of Ford did she drive?"

Andrew bobbed his head. "A Taurus."

Chills. "Color?"

"White."

"Mom, what's wrong?"

"Can you describe the woman, Sam?"

"Uh, yeah, but you're kind of freaking me out." He paused, but I just waited for him to answer me. "She was old, you know, a little older than you, but she looked way older because—"

"Because you're, like, way hot, Mrs. Hanson." Andrew looked to Ted for confirmation.

"Totally."

I shot Andrew a look. "So you guys didn't find her attractive. What kind of clothes?"

Sam shrugged a shoulder. "Sweats, maybe?"

Andrew took a seat at one of the bar stools. "Yeah, man, gray and navy sweats that said Rice University on them. And dirty, like, gross."

This didn't sound like Rhonda, but it could be a disguise. "Hair color?"

Sam shook his head. "Her hair was basically no color at all. What do girls call that?"

"Mousy?"

"Yep, exactly like a mouse."

"You're sure it wasn't blonde? Like, really, really blonde?"

"I'm sure. Why?"

"No reason." I dialed back on the paranoia. It was just a coincidence. "Have you ever seen her or her car before?"

"No—"

Andrew cut in. "I have." He turned to Sam. "She sits in her car where you work, man. I've seen her there a couple of times."

The needle on my tension meter quivered just below 10. "Really? Could you tell what she was doing there, Andrew?"

"I dunno. Maybe she's got a kid that goes there. Haven't you seen her, guys?"

Two head shakes.

Sam was the common denominator. My head spun. It had to be the same person, and everything inside me screamed Rhonda. Crazy didn't mean stupid. Of course she would change her appearance to do something creepy like stalk my husband and son. Dios mío. I reached my hand up to touch Sam's arm and saw myself shake. I dropped it and clasped my hands together. I had to figure out what to do.

"Did you get her license plate number?" My voice had a tremor like my hands.

More head shakes.

"All right." I crossed the kitchen, then stopped short. How could I warn Sam without panicking him? Maybe I couldn't. I needed him to get it, really get it. "Sam, that's not normal, what she did."

"It's not that weird. What's *up?*"

Think fast, Michele, I told myself. "I'm paranoid, ever since Adrian got hit. I don't mean to scare you, but just humor me, okay?"

"Okay, I guess," he said.

I made eye contact with each boy in turn. "I want you guys to tell me if you see her again. All of you. Can you do that?"

They okayed in chorus.

I hardened my voice. "Take pictures of her and her license plate with your phone, and get away from her. Call or text me immediately, or call 911, and go someplace safe."

They stared at me. Andrew half-laughed. "Whoa, you're really freaking me out, Mrs. Hanson."

I nodded. Good.

Sam had a funny look on his face. "Yeah, Mom, no problem." He changed gears, stepping between his friends and me toward the oven. "Hey, what's that smell? Is that tater tot casserole?" He peeked inside. "Guys, this is like the best stuff *ever.* You've got to try it."

Ted shifted from foot to foot. "We were gonna pick up some Taco Bell, dude."

Sam went to the breakfast table and grabbed one of the plates. "Suit yourself, but I'm eating this, and I'm your ride."

Sam's normalcy brought me partway around. I grabbed a mitt and pulled the casserole from the oven. "There's enough for all of you. I'm going to put the bicycle on the training stand and ride for a few hours. I'm watching *Miracle on Ice* if you guys want to watch it, too."

Sam loved *Miracle on Ice,* and I knew it. He still cried when the US won the gold. He started telling his friends about it as he scooped an enormous portion onto his plate. I had planned to eat with him, but his friends provided me with a great cover-up for a shift of gears. I needed to figure out what to do about the stalker.

"Hey, Mom, do you want any of this?" Sam asked, holding up the nearly empty dish. Ted and Andrew had full plates now, too.

"No, you guys finish it off."

I changed clothes and jumped on my bicycle. I pedaled to the sounds of teenage boy voices cheering on hockey players. I was too stressed to connect with Adrian, but I didn't have time for self-indulgence anymore. My son was in danger.

Chapter Seventeen

Sam brought my phone to me from the kitchen about fifteen minutes before the end of my ride—about the time I was ignoring the fact that my knee was cursing at me in all the words my mother had never allowed me to say. Sam was chatting brightly as he brought it to me.

"It's Gigi for you." He held it out to me.

I groaned very softly. "Hello, Mother." I pulled the phone away from my ear out of habit.

"Robert called us. He told us some really disturbing things about Sam, and he said you're never around when Sam needs you."

I stopped pedaling. "What?"

"Sam has always been such a good boy, but he needs more parental supervision than he is getting."

"Sam used to have two parents in our household. I can't bring Adrian back from the dead. He's going to have to make do with one parental supervisor." I clipped out and sat on the floor to take off my cleats.

"Well, his father said—"

"His father only involves himself enough to complain about me to my parents when things aren't going well, but not enough to help me." I jumped up, barefoot, in my sweaty bicycle clothes. "Sam is fine."

The subject in question poked his head around the door, looking sheepish. "I'm going to take Andrew and Ted home, okay?"

I waved and he left. Poor kid had just gotten an earful.

"Robert told us about last weekend, and you know what the police said."

I grabbed a can of Endust and a rag from the laundry room and stomped to my office while I talked. "Why the hell does he call you guys, and why do you even talk to him? I'm your family. Robert isn't." I sprayed a shelf and wiped harder than necessary.

"You were married to him for ten years. We've known him since he was a boy. We can't stop caring about him."

"You don't have to talk to him. It isn't normal. It isn't right." I stopped myself. I'd lose this old argument. Robert still dropped in on not only my parents but my aunts, uncles, and cousins—all of whom, it seemed to me, preferred charming Robert to tightly wound Michele. Mine was a cautionary tale about marrying someone from your hometown. My family found Robert no less charming after he met the love of his life while he was married to me. I didn't blame him completely. I didn't love him, and he knew it. But how could I love someone who didn't even like me?

"Mom, Robert hasn't offered to help me or Sam. Sam or me. All he's done is call you and tattle on us."

There was silence on the phone for a few long beats. "He asked us for advice on whether he should take custody of Sam."

"He what?" I slammed the Endust down with a sharp thud.

She spoke louder and enunciated. "He wanted to know if we thought it best that he took over with Sam."

"I hope you told him to go to hell, Mother."

"Sometimes in life—"

"What you did not hear from him is how much better Sam is doing. Sam and I got things worked out between us. I am very pleased with his changes, and I am here. I live with him. I see him every day. I am his MOTHER."

"Robert said those detectives told him that Sam was hanging out with boys that buy drugs, and that he lied to the police."

I put Detective Young on my shit list for yapping to Robert. I had to make this stop. There was no Adrian to help me. I had to do this on my own. I pictured the bluebonnet sky from the first day Adrian came back to me, when I was bicycling near Waller. I closed my eyes and held the image in my mind. I started to count backwards from ten, but it was my husband's voice I heard, and I felt tears running down my face. He reached one. *You can do this, Butterfly.*

I licked the tears from my lips and spoke in my most authoritative voice. "Mother, Sam lied to the police because he didn't want to get in trouble for skipping baseball practice to hang out with Billy Mays. That is a closed issue. He is not a suspect. And I like his new friends. Robert hasn't met them." My hands weren't shaking anymore.

"Still, it troubles your father and I that you left town to go on your exercise trip without making sure that Sam went to his father's. You won't like hearing this, but we think you're spending too much time on yourself, and not enough time on your son. I've researched this issue."

Your father and ME, I wanted to scream, but I didn't, and it wasn't even the point. She'd uttered her magic words: *researched the issue.* When my mother utters the word *research* in relation to any issue, she's saying she speaks God's only truth.

I stayed calm. I breathed. I thought about how unlikely it was that my father had expressed a thought about my trip to Huntsville. A strong and proud man, Papa said my abuelo knew when to speak and when to act, like when he moved my abuela over her vocal objections away from her family in the Valley all the way to Midland so he could get a higher-paying job in the oil field and help send Papa to Texas A&M. Like him, Papa rarely does more than nod his head when my mother goes on about something.

She was still talking. "And I know you're spending as much time preparing for your race each week as you are going on TV and at work. There's no time left for Sam. You're being selfish. You need to—"

I threw the dust rag across the room and picked up the Endust can and chunked it after it. The can smashed against the floor and clattered into the wall.

"Selfish? I'm being selfish because I don't sit at home waiting on a son who isn't here because he's sixteen years old and would rather hang out with his friends and go to his job and play baseball? I'm selfish because all my non-work and non-training hours go to my son? Meanwhile, my heart is breaking in two, I miss my husband, I miss Belle, and I don't see Sam's dad saying, 'How can I help, Michele?'

Instead, he calls my parents and suggests I'm not fit to have custody of Sam."

"We think you should save the race for next year, or when Sam is off to college."

I wanted to scream at the top of my lungs and spin until I fell down, I wanted to be the knife-winged butterfly my father had named me after, but I tightened my jaw. "I am doing this race, this year. I am doing it for Adrian." With Adrian, I thought. With Adrian.

"Adrian is dead, Michele. Sam isn't."

Her words stabbed me through the heart with a knife of ice. Now I did scream. "This race meant the world to Adrian. If I don't go, he doesn't go. And guess what? It's part of my job, the job that puts food on the table for Sam twelve days out of every fourteen."

"If Adrian were here, he would understand."

I was panting with rage. "If Adrian were here, he would tell you that I can do both. Quitting this race wouldn't make me any more 'here' than I already am."

"You could—"

"Enough, Mom. Do whatever you think you need to do. We're done here."

"We just want you to think about it. We love you."

"I'll think about it. I just won't talk about it. Not another word."

I ended the call, lightheaded. I leaned over and put my hands on my knees.

"Mom? I'm home and going to bed." Sam stood in the doorway to the kitchen.

"Okay, hon. I'm sorry about that."

"It's okay." He hesitated, looking at me. "I love you."

His words nearly knocked me over. "I love you too, Sam."

He headed toward the stairs, and I sat down on the wood floor in the office and put my head between my knees. Why did it have to be that hard? I needed a break, just a tiny little breather. A moment. I needed everything to stop. My light head returned to normal, and I stood up. I needed to run, but I wasn't going to leave Sam alone right then.

So I started to pace, making laps around the house. I had walked so many miles that way over the years. I need action, motion, when my emotions kick in. I always had. Adrian liked to go off by himself when he was upset. Not me. I wanted a fight, a dramatic fight with hands in the air, voices high, and full use of all available real estate. More than once when we'd holed up in our room to resolve an issue, he left with me hot on his heels—even, once, out onto the sidewalk when he tried to take a run to clear his head. That hadn't made him very happy, and I'd given the old Jewish couple catty-corner across the street an earful.

Passion. Adrian and I had passion. I walked faster. It drove our marriage and my life. At first it scared me that our incredible lows offset the incredible highs of our emotional connection. When we got crossways, we lived out a one-act Greek tragedy. We didn't bicker or pick at each other. We agreed on life's big issues. Then we duked it out over minutiae we couldn't remember five minutes into the battle, because the fight was about the passion. I had needed it. I still needed it. It was childish. It was exhausting. But it was love. What we had was real, it was glorious, and it was love.

One childless night when we had only to choose how to spend the evening together, Adrian had kissed my ear. "What do you want to do?"

"Oh, I like it when you pick," I cooed, and snuggled up to him on the couch.

"I just want to make you happy."

"It will make me happy if you choose."

"I want you to choose because I don't want to disappoint you."

"You're not going to disappoint me."

"If you're disappointed, it will ruin the whole night."

"What are you saying? That I'll pout or throw a tantrum? When exactly have I done that before? When have I ever ruined an evening because you disappointed me?"

"You got upset when we went to the Astros game that time and got kicked out of our seats."

"Of course I got upset! Security escorted us to the door, Adrian. We used stolen tickets—not stolen by you, but you know what I mean. I didn't get upset at you, though. You didn't disappoint me."

"Well, the way you acted, I felt like I had let you down."

"You didn't let me down. The experience frustrated me."

"You can put lipstick on a pig, but it's still a pig."

"What did you say?"

"What? You mean lipstick on a pig?"

"Yes, I do. What exactly does that mean, Adrian?"

"That you can dress something up, but still, it is what it is. You can say you got upset for one reason, but bottom line is that I made the plans for our evening and you got upset."

"So, in this story, who is the pig?"

"No one is the pig. The pig is just a, a—"

"A what?"

"A—"

Eruption.

Irrationality.

Passion.

I paced a lot then, too, but we'd generated fireworks that lasted all night as we made love on the couch, in the shower, and finally in bed, where we woke up the next day starry-eyed and holding hands. It hadn't always made sense, but it was perfect.

Perfect comes in different shapes and sizes. Like my Sam, no matter what his father said or what my mother thought. I paced through the dining room, perfection in motion, cursing Robert, my mother, and fate. I paced past the kitchen island, cursing the woman in the Taurus who had me so shaken up. I paced past my hand-me-down piano that I hadn't played since Adrian died, cursing Detectives Young and Marchetti, who couldn't figure out who killed my husband but could terrorize my son. I paced back through the living room, looking out through the floor-to-ceiling windows at the tropical backyard—"Like

Kona," Adrian had said when we planted a dwarf palm together—cursing Diane for taking Annabelle, Scarlett for pushing me, and Brian for his expectations. And around the corner and back into the dining room, cursing Adrian for leaving me there without him.

And repeat.

Repeat.

Repeat.

All the while unwinding, remembering, coming somewhat to terms with my life, and, finally thinking. Planning my attack on the world, on the driver of the Ford who was stalking my son, until I collapsed into bed, the pieces of the puzzle in my mind finally in place. I knew what to do, and I would make it happen.

Chapter Eighteen

I'd never been in a police station before. What a depressing gunmetal-gray place it was: gray floors, gray chairs, and gray doors. It smelled gray, too, like someone had mopped it with dirty water. Detectives Young and Marchetti sat across from me in the gray interview room at eight a.m. because I had requested help.

The number from Blake's office appeared on my screen, calling me. Skipping my appointment that morning probably wasn't the most auspicious start to my recovery, but in a battle between my knee and Sam, even Kona and Sam, there was no real contest. I turned my phone face down.

Detective Young looked at me with something in his eyes. I couldn't tell what it was at first, because it was so different than what I usually saw from him. Then I recognized it. Pity. Pity brimmed over his brown eyes, oozed from the pores in his dark skin. He pitied me. I liked that even less than the look of challenge he'd always pointed my way before. I didn't need pity. I had my fighter on.

He cleared his throat and glanced at the impassive Marchetti before speaking. "I'm glad you brought this to our attention, Michele. However, we have an eyewitness, remember?"

"Mrs. Hanson. But you haven't found the car that killed Adrian. You have an eyewitness to a car that you have never been able to find."

"Yes, but—"

"I have a suspicious person in a suspicious car following my son. A suspicious car that also showed up in Adrian's life—even on the last day of his life, Detective."

"We have a reliable eyewitness to a young man driving a white late-model Ford F150."

I ticked on my fingers. "You don't have a license plate number, a car, or a suspect. Unless you count 'persons of interest' like my son."

"You don't have a license plate number or a suspect, either."

"I have a description of a suspect, and I have Texas plates. And I have suspicious circumstances."

"Except you don't have any motive, or a way to identify the person, or to tie the person to your husband or son."

"Other than she stalks them. And that's why you investigate, right? To find all this stuff out."

"What you told me bears looking into, but it's more than likely a series of coincidences. I can promise you, though, we'll look into it."

Damn him for brushing me off. Didn't he see me in front of him, *me*, Michele Lopez Hanson, fully convicted, and ready to storm the Alamo? "It's just not as high a priority as interrogating my boss, my papa, and my son, or as calling my ex-husband to feed him your low opinion of my parenting skills, is it?"

He held my gaze. "If you're concerned with how we've handled things, you should file a complaint."

"Of what?" Did he mean a complaint against him? I considered it, and the thought gave me a tiny thrill.

"Texas has an anti-stalking law. I could put you with an officer who could help you write up a complaint and you could file for a restraining order."

Ah, not against him. Against the stalker. I tucked my hand under my thigh to keep my nails out of my mouth. I knew that at some level he wanted to help me. I didn't like his methods, but I would do whatever I had to do to get this started. "Okay. But it's important to me that this goes on the record as part of *Adrian's* case. What you call a 'series of coincidences' is more than that to me."

"I understand." He paused several beats. "I'll go get an officer to take your complaint now."

Marchetti stayed to babysit me and fiddled with his mobile phone. I bit my thumbnail. To hell with my mother. I jiggled my aching knee. To hell with everyone. I needed to get out of the station to start the next phase of my plan. This visit was taking too long. At least I had doubled my workout that morning—and gotten much-needed connection and time with Adrian—so I had no other road blocks in front of me.

A reedy female voice sounded from the doorway. "Mrs. Hanson?"

A pale, freckled officer walked in. My mind redressed her in a plaid school uniform and knee socks that worked on her better than the creased police blues. "Here."

"I'm Officer Nickels. N-I-C-K-E-L-S." I felt a flicker of common-name-spelled-uncommonly kinship.

Marchetti left without a word, custody of the miscreant passed.

Nickels sat in the chair he vacated and spread some forms out in front of her. "You want to make out a complaint against a stalker and file for a restraining order, right?"

"Yes." I leaned forward.

"Um, so what is the name of the individual?" She looked down at her form, pencil poised.

"I'm not sure. I know the car, though."

She nodded. "That will help. License plate number?"

"It's an old white Ford Taurus with Texas plates. I don't have the number."

She opened her mouth, then shut it.

"I think the stalker is a woman named Rhonda Dale, but I'm not certain. It's at least a Caucasian woman, thirty-five or older, but I'd say younger than sixty-five. Can we see if Rhonda Dale has an old white Ford Taurus? If she does, then we'll know it's her."

"I—" She stopped. Her eyes clouded over.

Come on, I wanted to shout, but I needed her help. I imagined what supportive would sound like, and tried to match it with my voice. "Or maybe we could just find all the women thirty-five to sixty-five in Houston within driving range of my home that have older white Tauruses." I gave her our zip code.

"I'm not sure."

I gave her the most encouraging smile I could muster. "Is there someone who can help you?"

She stood up. "One moment, okay?"

I smiled again, my cheeks tight. "Of course."

I chewed off another fingernail.

Five minutes later, she returned. "Okay, we're looking for white Ford Tauruses, older models, registered to Caucasian women aged thirty-five to sixty-five."

"That's great."

"We should have the information within a week, and we can finish this paperwork then."

Seven twenty-four-hour days. A lifetime away. "That's not great."

"What?"

"A woman is following my son in this car, and a month ago a woman in a car like this one followed my husband, and then a hit-and-run-driver killed him. Next week is not great. Tomorrow is not even great. *Right now* is great."

"Well, I'm not sure what else we can do if you can't identify her." A fleeting image of Detective Young and Officer Nickels covered in honey and tied to aspen trees in bear country appeared to me.

"Maybe there are things I can do." It was past time to picture Michele in her happy place, and my knee started bouncing again. I didn't have the time to visualize bluebonnet skies or run to the pool.

She frowned, casting shadows in the pale skin on either side of the gap between her mouth and nose. "You shouldn't take the law into your own hands, ma'am. You could put yourself in danger."

"So, what should my son and I do in the meantime?"

"Well, you should stay away from her."

Not helpful, young lady, I thought, shaking my finger at her inside my head. "Maybe I could keep a log of the times and places we do see her?"

"That's a good idea."

"And I could review all my husband's papers and records. Maybe I'll see something that connects him or us to the car or some woman— maybe even Rhonda Dale?"

"Yes, that would be great."

"Bank records, credit cards, fan mail, old Day-Timers, computer files, all that kind of stuff."

Her face relaxed, and she exhaled. Great. Well, at least she was easy to guide, if not highly self-directed. "All good ideas."

"And you'll call me when you have the information?"

"Yes, ma'am."

"And then maybe my son and I can come in and you can show me drivers' license photos and see if we can identify her?"

"Yes, ma'am."

"Excellent. So, I'll have Adrian's information assembled within three days. To whose attention shall I bring it?"

"What do you mean?"

"I mean who will be the lead investigator?"

"That would be me, ma'am."

"Well, then, here's my card." I held mine out while she fumbled for hers.

"If you could sign the complaint for me, I can get things started, Mrs. Hanson."

I scribbled my name and left, knowing one thing now for sure: it was up to me to protect Sam and find this woman.

Chapter Nineteen

I logged in to the desktop at home and pulled up my email, typed the name of my long-ago roommate in the search box, and scrolled through the results. I clicked on her last Christmas email and scanned it for the name of the private eye service she and her husband started that year: Stingray Investigations.

Adrian had said there was something off about the driver of the Taurus, so he must have been connected to her in some way, however small, and I had to find it. I hoped the connection wasn't a night in a New Orleans hotel room after a half Ironman, yet Rhonda Dale had popped up as frequently as the car, and no doubt she'd followed Adrian, stalked him, across Louisiana and Texas. I just couldn't imagine why she'd have an interest in Sam now.

I dialed my phone, checking the 340 area code twice. I'd never called anyone in the Virgin Islands before. She answered right away, and her voice hadn't changed since our ten-year law school reunion. I loved her voice. Whether she was talking or singing, it was beautiful, with a timbre like handbells. I missed that voice.

"Katie? This is Michele Lopez."

"Michele! I'm so glad to hear from you. I've been so worried about you, and I am so sorry about Adrian. I think about you all the time. I hope you got our flowers. I've emailed you too, but I'm not sure I'm using the right address. Oh, God, I'm rambling. How are you?"

She had my email address right. I just hadn't answered it yet. I looked at my desk blotter and saw I had doodled Adrian's name. I ran my finger across it. "Thank you, I got them. I'm surviving, sort of. It's hard."

"I can't imagine."

"He's actually the reason I called. I need your help—both of you, I think."

"Absolutely. He's right here. Should I put him on the phone with us?"

I agreed, and Katie put Nick on speakerphone. When he said hello, I was flooded with relief. He sounded helpful and confident, and just right. So unlike Detectives Young and Marchetti. I was glad I called.

"I want to hire the two of you for a consultation. I've got a big problem."

I told them the story and briefly sketched out my theories. Nick took the lead, but he and Katie traded off talking for half an hour. They prompted me with more questions and answered mine, and together we fleshed out my plan. My heart raced—but not with tension this time. With anticipation, with confidence and determination.

"Thank you so much, guys." My voice caught. "You can't imagine how much you've helped me."

Katie said. "Call us if you need anything, Michele. You're a forever friend to me."

Her words warmed a lonely place in me. "You're a forever friend to me, Katie."

Nick cleared his throat. "Be careful, Michele. And be sure about this before you start. Sometimes you find out things you're better off not knowing about your loved ones. Don't let anything you find take away what you know is real."

"I won't. I mean, I'll try not to." We ended the call.

I understood Nick meant well, but I knew Adrian, the good and the bad. There was plenty of bad, of course. He was a bear if he didn't get enough exercise, he never arrived anywhere on time, and his sarcasm drew blood. Adrian was vain. Dios mío, was he vain. His scraggly blond hair hung perfectly scraggly, he chose clothes that said "I don't care" when he did, and he worked hard to maintain an exact balance of lean to muscle. He talked endlessly about the minutiae of his training schedule. And when he got down and lost sight of his half-full glass, he saw an empty glass crushed and ground back into sand.

Yet for all his faults (and mine, for that matter), he was open with me, and I with him. We read each other's email and blind-copied each other on personal correspondence. We shared a desktop at home. We opened each other's mail. I picked up his phone and read his texts and he mine sometimes. He couldn't be that open with me and yet hide something that would hurt me. He just couldn't.

Yet still a connection existed between him and Rhonda, and I didn't know what it was. There were secrets Adrian hadn't shared. Nick was right to caution me. Suddenly, a chill shook me and my empty house shrieked like there were banshees in the corners.

No, not banshees. Banshee. One of them. Only one had appeared before Adrian died, and I would find that hag, platinum blonde or not, and she would regret she ever came to know Adrian Hanson and his little clawed butterfly.

A clawed butterfly wouldn't sit in an office with the blinds drawn and hug herself. She would get up and fight. I whirled my chair back to the computer and my list. Time to do battle.

Chapter Twenty

The first item on my plan involved figuring out what Adrian had last worked on, and who with. I added fan mail to this item and started searching. After I'd exhausted the desktop files, I moved to his laptop, jump drives, and the files and papers in every drawer in the house.

The desk files were interesting. In an overflowing file Adrian had marked as Mail in blue highlighter, I found some pictures from fans showing off their assets. A woman in a tiny red Brazilian bikini. A man in a silver Speedo. Heat rose in my cheeks. He should have shown me these, I thought. But I wondered what good it would have done. I knew the groupies were out there. I also knew Adrian didn't pay them much attention. Nick's warning filled my head again: Sometimes you find out things you're better off not knowing.

Most of the mail was from lonely people sending hopeful letters to a handsome athlete who wrote about what they wished they had. I found a few from Connor Dunn, all very friendly, thanking Adrian for his inspiration and for his "My Personal Best" piece. No bug-eyed lunatics or obsessed schizophrenics jumped out at me, and no Rhonda Dale or Ford Tauruses.

I got lost in some of his old articles and columns. I clicked on the links, hypertexting my way back in time. "Endurance Eating, Despite Your Spouse" popped up on the screen, a tongue-in-cheek comparison of the ideal triathlete's pre-race diet to the food served in our home. He exaggerated our household idiosyncrasies, but it made him accessible, and better than someone writing dry "10 Foods To Avoid During Triathlon Training" articles. I clicked the "You Might Also Like" suggestion at the bottom of the article. "My Personal Best." The one Connor mentioned. I read the opening paragraph:

> *The beauty of triathlon is that anyone can reach a personal best at any age, on any day, on any course. I'm 41, and this year I set a personal best for the Half Iron distance, when I had always thought of myself as a*

sprinter, first as a college freestyler and then as a triathlete who just missed the Olympics in both. It's the same with life. At any age, on any day, in any situation, you can reach further than you thought possible. At 41, I discovered I was made to go the distance, and I married my Butterfly— she's my partner and my personal best, no matter what the contest.

Damn this man. Damn him for coming along and ruining me for anyone else. For making himself a liar, not just about forever, but about personal bests. He was wrong. I had nothing left to strive for, no expectations to exceed. I *was* my personal best with him, and there was nothing to reach for now. Butterflies migrate south, to a better place, but that's where it ends. It just ends.

I jumped up and shoved my rolling chair back from the desk so violently it tipped over backwards and crashed to the floor. Chingase. I couldn't wallow. That woman could be following Sam right now. I didn't have the luxury of wallowing. Claws out, girl. Claws out.

My next item was Adrian's pockets. Dios mío. I was already in hell, and the only way out was through Adrian's closet. I stomped into our bedroom and opened the closet door with my eyes closed.

The Adrian smell—Old Spice, sunscreen, rubber swim caps and tennis shoes—enveloped me. I straightened my back and started on the right-hand side with his shirts. I moved as fast as I could, trying to keep it clinical. Then I came to the linen shirt he wore at our La Grange wedding. I rubbed my cheek against it before I checked its pocket. That was enough to draw me into my task, and I began to swim through the clothes, gliding from one sensation and memory to another. I pressed my lips on the burnt-orange stitched "Hanson" on the breast pocket of a threadbare white shirt. I caressed the camouflage board shorts he loved to wear after a shower. I squeezed the dry mesh of his racing flats in my fingers, remembering their heat and dampness when he would throw them triumphantly in the back of the 4Runner, with me on his heels transferring them to the dirties bag.

I moved on in a trance, plunging my hands into memories I'd avoided for a month and coming up with little treasures: dry-cleaner receipts, gum wrappers, and in the pocket of the khaki shorts he had on when he met me for lunch at Beaver's on the last day of his life, a note about a paintball location for Sam's birthday, hard to read after its tumble in the washing machine. When I'd dried the last of my tears on the Baylor hoodie he wore to Bears games with me, I walked out of the closet. No hotel receipts. No threatening notes from jealous husbands. No phone numbers in lipstick on bar tabs. I gently pulled the door shut behind me until it met the frame, then gave it a firm tug. The finality of the soft clunk as it latched into place set me off again.

I snagged a box of Kleenex on my way back to the office and set it by the monitor. I looked down at my plan as I dabbed my eyes. Internet searches were next.

For the next hour, I Googled Adrian's name and mine, but it proved futile. With so much publicity since the book launch and his death, the volume of material overwhelmed me. I didn't have anything useful that could narrow my search, either. Certainly adding *Rhonda Dale* didn't help my results or my attitude. I eyed the search results and imagined slicing each article out of the Internet with my obsidian-tipped wings. It helped a little. I tried using the word *Taurus* with Adrian, but got only horoscopes and astrological charts. I switched search engines again and again, but Yahoo et al yielded nothing more than Google.

I checked the time. I had four hours before my three o'clock meeting with Scarlett at Juniper, when ESPN would be taping footage of me for their Kona coverage. I decided to tackle finances. My knee hurt something fierce, so I popped some Aleve and propped my foot on a chair, balanced an ice pack on my knee, then got to work.

The first two hours yielded nada except a headache. Adrian managed our money well. It never came easily to me, but he'd studied finance and accounting in college and worked in audit for nearly ten years. He turned to writing because he discovered a love for connecting with people, for saying the right thing, just right. It became a passion for him, like triathlon. I combed through our accounts from the past six months, on money in and money out, unfamiliar names, unusual transactions.

As I started to understand his system better, I adjusted my approach. We kept joint checking and savings accounts, but we had separate retirement accounts and premarital accounts. Adrian had a savings account for what was left of his inheritance from his former wife after we bought our Meyerland house. I knew this because we'd gone over our assets when we did our wills. We never touched that account or my premarital savings; they were emergency funds.

I found all the records for our modest joint savings account and my premarital savings account, but I couldn't find any trace of his. Nothing at all. No statements. Nothing online. Two hundred thousand dollars had vanished like it never existed.

I called the bank. Adrian closed that account three months ago.

The news exploded like a shotgun blast in my brain. Closed? Adrian closed a $200,000 savings account without telling me? I scanned the bank statements arrayed before me. Nothing. There was just nothing about it in the last three months. As I pawed through file folders it got worse. There was nothing about this account anywhere. Never. Not even before June.

It had existed, though. We'd talked about it. I'd seen it. Its tax statement came in the mail every January. So either my husband destroyed the file or he hadn't kept one. But of course he kept one. He even had files for closed credit cards. There had been an account, and there had been a file, but they were just gone, like every other damn thing I'd counted on.

"Oh, Adrian, what the hell did you do?" I wailed.

I had to think, not act like a scorned little woman. This could be significant, it could be my first big clue that could break this whole thing wide open. And that meant I could prevent Sam from ending up a victim, too. So, how did the money disappear? Drugs? Gambling? I didn't think so. A woman? Not unless you counted Rhonda Dale's story, which I didn't. Blackmail? I couldn't imagine what for. As I chased theories, a tiny, weak place in me whispered, "What if he was planning to leave you?"

Nick was right. Sometimes you don't want to know. My husband, my shiny blond Adonis, looked tarnished now.

When my phone rang, I jumped out of my chair. I'd lost time again. I felt like I was fighting for traction in slimy mud, sliding backwards down a hillside toward a deep, black, bottomless hole. I fought harder. I snatched up the phone and read the display: 3:15, Scarlett calling.

I skipped hello. "Shit, Scarlett, I'm sorry, I just saw the time."

Her voice hissed. "Michele, this is ESPN. They are not happy."

If they're unhappy, they might not give me the airtime Brian needs to sell books and you need to justify your fee, I thought. "I can be there in fifteen minutes. Can you stall them?"

"I'll try. Is your makeup done?"

"It will be when I get there."

She hung up.

I grabbed my makeup bag and purse and sprinted for the Jetta, painting my face at every red light between my house and Juniper with trembling hands. I parked and hurried in, trying not to limp, hoping my makeup wouldn't melt before I got inside. The door opened right before I reached it.

"Thank you." I ran through without looking to see who opened it—then screeched to a stop so fast I thought I heard brakes squeal.

The reception area looked like a lunar landing pad under a ray beam. Light kits angled overhead were trapping everything beneath them in a hot yellow light. The couch and chairs had disappeared and in their place loomed tall chrome stools. Ten feet away from them, a faux office had been set up with a black metal desk, black metal chair, and computer monitor. A big black camera on a truck pointed at me and I flinched.

"Michele's here," Marsha shouted, then lowered her voice to a normal timbre. "Scarlett and the producer are in your office. And I hate to bother you with this, but Connor Dunn called again. He said it's important."

"Thanks." I tried to walk sedately through the strange set, but I couldn't. I started running again, down the hall and to my office, even though the starts and stops had my knee screaming in protest. Shut up, knee, I told it.

Ten feet short of my office door, I stopped and smoothed my wavy hair and was comforted by the fact that it always looks the same no matter what I do. I patted my face, trying to remember if I'd finished my makeup. I slowed my breathing and straightened the top of the sleeveless embroidered pantsuit I'd thrown on that morning before I went to the police station. White linen. A little rumpled. But couldn't they do amazing things in editing?

I reached the door to my office, and I heard Scarlett before I saw her.

"Don't you love these photos from their book launch? Adrian was a gorgeous man, and Michele has that underdog ethnic thing going for her. You know your business best, but if it were me, I'd consider this one."

I stood in the doorway and watched her as she talked to a short man with a shiny bald head. He didn't look familiar to me. He had to be with ESPN.

I caught a glimpse of the picture in question. Three people in the frame. Me, Adrian, and clinging to him from the side, Rhonda Dale. Scarlett was gripping it with blood-red talons. I heard a roaring noise in my head, like one of the brush fires that raced across the pastures near our house one hot, dry summer in my childhood. I couldn't understand what I was seeing. I smelled smoke.

Scarlett spoke in a half whisper. Colleagues in the biz. Conspirators. "We got such a great sales and media pop when we released this picture before. You could crop Michele out—that's what we did—it has a lurid appeal that keeps people glued to the story."

The desk in my office burst into flames. The pictures caught fire, their edges curled, the paper twisted as the fire animated them, shrank them, and turned them to ash. The fire reached for Scarlett's fingers. I shook my head to dislodge my fantasy.

"Scarlett?"

She whirled. "Michele, you're here! So sorry you got stuck in traffic. Let's head down to the set and I'll introduce you to everyone." She tilted her head to the man. "This is—"

"You bitch."

"Michele!"

"It was you. I don't know how I could have been so stupid. Of course it was you."

"What are you talking about?"

"The email to the media. The picture that was attached to it. Your picture. That one." I pointed at her hand, and she turned the picture so that the print faced the floor.

The fire reached for me now, and I wanted to fly away, far away, away from Scarlett and the fire and this office. That or stay and claw the bitch's eyes out.

"What's going on here?" Brian asked, walking up behind me.

I turned to him with my claws unsheathed. "Ask Scarlett, and find my replacement."

My feet retraced their earlier path. I gathered speed down the hall of pain, flames chasing me faster, faster, until the edges blurred and my feet lifted from the ground.

Chapter Twenty-one

I drove the Jetta away from Juniper like a woman possessed, my tires screeching as I left the parking lot. All I remember from the drive was pressing my foot hard against the gas pedal, and the squeal as I turned into my driveway. I stomped hard on the brakes and was thrown forward into the steering wheel when the car jerked to a stop inches from the house. I rubbed my forehead. I hadn't even put on my seatbelt. While I huffed breaths to calm myself, I slammed the Jetta into park and turned it off. Silence wrapped around me like an embrace, and I held myself perfectly still.

When I realized sweat was rolling down my face, I got out of the car and walked into the house. I shut the door gently behind me. I tiptoed into the office, leaving the lights out and drawing the blinds as I went, and slumped into the black office chair. I tucked my wings in tight, cradling my body, rocking, slowly rocking in my chair.

A sob broke free from my chest, then another and another. I rocked and sobbed for I don't know how long, my brain emitting a low hum, a buzzing that rose and fell with the rhythm of the needle at the end of one of Papa's vinyl Everly Brothers records. I had nothing left, nothing except Sam. A harsher sob dragged my chest toward my knees. No one to help me. No one who believed in me. I started to sob again, but I swallowed it, and pictured my son. I scrubbed at my eyes. I couldn't let Scarlett derail me like this. I couldn't let anything happen to Sam. I had to think. I had to quiet the buzzing in my head, I had to use my brain. I rotated my shoulders back, and my arms rose and fell by my sides. Because that's all they were. Just arms again, not wings. I stretched them out in front of me. Short brown arms.

My bag lay at my feet. I leaned over and retrieved my phone, cleared my throat, and pressed a number on speed dial. It went to voice mail, and I kept my message short and sweet. "Robert, I'm going to need your help with Sam, immediately."

***

An hour later, Robert had returned my call. He'd agreed to drop Sam at my parents' in Seguin the next day for a long weekend of Dr Pepper, four-wheelers, and Seguin grandparents—maternal and paternal. I billed it as time away from his new friends before the start of his junior year. The grandparents would see firsthand that Sam had not sprouted horns living alone with me, and he would be safe, away from whoever the hell had him in her sights.

He would pick Sam up after baseball in a few hours. I glanced at my watch. Six p.m. I grabbed two Tylenol PM from the bathroom and chased them with water before burying myself in my bed.

***

Jobless, husbandless, and now temporarily childless, I woke at four a.m. the next day and took Precious by surprise. She didn't object. She was more concerned that Sam wasn't in his room, and as I got ready, she yowled at me.

"Got issues with me, cat? Get in line." I emptied a small can of Fancy Feast into her dish. She shut up and ate. Today Michele would kick butt, take names, and save the day.

I checked my phone for messages from the kids. Nothing. A twinge of sadness surfaced. I had tried to get in touch with Annabelle several times over the past few days, and she was still ignoring me. I needed to fix whatever was broken there soon. Soon. I scanned the messages I did have. Just a few from Brian, which I skipped, and another one from Blake's clinic: "You missed your Wednesday appointment. We have you down for eight a.m. on Friday. Let us know if you can't make it."

"I'm sorry, Adrian," I whispered in my head. *"I know you understand, but I promise I'll take care of my knee, too, just not yet. I won't let anything keep me from Kona. Not if I can help it."*

I packed up for my predawn swim and aqua jog. I reached down and stroked the cat's head. "Good girl, Precious. See you in a few hours." I was meeting my husband at the pool, and missing savings account or not, I'd loved the man a month ago, and I loved him still. That was what I knew was real.

***

At nine thirty I returned to the land of the living. Just in case, I checked in with Officer Nickels. Because who knew? Miracles could happen. Today was special. I could feel it.

"This is Mrs. Hanson. I wanted to see if you had any drivers' license photos for my son and me to look at yet?"

"No, ma'am. Um, it's only been one day. I have put in all the paperwork ordering the records, though, and I asked for a rush, so maybe on Tuesday."

"Wow, that's much faster than a week." And still way too slow.

I thanked her and hung up. So no miracle yet. Time for DIY. Ironically, since I hated the media, I had a journalist badge through Juniper Media. I decided to use my creds to find the driver myself. Well, that's not the whole truth. I called my friend Manny in the records department for Harris County and asked him do me a favor, since we went way all the way back to Vogel Elementary School in Seguin.

"Hey, Michele, how are your parents?"

"My father is a saint and my mother is a harpy."

"No, your mother is an angel. A beautiful woman, like you."

Manny had helped me many times for legitimate articles. I pitched him what I needed, attempting to make it sound legit, but he saw through my ruse. "I'm not supposed to do this. You could get me in trouble."

"Manny, the person that drives this car is stalking my son. It may be the same person that killed my husband. I need a restraining order, and the police can't get the records for a week. I can't wait that long."

"Dios mío! Why didn't you say so?" Manny had three young children. Keys began to click. I kept my mouth shut and let him work his magic. "It's a big number, Michele. There are thirteen hundred and one white Ford Tauruses registered in Houston that are five years or older. Ouch, mamí. This is a popular car."

"How about within ten miles of my house?" I gave him the address.

"Two twenty-nine."

"Female owners?"

Click click click click. "Thirty-six."

"How else can I narrow the information? What can you search by?"

"Well, we can pull some DMV information, you know, the stuff from drivers' licenses. Do you know anything else about her?"

"She's white, and she's at least thirty-five."

"White can be tricky. I don't want to limit you too much. How about I rule out anyone of Asian or African descent?"

"Okay."

That got us down to seventeen. By eliminating owners under thirty-five, we ended up with twelve, and I could work with that. He read the names and addresses to me over the phone in a low voice.

"Are there any more?"

"That's the whole list."

"There's not a Rhonda Dale?"

"Sorry, no."

How was that possible? I pulled up one of the articles about her and scanned for her age. Thirty-seven. Manny's search should have pulled her in if she owned an old Taurus. If it was registered in Harris County and not somewhere else. If it was registered as white and hadn't been repainted. If a man didn't own it and let her drive it. The possibilities started spinning through my head and anxiety rippled through me. But no, I told myself, I couldn't get sidetracked. I had to pursue the most logical leads first.

"Can you look her up and tell me what she drives?"

"Sure." Click click clickety click. "Hmm. I don't show any vehicles registered to Rhonda Dale in Harris County."

Mierda. She could have come from anywhere.

"Thanks, Manny. Are there pictures?"

"Not that I can get to you without getting fired. Seriously. They check to see if we send out that kind of stuff. Would it do any good for me to look at them and tell you what I see?"

"I don't think so. Thanks. I owe you. I don't even know what to offer, this is such a big favor."

"You don't owe me nothing. I'm going to pray for you guys."

I knew he would, too. I would pray for him in return, and I would try not to make it about his grammar.

So, now I had twelve names and twelve cars. No Rhonda left me stymied.

The front doorbell rang. I peeked out the side window at the thinner of Sam's two new friends. I opened the door.

"Hey, Mrs. Hanson. Is Sam here?"

"No, he's out of town. Well, you're not heavy enough to be Ted, so you must be . . . ?"

The kid had a great smile. "Andrew. I left my wallet in Sam's car, and he didn't answer my texts, so I thought I'd see if he was here."

"No, sorry. His car isn't here, either." Car. Sam's car. "Andrew, could I ask you a favor?"

He stood up taller. "Sure."

"I am trying to identify the woman Sam hit the other day and I have twelve names, and I wanted to Google some pictures. Could you come see if you recognize any of them?"

"Uh, yeah. Like, right now?"

"Please."

He wiped his hands on the thighs of his pants and stepped through the door.

"I'm making myself a sandwich. Would you like one?"

"Yeah. I mean, yes, please."

"The list is by the computer in the office." I pointed. "They all live in Houston, and they should all be Caucasian and about my age or older. If you get pictures that look nothing like that, it's the wrong person, because—"

He smiled and cut in. "Because there could be like fifty people named Andrew Ellory."

"Exactly."

I walked into the kitchen and pulled out ham, cheese, Miracle Whip, and Wonder Bread for Andrew, and brown-rice bread, turkey slices, Swiss cheese, lettuce, tomato, and German mustard for me. I raised my voice. "Ham, cheese, and mayo on white?"

"Okay, thanks."

I assembled sandwiches and grabbed a bag of carrots for me and Doritos for Andrew, a Dr. Zevia and a Coca-Cola, and tucked a roll of paper towels under my arm. I set everything out on the long desk surface and carried a chair in from the dining room. "I forgot to tell you to print any pictures that look promising."

"Okay, but I haven't found her yet. These with the check marks by them," he pointed at my list, "are definitely not her. Some of them I can't find, which is weird. Who's not online these days?"

"Old people. Private people. People that don't have computers. People that like to do other things instead of get online."

"Weird people."

"Those, too."

"Well, I've looked for all of them—and I don't mean to brag, but I'm pretty good at finding stuff about people. I found eight of them, and none of them are her. I couldn't find these four, though." He touched his index finger on the unchecked names of Rebecca Holden, Elizabeth Copeland, Nan Weaver, and Stephanie Willis.

My heart leaped. I could do handle four. "Wow, that's great! Thanks!"

"Yeah, and do you want me to print out the pictures of the other women? I have them open in all these tabs." He pointed at the screen.

"No, that's okay, Andrew. I couldn't have done this without you."

He jumped up. "No problem. I work at a computer store. This stuff is easy." He walked toward the door then turned around and walked backwards. "One thing, Mrs. Hanson. About that lady. I think you'll know it's her when you find her. She's really creepy."

The door slammed behind him.

Chapter Twenty-two

Four women. Four home addresses. A wide-open afternoon. I mapped their addresses, one to another, printed the results, and slung my zebra bag over my shoulder. I had more than enough time to run them down.

Rebecca Holden's address mapped closest to mine. I pointed the Jetta toward Reliant Stadium and cruised her street, mid-1900 teardowns interspersed with new construction pressing hard on the height and property-line setback requirements of the neighborhood. Box after box went by until I came to a T intersection. A white Taurus was parked in the driveway, and my adrenaline surged. As I rolled along the street, I got an eyeful of Rebecca's bumper stickers, crammed edge to edge on every square inch of its rear exterior. "Snowmen against global warming." "War is not pro-life." "Quiet women seldom make history." I grabbed a pencil from my console and scratched Rebecca off my list.

One down. Three to go.

The next Taurus belonged to Elizabeth Copeland at an address off Beechnut and Highway 59. I made it there in fifteen minutes. The rundown wooden house was on the rough fringe of a declining neighborhood, and the Taurus backed into the driveway looked promising. I couldn't tell if it was *the* Taurus, but I couldn't rule it out. I parked two houses down, taking care not to lock the Jetta. My running shoes made little squeegee sounds on the sidewalk, but the roar of Highway 59 blocked out life itself. It was like walking alone at the edge of the earth, cocooned inside myself with only my thoughts real. I turned up the sidewalk between weed-edged brown squares of lawn. The street number on the door hung askew by one nail: 7306. I pressed the doorbell and heard it chime inside. Ding dong ding dong. Dong ding ding dong. No answer. I knocked. Still nothing.

I did a visual sweep of the neighborhood. Satisfied no one was watching me, I opened the mailbox. Nada. When I talked to Nick and Katie, we hadn't covered physical sleuthing, but I had some experience from when I dated an older guy at Trinity. I heard he was cheating on me and I broke into his house and searched it. It went off without a hitch, although it spelled the end of the relationship. Unfaithful bastardo.

I'll just take a quick peek inside, I thought. One minute, maybe two. Adrian wouldn't approve, but he wasn't there. I opened the side gate to the yard and tensed, listening for barking and growling and slobbering. Nothing. I crept around to the back door. I put my hands around my eyes to block the sun and pressed my nose against the window. The lights were out and I couldn't see much. I pressed harder against the glass.

A nasally male voice far too close to my left ear sent chill bumps racing up my arms. "Who the fuck are you, lady?"

Without turning, I raised my arms high in the air. "My name is Michele Lopez Hanson. I'm looking for Elizabeth Copeland."

The guy spat by my foot. I kept my eyes up. "If you find the bitch, tell her I took all her shit to the dump."

I turned slowly to face him. Hispanic. Skinny but strong-looking, and at least six inches taller than me. "So you haven't seen her?"

"That's what I said, isn't it?" His gold front tooth reflected sun into my eyes. He shook his head and looked past me. "She ran off with some pendejo a month ago, and I ain't seen her since."

I kept my guard up and lowered my hands. "I'm sorry. I saw her car out front and thought she might be here."

"It's my car now." He laughed, enveloping me in at least a twelve-pack of beer breath. He narrowed his eyes. "Anything of hers is mine now. Friends, too. What do you say, pretty lady?"

"I'm not her friend."

"That's okay, I think we can work something out." He reached toward my hair.

I whirled and ran for the gate, his cackle following me but not his footsteps. I didn't bother to confirm he wasn't chasing me, just sprinted for the Jetta.

Probably safe to cross Elizabeth off the list.

Two names to go.

The next address in the Galleria area was a bust. No Taurus, no Nan Weaver. Well, people had jobs, and it was a weekday afternoon. I could come back at night.

The last address belonged to Stephanie Willis. It was at the far edge of the ten-mile radius Manny searched for me, north of 610 and west of 290. And it was a dump. The small 1950s ranch was missing a few shutters, and cardboard and duct tape covered holes that used to be windows in the garage door. Weeds and dirt served as the front yard. If Adrian's $200,000 went to Stephanie, she hadn't used it on the house.

An old white Taurus was just turning into the driveway, and it rolled until its front bumper nearly touched the garage door. I sucked in a breath. Perfect. When its taillights went out, I pulled in tight behind it and jumped out. My feet barely made a sound on the smooth concrete drive. I moved quickly and stood even with the backseat on the driver's side, ready. When the door opened, a woman got out and shut it, and I took a quick step between her and the house. Her mouth fell slack and she stepped back against her car.

The haggard woman pinched her mouth shut, crone-like, and squinted at me with small brown eyes. Limp, colorless hair hung down her forehead, with the rest scraped away from her face in a band. Her Yellowstone t-shirt was crusted and stained with something that probably started out red. For a moment, she seemed lost to me, like someone had turned the lights out around her and she was trying to adjust. Years fell away from her age before my eyes.

I leaned into her personal space and her smell almost gagged me. "Hello, are you Stephanie?"

She nodded, unblinking.

Anger rose inside me, and I went on the offensive. "I'm Michele Lopez Hanson. I thought we should meet face-to-face so you could tell me why you are following my son before I turn you over to the police." I crossed my arms and my chin jutted forward of its own volition.

When she spoke, her voice was atonal, flat with no affect. "I don't know what you're talking about."

I shook my head. "Whatever. I saw you following Adrian—who's dead, but you already knew that. And I've seen you following my son, and me, too. All I want to know is why."

She stared at me, zombie-esque.

I fought the urge to scramble backwards. "No comment?"

"I don't know what you're talking about."

"Well, if you don't have anything to say to me, then I guess I'll just finish up with what I have to say to you."

Suddenly she looked like a creature that *belonged* in the dark. But I lived half my life in the dark those days, too.

"Sam is out of your reach now, so stay the hell away from us." I closed my eyes for a nanosecond, picturing Sam in Seguin. When I opened them, my arms raised themselves, and I stretched them to their complete length. I flexed my claws and shook the air with a tremendous flap of my orange and black wings, their obsidian tips shooting flashes of light ricocheting through the air. "The police will be here soon, Stephanie, or whoever you are. I'd suggest you cooperate, because if they don't lock you up, you'll have to deal with me."

"You're nuts."

We stared into each other's eyes for another ten seconds. She didn't budge, but neither did I. Violent scenes played in my mind, satisfying scenes: my claws around her neck, squeezing, tearing; her, scratching at my face; me, beating her head against the ground until she couldn't get up, ever again. Orange and black dust on her fingers and face.

Finally, her façade cracked. She giggled like a sorority girl with very bad breath. "If I don't have anything left, neither can she." She wriggled her fingers at me. "Toodaloo."

Back in my car, I put a big fat double star by Stephanie's name, started the Jetta and backed out of her driveway, but only made it three blocks when the Jetta shut down and coasted to a stop.

And then a thought hit me. I forgot to check Stephanie's car for a dent. "Ay chingada," I muttered.

I paced around my car, opened the hood, and looked inside, then slammed it shut and sat down on the curb. Cars whizzed past me, but none stopped. Think, think, think. I couldn't afford to slow down. The 4Runnner was at Robert's, but he and Sam were gone. Brian and I weren't on speaking terms. I didn't have girlfriends. For the last five years, I'd had Adrian. His name on speed dial. His "Hey, Butterfly, I can be there in fifteen minutes. Hold tight."

I didn't have anyone now. I shook my head, hard. All I had was me. Come on, Michele. Broken cars aren't the end of the world. They get fixed. Call the dealership and have them fix it.

The number was in my contacts, and I pressed call. After a few transfers, service picked up.

"Yallow."

I told the man about the Jetta's many problems.

His laugh was a loud har har har. "Sounds like you need an exorcism, darlin.'"

My sense of humor wasn't great, but some of my mother's lessons took, so I used honey instead of vinegar. "I don't suppose you offer those?"

"I ain't a priest." He har harred again. "Bring it on in, honey."

"It won't start."

"Does your insurance cover a tow?"

"If they won't, I will. Can you arrange for one to pick me up? I'm on the side of the road. No Yellow Pages."

We worked out the details, and I moved into the shade of a treed front yard to wait. My next call was to my insurance company. Yes on the tow. And a rental car, if I wanted it. If? Ha.

***

Two hours later, I turned onto my street in a sage green Toyota Camry rental. As I pulled close to my house, an old white Taurus passed it slowly in my direction. Jesús Cristo. Had I spooked Stephanie out of her lair? I craned forward.

"God in heaven, it's her," I breathed.

No bumper stickers. The car looked just like the one I remembered from the month before, then the week before. Only it wasn't Stephanie. It was Rhonda Dale.

I pounded the steering wheel over and over and sped up the street to turn around in a neighbor's driveway. "Now who's following who, bitch?" I shouted.

The woman who had made our lives a living hell, who scared my husband by showing up everywhere he went in the last few days of his life, was casing our house. At the first traffic light, I pulled up behind her and snapped a picture of her license plate. I rolled on behind her, invisible in my green Camry and sunglasses. She cruised just below the speed limit along Brays Bayou, where I would have been running at that moment if not for my knee.

Vindication was burbling through my rage. "Take that, Detective Young!" I knew I should go to the police. They could question her. They could take my statement and process my complaint and give me my restraining order. It's what Adrian would want, and it might get Young and Marchetti to look harder at her.

When I thought about it, though—Nickels' inexperience, Young's resistance, and Marchetti's diffidence, and pictured the pity on Young's face as he poo-poo'ed my suspicions—anger crashed in waves inside me.

I would do this myself.

Rhonda stopped for gas at the Chevron Detective Young told me about, went through their Burger King drive-through, then headed west on 610 and north on 288. Traffic was horrible, and I struggled to stay within a car's length behind her. She took the MacGregor exit west, a right on Almeda, a left on Hermann. When she parallel-parked next to some yuppie apartments, I lifted my eyes and my pointer finger toward heaven. "Muchas gracias."

Then I shook my head and smiled a little, because my papa did the same thing three or four times a day.

I parked behind her and jumped out, triumphant.

Rhonda was wearing her usual hot pink, this time a spandex workout top and black yoga pants. She walked toward an entrance to some interior hallways, and I ran to catch up with her.

"Excuse me." She turned around. "Are you the slut who was driving by my house half an hour ago?"

She stumbled backwards and whimpered.

I moved closer. "Rhonda, you're busted. I know you've been following my son and me, and before that, Adrian. I'm taking everything I know to the police."

Her forehead smashed in on itself and she answered in a high, strained voice. "What? No! I mean, yes, I drove by your house today. I shouldn't have, but—Scarlett told me you found out she was behind the story about Adrian, and I just, I don't know. I just drove by. But I haven't been following you—or your kid."

"You can explain it all to Detective Young when he calls."

I didn't wait for her answer, just got in the car and drove away.

Chapter Twenty-three

The next morning, Precious anticipated my four a.m. alarm and walked on my face five minutes early.

"You're too damn smart," I muttered, shoving her off. I lay in the dark, knowing I wouldn't go back to sleep, that it was a miracle I'd slept at all. I had left three messages for Detective Young. When he didn't call back, I tried Marchetti and Nickels. Voice mail for both. I knew Sam was safe with my parents, but, still, I wanted a little backup.

No dice. I was, as usual, completely alone.

The last few days had crushed my tension meter like a stinkbug under a boot heel. I needed a pounding run and the presence of my husband. If only I could lace up my shoes and fly across the trails. Aqua jogging didn't give me quite the same high, and the thought of pedaling in my living room in the dark wasn't doing it for me, either. I'd missed a workout that week and had to ride twice as long to make up for it. Rhonda Dale be damned, I had to fly.

***

Thirty minutes later, with La Mariposa loaded on the bike rack, I was on my way northwest out of Houston to Waller. I couldn't get the miles I needed in the city. I had given the police everything I had on Rhonda in my messages, and I could be at the station by ten a.m. if I hurried. I'd brought Adrian's Old Spice sports wipes and a change of clothes, so I might even have time to stop for a few dozen doughnuts and a gallon of Starbucks on the way.

"I'm coming, my love," I said to Adrian.

My heartbeat quickened as I exited Highway 290 at Fields Store Road and saw that my timing was perfect. Fog hugs the ground any time the morning temperature out in the Waller area dips below 90 degrees, and it doesn't roll away until after sunrise. Flying down the highway through the dark fog with Adrian, feeling the wind through my helmet and moisture on my face and glasses, was just what I needed. I parked the Camry, zipped up my yellow reflector vest over my sleeveless white bike shirt and shorts, and prepped my bicycle. Sweat dripped off my forehead. August in Waller, even before first light, is like my un-air-conditioned middle-school gym after boys' PE. I drank a bottle of 5-Hour Energy from the stash in my console, then clicked the key fob to lock the rented Camry—such luxury. I pushed off at five thirty, just as I'd hoped.

"Adrian?"

No response, but I'd barely started, so I didn't let it bother me. I had tried to summon him countless times in the last few weeks, but he never came to me on demand, or any time other than when I trained. He would show up when he was ready. I stood in the pedals and coasted. My bicycle seat had absorbed half a bayou of water and it took some getting used to.

"I quit my job, Adrian. Brian let Scarlett get out of control. She really hurt me and the kids. And Rhonda is even worse."

Nothing from Adrian. In all the times he'd appeared to me while I was training over the past month, we'd never talked about his accident, or the stories in the paper, or anything else except us. It just never came up, never felt right, so I'd avoided the missing money. I hadn't told him about Annabelle leaving. I just enjoyed him when I had the chance. Maybe we could talk about what happened, what *was* happening, though, just this once? I could at least try.

"I think she's the one who hit you and has been following Sam. Maybe sometime when you're ready, you can tell me what happened. Somehow." I swallowed, hard. *"Adrian, I know she's lying. I don't understand about the money, but maybe I don't have to. I'm trying to believe that."*

La Mariposa flew through the fog as if through clouds, a brilliant flame breaking through with the sunrise. The air rushed beneath me, around me, above me, and my heart soared—with joy that I could protect my son. With hope.

"There's my Butterfly." Adrian's voice came from far, far away. The tips of his fingers touched my nose. *"You are the most loved, the most beautiful woman in the world. You know that, don't you?"* And then he did the thing I loved the most, slipping his arms around me from behind and staying there, just holding onto me.

"I do. And you are the most gorgeous, most loved man ever. You know that, too, right?"

But he didn't answer. I don't know if he heard me. Did he hear me enough when he was alive? Had I made sure he really knew how much I loved him, what he had done for me? I regretted every second of discord, every grumpy moment. I wished I'd given him nothing but happiness every chance I had. That I had complained less, criticized less, lost my temper less. I streaked through the fog with tears in the corners of my eyes.

The ride passed quickly. The mist started to lift. I checked my Garmin. Eight thirty. I would be back at my car by eight forty-five as planned. I didn't want to be, though. I didn't want to let this warmth go, to let the feeling of Adrian's arms around me end. I had so little of him. I didn't want to stop.

As I came around a downhill right-hand curve that cut through thick forest, a car careened straight toward me on the wrong side of the road. For a split second, I thought I was dreaming it. I blinked.

The car was really there.

I could veer to the right, like last time. Only we were about to cross Little Fall Creek and a low concrete wall blocked my way.

Adrian's breath puffed hot against my neck. *"You can't ditch to the right, and you can't let yourself go under. You have to aim for the car, and jump your bike over it, and fly."*

Oh, how I wanted to stay there with him. I nestled into the sound of his voice and steered straight for the car on the damp road, cranking the pedals as fast and hard as I could. But I didn't crouch. I didn't prepare to pull up and jump. I pulled in my wings and wrapped them around myself, and right before I closed my eyes, I saw the driver. Limp mousy hair, squinty eyes.

Tires squealed. Air rushed behind and beside me. Shock waves from an impact to my left crashed into my eardrums. Then, nothing.

Something warm covered my face, and I smelled dirt. Was I dead?

My eyes opened. Seconds later? Minutes later? I didn't know.

Sun. It was sun I felt on my face. No God. No angels. No Adrian. Just me, sprawled in fog-wet grass, by myself on the side of the road. Alive.

I looked around me. La Mariposa lay crumpled ten yards behind me. I groaned. Not my beautiful bicycle. It was like another piece of Adrian had been ripped from me.

I probed along my body. Grass and gravel on my right, wet dirt on the left. Scrapes. A few sore spots, but that was it. I glanced to my left and saw my butterfly locket on the ground, its chain broken. I rolled over and grabbed it and curled around it, fetal, whimpering.

I heard sounds off to my left and pushed myself up to a sitting position, then rolled forward to my hands and knees and stood up one leg at a time. I kept still until the black spots in front of my eyes went away, then I walked about fifteen yards back to the road. A large truck pulling a horse trailer was stopped there. The car wasn't. The truck had a badly mangled front fender, but no more damage. A man was talking loudly on his mobile phone, and when he saw me, he kept talking and headed toward me. He put his hand over the mouthpiece.

"You all right?"

I nodded. Sort of, I thought.

He moved his hand and resumed his call. "I slammed on my brakes, but I kinda skidded. I just prayed to God to save us all and kept it straight with the brakes locked down." He closed his eyes. "The Taurus is upside down in the creek, and ain't nobody got out yet. I'm looking at the lady on the bike, and she's scraped up real bad, but she's walking and she says she's all right." He gave the location and got off the phone.

I ran down the embankment to the creek bed behind him, slipping in my bike cleats. We peered inside the car, a white Taurus, and I saw her. Stephanie, on the ceiling with her head trapped between the roof and the steering wheel.

The truck driver felt for a pulse, then shook his head and walked away from the wreckage, talking into his phone. "Looks like the other driver didn't make it."

I started shaking. Pain shot through my head. I sank to my knees.

"Miss, you okay?"

"I think so. I—I just realized how lucky I am."

"You shore are. Somebody upstairs must be looking out for you."

"Maybe so."

"I ain't never seen no dead person before. Plenty'a dead animals . . . I'm feeling a little queasy." He stared at the horizon. "I'm gonna check on my horses."

As soon as he was gone, I stuck my head into the Taurus, looking for something, anything, to help me understand. Stephanie's purse lay on the ceiling of the car by her head. I tried not to look at her as I grabbed it. I sat down on the creek bed and pawed through the contents as quickly as I could. The police would arrive soon. I grabbed her driver's license first: Stephanie Willis, at the address I followed her to the day before. I pulled out a cracked and soiled ID badge for the Houston Independent School District. I found a package of photographs of Adrian taken over the past few weeks, even months—some with me, some with Sam, some with Annabelle, and some with all of us and even other people. That was it for the purse, but the papers, spattered with Stephanie's blood and brain tissue, included a sheaf of Adrian's articles.

I slid one out and a sob caught in my throat: "My Personal Best." It was highlighted in yellow and underlined in black pen so hard the paper had ripped. This time I read past where I'd stopped last time.

I was married before, and I've been a triathlete for years, but now I have a partner, a partner in life and a partner in sport. This makes all the difference to me. My life has purpose, and triathlon is a joy again. Training is a time we can spend together, achieving shared goals and attaining dual victories. Becoming her coach has rounded me out as an ath-

lete. From the first race we trained for and competed in together, I set personal-best times. Yes, I got faster in my mid-forties, thanks to my partner—but best of all, I became whole, even though I never knew I was incomplete.

I was so proud of him when that article came out. It really touched his readers, and even now, it made my tears roll. What had it meant to this woman, though, that she had carried it in her car, marked to bits? I stared at the documents in front of me, no closer to understanding why she had ruined my life, until I heard sirens approaching.

I needed to get out of this woman's things before the police drove up, so I shoved the purse and papers back into the Taurus with what was left of my husband's killer.

Chapter Twenty-four

I perched gingerly on the seat of the squad car, trying to keep my bare thighs off of the sticky vinyl seat that bounced under me. The car smelled of sweat and cigarettes. I fought nausea. The officer pulled away from the accident and I felt a visceral tug at my heart—I turned back and saw La Mariposa. I wanted to jump out of the car and run back, to throw myself over the bicycle and weep.

"You okay back there?"

"I'm good." I had popped two Aleve at the scene and declined medical attention. The pain settled into me, worse than I'd expected.

"Your car's parked by the old stadium?"

"Yes, thank you."

"You're welcome. I called that HPD detective. Just wanted you to know."

My phone rang: Robert. As tempted as I was to put him off, I'd have to tell him what happened sooner or later. "Hello?"

"Sam's missing, Michele. He stayed in the barn apartment at your parents' place last night, and we couldn't find him this morning. We searched the whole property. Please tell me you've heard from him."

"What? No! I'm in a police car, riding away from an accident. I haven't heard from him, or anyone at all." I scrolled through my missed calls and messages. Nothing.

"Shit! I can't believe he would take off."

"He wouldn't, Robert. Sam wouldn't do that."

I stared down at the bloodstains on my clenched fists, trying to figure out where I was bleeding, then realized it was Stephanie's blood. I wanted to scrub my skin with a wire brush, scrub myself clean of her, the crash, that damn Taurus.

The Taurus.

I screamed at the officer. "Turn the car around!"

I heard "What?" in one ear from Robert and "What?" in the other from the officer.

I was screaming and sobbing, "My son is in that car. I think my son is in that car. Please turn around!"

Firing questions at me, the officer turned on his flashers, wheeled the car around, and radioed ahead all at the same time. Robert's voice rang out from the phone in my lap.

I hit speaker and leaned as close as I could to the front seat, holding my phone where the officer could hear it. "Officer, I have you on speaker. My son's father is on the phone, and he said our son Sam is missing. This woman, the dead woman from the accident, has been following Sam for a few weeks, maybe longer. I told you earlier but I'll repeat it for my ex-husband now—I believe she killed my husband a month ago, after stalking him. I just didn't figure out her identity until yesterday when I confronted her. Sam was visiting his grandparents in Seguin. I told her he was far away and safe from her. Twelve hours later, she tried to kill me, and my son is missing."

"Did you see your son in the car, Mrs. Hanson?"

"No, but I know he's there somewhere. He didn't have a car in Seguin. He wouldn't have run off. He had nowhere to go. Stephanie took him. I know it."

"Houston is a long way from Seguin, let alone from Waller."

"Two hours to my parents' place, and the same back to Houston. One hour to kidnap my son. She had more than enough time."

"Well, ma'am, the fellas on the scene didn't see a kid."

"Did they check the trunk?"

He radioed my question. A crackly response came back through. The officer translated. "The car left on the back of a wrecker at the same time we did. They're trying to raise the driver on his cell phone now." He glanced back at me and the car swerved. He corrected it. "They couldn't get the trunk open."

"He could be injured! Can we catch the tow truck?"

"They're en route, but I can head in their direction." He slowed down and turned the car around again. "Young and Marchetti with

HPD said this wreck is part of their homicide investigation. They've got more resources than us, so we sent the vehicle to a yard north of downtown Houston. It'll take 'em about forty minutes to get it over there and take us about the same from here. If he is even in there, which he may not be, ma'am. Maybe you should call the police in Seguin, too."

Robert yelled something I couldn't understand.

I took the phone off speaker and put it to my ear. "What's that?"

"Your parents are calling the police on the other line. What in the hell have you gotten him into, Michele?"

"Now is not the time to point a finger at me, Robert. Luckily, I am alive to help you figure out where Sam is. There was a stalker, a killer—not to be confused with Michele, a mother, and the person who figured all this out."

I dropped the phone. "Sir, I had a thought. She had time to go by her house, so she could have left my son there. Could someone go check?"

"That's a great idea."

He got back on the radio and in minutes had ushered up assistance in Houston. "Give 'em about thirty minutes, ma'am. HPD said they have officers close by."

I closed my eyes and pictured Sam. I held his face in my mind. The pull I'd felt not to leave the accident. I held back another sob. "Hold on, Sam. I'm coming."

"Still no answer from the driver of that tow truck, ma'am. We'll get there soon, though."

I put my phone to my ear again. "Robert, are you there?"

"Yes."

"Do you want to stay on the phone while we're en route?"

"I do. And Michele, I'm sorry for what I said earlier. That was out of line. I'm scared about Sam."

"I understand. I'm scared, too."

The drive seemed to take forever, but twenty minutes later we pulled into an impound lot on Dart Street, with downtown Houston looming over us in the near distance.

The tow truck and the old Taurus had an ambulance parked beside it.

Just then, the radio crackled to life. Garble, garble, garble.

"What did they say?"

"It's the officers at the suspect's home. They didn't receive an answer to the knock on the door. They have entered and are searching. No sign of anyone yet."

In the office, the driver was logging in the Taurus. I was in his face in a split second. "Why don't you answer your phone?"

He scowled at me. "Who the hell are you, and what's it to you?"

The officer held his hand up to quiet me. "Sir, I'm Officer Dodge, and we called ahead. That's our ambulance. We have reason to believe there's someone in the trunk of the vehicle you towed in. We need to search it." He turned to the desk officer and flashed his badge. "This accident occurred in my jurisdiction, and I am working in cooperation with Detectives Young and Marchetti of HPD. Can I get some help opening the trunk, please? It's an emergency."

The man at the desk nodded and talked into an intercom.

I went outside and started pacing in front of the building, where the scents of urine and gasoline assaulted me. I breathed through my mouth, trying not to hyperventilate. The tow truck driver came back out with a large man in greasy clothes wielding a crowbar and some other tool. They took Officer Dodge and me back out to the Taurus.

The two men worked together on the trunk, grunting and straining as one worked on the lock and the other levered with the pry bar. The ambulance attendants stood beside them.

"Sam, honey, Sam, are you in there?"

Officer Dodge's radio crackled to life again. This time, without the highway noise, I could understand the voices clearly.

"No sign of anyone at the residence of Ms. Willis. The officers have completed their search. Detective Young was on the scene, and he identified pictures of the boy and his family in her things."

I swallowed hard and looked back at the Taurus. The roof and front end had sustained the worst damage, but two strong men couldn't get the crumpled trunk to budge.

I spoke into my phone. "Robert, are you there?"

"I'm here, I heard."

A popping noise drew my attention to the officer working on the trunk. "I think we've got it. Stand clear."

I couldn't swallow the enormous lump in my throat. Tears stung my eyes as I prayed, "Please, God, let him be all right. If he's in there, let him be all right. If he's not, let him please come home and be all right. Just please let my Sam be okay."

The trunk latch released, but it didn't pop open. The officer bent his legs and positioned himself low with his hands around the bottom of the trunk lid. He pushed with his legs in a dead lift, crying out with the strain until the lid groaned, then with a long, loud creak, opened.

My son lay motionless inside.

I yelled so loud my voice hurt my own ears. "It's him!"

Robert's voice crackled from my phone. "Michele, is he okay?"

I didn't answer. I didn't know the answer. I watched the two paramedics as they reached into the trunk to do their work. He was wrapped in a wool blanket, with a strip of something white through his mouth. His forehead had a gash, and there was blood, a lot of blood, but I couldn't tell how bad it was.

One of the paramedics turned his head toward me. "We've got a pulse. His respiration is slow, though. We're going to move him out of here. Please stand clear."

"Robert, he's alive. They're getting him out now." The phone fell from my hand, and

I dropped my head into my hands and sobbed.

Chapter Twenty-five

I woke with a start in a strange place. The smells were strange: antiseptic, coffee, and something vaguely unpleasant. My forehead was resting on a flat, hard surface. I lifted it and looked down. A table. A cup of coffee of suspicious origins in front of me. I sniffed. Definitely not Kona.

An efficient female voice interrupted my thoughts. "I'm Dr. Smith. Are you Sam's mother?"

Hope surged in me and I leaped to my feet. "Yes, I'm Michele Lopez Hanson."

She waved her hand "no." "Please, have a seat. I just wanted to update you on Sam's condition."

I lowered myself back into my chair and put one hand around my cold coffee, the other in my lap. "Thank you very much. Please, how is he?"

"Lucky, for one. Really, we can't find any serious injuries."

"His head?"

She smiled. "A concussion, but that's it. We'd like to watch him overnight, but if all is well in the morning, you can take him home then."

"Oh, thank you!" I rose so quickly I jarred the table and knocked my coffee over. "I'm so sorry!" Coffee ran in every direction and soaked the tiny napkin underneath the cup.

Dr. Smith went to the condiments bar and brought back a stack of paper towels and we both started blotting. "He woke up while we were stitching up his forehead. His head hurts and he's pretty nauseous, but that's to be expected. He's on his way to a room now. You can go see him." She gave me the room number. "I'll finish this up."

"You're sure?"

"Of course. Go."

"Thank you, Doctor," I said over my shoulder. I was already halfway to the door.

I rounded the corner of the cafeteria into the hallway, where my body met a solid object. Large, unyielding, but not hard. A familiar scent. Two large hands reached for my upper arms. They were gentle.

"Sorry."

"Just the person I came to see." It was Detective Young.

"I'm on my way to Sam." I stepped back and started around him.

He reversed course and fell in step with me. "Good. I'd like to see him, too."

I bristled. "He has a concussion. He's in no condition for questioning."

"I only want to see him, to tell him I'm glad he's okay. That I'm glad this is over, and I'm sorry."

"Okay. Is Marchetti with you?"

"He's back at the station doing all the paperwork. He'll be with me when we take Sam's statement. Yours, too."

"But—"

"Slow down, Michele. When Sam is ready."

"Good."

I pushed the call button when we reached the elevators and the doors opened immediately. We got in together and ascended, jerking and dinging, to the third floor. When the doors opened and we stepped out, I said, "Thank you. For taking it seriously this morning about Sam."

"I got your messages last night about Rhonda Dale and the other women, and what you'd done. That was pretty damn stupid, you know."

"Someone had to do something. I was right about the Taurus. And that woman won't get the chance to kill my son like she did my husband."

"Point taken."

We turned onto Sam's hall and I pushed ahead of Young into Sam's room. My eyes pulled my son into me. Tall, dark, and handsome, that was my boy, even in a hospital bed. A blue flowered gown hung from his frame, and his forelock hung over his bandaged forehead. He was sitting with the head of the bed raised, clicking a remote control.

"Sam."

He tracked my voice, and grinned, or tried to. His eyes were sunken and black-rimmed. "Mom." His voice was scratchy and young.

"How are you feeling, kiddo?"

"Weird. Not great."

"You've got a concussion, I'm sorry to say, so it may be a long night." I leaned over and kissed his cheek. "I love you. I'm so happy you're okay." I sat down in the stuffed leather chair beside the bed and took his hand. He didn't resist.

Young moved close to the bed. "Hi, Sam."

Sam looked at me. I smiled. "He's just here to say hello."

Sam said, "Hello," in a deeper voice than he'd used with me.

"It's good to see you're all right. When you're feeling a little better, I'll come back and talk to you about what happened, but it's all going to be okay." Young stepped up to the bed. "Has anyone told you yet that your mother saved your life?"

Sam shook his head, just a little, and grimaced. "No, nobody's told me anything."

I patted his hand. "Do you remember what happened, honey?"

"Uh—" He stopped and looked at the door as Robert, Papa, and Mom walked in, erupting with noise. Sam winced but smiled.

I stood up. "Easy guys. Concussion."

Papa stepped in front of Robert and Mom and peered into Sam's eyes. His hand reached into his pocket for his pen light, ever the man of medicine, even if usually with animals. He came up empty.

My father hugged me. "Itzpa, we were worried."

I stood and slipped my arm around him. "He's going to be fine, Papa."

Young made an "ahem" sound. Papa released me. "Tough kid you've got here. Good kid."

All heads swiveled toward the interloper's voice.

I gestured toward Young. "Everyone remember the detective?"

"We've met over the phone." My mother's voice promised she had a lot to say about it, but she held it in. Robert and Papa just nodded.

"Good to see you all again." Young made a round of the group, shaking reluctantly proffered hands. "I have to get back to the station. Michele, Sam, I'll see you guys later."

I moved back to let my mother join Papa. An arm slipped around my shoulders, and Robert squeezed me, hard. It was the first time he'd touched me since I moved out of the house we'd lived in together. I wouldn't need a repeat for a long time, but I didn't resist. I put my arm around his midsection and squeezed him once, too. Sam was our son. Right now, the only person in the world who felt like I did was this man beside me.

My phone rang. I broke free of Robert and saw it was Annabelle. "Hello, Belle." I had sent her a message earlier that Sam was in the hospital, but I'd left out the details. It was the first time she'd called or texted me in days, and I was glad to hear her voice.

"It's all over the news, and Facebook." Her words ran together. "Is he all right, Michele? Is Sam going to be all right?"

"Yes, sweet pea, he is. He can go home in the morning. Let me hand him the phone." Smiling, I held it out to my son. "For you. It's your sister."

An hour later, we had worn Sam out. Papa and Robert leaned against the window ledge and stared at the TV, a preseason NFL game. The Texans and somebody. Mom and I sat on either side of Sam, patting him. The kid would have bruises soon, but I just couldn't stop.

"You don't have to talk about this if you don't want to, Sam, but do you remember what happened?" I bit a fingernail on my non-patting hand.

"Michele." My mother shook her head, miming biting a fingernail. I pulled it away from my mouth, then hated myself for doing it.

Sam touched the bandage on his forehead. "Yeah, umm, not a lot. I went to bed, and then I woke up because I heard something. A woman was in my room, and she had a gun. She told me to stay quiet or she'd kill my grandparents. She made me get in the trunk of her car, then she jabbed my arm with something, and I don't remember anything after that."

"Well, kiddo, let me tell you the rest." My mother's version? I stiffened. "That same woman ran your mother off the road on her bicycle, and the car flipped and the woman died. We discovered you were missing, and no one had a clue what to do. Except your mom. She told the police you were in the trunk of that car. Nobody believed her at first. But she didn't stop until they'd found you, right where she said you'd be."

I couldn't remember the last time I'd heard my mother talk like that about me. I put my fist to my mouth to hold in a sob.

"Mom? How'd you know?"

I lowered my fist slowly and relaxed my hand. "I don't know. I just knew."

"She was the same woman I hit with Adrian's car, wasn't she?"

I nodded but I couldn't speak. Sam still called it Adrian's car. He hung on to Adrian, too. Something zinged my heart. Adrian should be here.

Mom took over the conversation and Sam hung on her words, letting her fill in the blanks for him. As much as it soothed my soul to see my boy's brown eyes clear and my mother take rare pride in me, my mind was adrift. Adrian wasn't with me anymore, and I wasn't sure when I'd lost him.

When I came to my senses after the wreck, he was gone. I thought back to the moments before the crash, to his arms around me, to his breath on my neck. To the moment I didn't jump my bicycle.

I hadn't jumped my bike because I wanted to stay with Adrian, and I'd almost joined him. Instead, I lived, and because of that, my son was alive. A horror swept through me. If I'd died, no one would have found Sam. Somehow, God or fate or—who knows, maybe even Adrian— had intervened, and because of it Sam lived. Jesús Cristo, I had made a choice that almost cost Sam his life.

Like a bulldozer, a thought crushed me: Adrian vanished when Stephanie died. I found his killer, and he was gone. The sobs I held in almost strangled me, but I could not fall apart again, not when Sam needed me, not when everyone thought I was finally back to acting like a real mother. Oh, what they didn't know. What they didn't know.

And then the warmth slipped over me, the warmth of my husband. Maybe he wasn't gone. I focused on the feeling, listening for his voice. I strained, but there was nothing. Something inside told me to me look up, look UP, and when I did, there he was, standing in the doorway to Sam's room, right where he should be. I stretched my hand toward him. He was so beautiful. His blond wavy hair, his sparkling green eyes. I could even smell him. He was real. The scent of tennis shoes, Old Spice, and him. Just him. I dove into his eyes, and his thoughts washed over me.

"You're not safe, Butterfly. It's not over." He disappeared.

"Take me with you!" The warmth faded and I felt a pop, and something inside me loosened and fluttered down, down, down. I spoke aloud. "Adrian? Adrian!"

But he was gone.

Chapter Twenty-six

I spent the night with Sam in the hospital, staring into the dark, unmoving, unwound, and untethered. I couldn't stop the images that blasted through my head one after another in an endless loop. Adrian, catapulting into the sky in a shower of sparks off the bumper of Stephanie's car. Sam, tiny and unconscious, wrapped in a burning wool blanket. Stephanie shoving Annabelle into the airport security line as the terminal around them ignited, Stephanie holding a lighter under Scarlett's red nails as they burst into flame, and me flying on La Mariposa toward Stephanie, a lance with a glowing hot tip gripped under my right arm and aimed for her head. The fire in my head robbed the heat from the rest of my body. I wrapped myself in every blanket I could beg from the nurses, but I couldn't get warm. The minutes ticked by, one second at a time, hours marked into halves by the visits of the night nurse to check on Sam.

At five fifteen the next morning, I heard a tap on the door. I jumped. My mother poked her head around the corner.

I tried to keep my voice down. "Do you know what time it is?"

"You don't have to whisper, Mom," Sam said. "Somebody comes in and wakes me up every ten seconds, so it's not like I'm asleep." He sounded tired and cranky.

Mother marched to the chair on the other side of Sam's bed and sat herself in it. "I'll handle it from here, Michele. Call when you're done, in case they've let us check Sam out."

"What?"

She made a little hrmph noise. "You only have six weeks of training left until you taper. Now's not the time to slack off."

Taper? Where in hell had my mother learned triathlon terminology?

Sam spoke in a slightly less grumpy voice. "Geez, Mom, don't just stand there. Gigi's got this."

They were right, of course, but something had come off its track inside me, like the belt from the flywheel on my abuela's antique sewing machine. I used all my strength to will my feet to move. I grabbed my bag as I passed it and left the room.

My condition was more than inertia, though. I dreaded facing the pool. Dreaded it more than death. Adrian's words replayed in my head. "You're not safe. It's not over," he'd said, then disappeared in a way that screamed "gone" at me all over again. Gone. Was Adrian really gone this time? I knew, but I didn't *know*, and I didn't want to find out. If I dove into that water and he wasn't there, what then?

I spent three and a half hours in the water aqua jogging and swimming without a flicker of connection with Adrian. Not the tiniest bit of signal. He was gone, truly, and a piece of me broke off and floated away.

***

From the gym I went to the police station. It hadn't changed since my last visit, but I had.

A text came in on my phone from Robert: *"Sam discharged. I have him."*

"It's not over," I said aloud. Sam would be safe with Robert, away from whatever it was that wasn't over. More safe than with me, at least, the woman that couldn't keep Stephanie Willis from getting to him. I shivered and put my hands around the warm Styrofoam cup in front of me and sniffed. The coffee smelled like weeds. I sipped. It tasted like weeds, too, but I knew I needed it.

Young, Marchetti, and Nickels entered together, and we exchanged greetings as they sat down. Marchetti's sweaty shirt stuck to his chest.

Young took charge. "Thanks for coming in. We got Sam's statement this morning with his father present. I think we're good there."

"Okay."

"I'm glad he's all right, Mrs. Hanson," Marchetti said.

I sighed. "Michele. And thank you."

Young grilled me for over an hour. They weren't happy I'd taken the investigation into my own hands, but I deflected their disapproval. I hadn't broken any laws, and we'd ended up in the right place. I could let them have this.

"We have evidence that suggests Ms. Willis killed your husband. She kept notes of every time she followed each of you. What you were doing. When. Where. What she did." He cleared his throat. "She made a note on August second that she 'took care of Adrian Hanson' near Meyerland Plaza at 4:05 p.m. And, of course, the paint on her car is a match for the paint on Adrian's bicycle."

I sat, stone-like, even my heart and lungs on pause. I had known this, but I hadn't had the proof. "So is this enough for you? I thought you had an eyewitness who told you different?"

He looked down and moistened his lips. "There's more. She also made a note that she contacted the police and gave an eyewitness statement that a white Ford F150 driven by a young man in his late teens had hit a bicyclist."

My heart restarted with a jolt. "She was your witness?"

"She was our witness." He held up his hand. "We had no way of knowing she had any connection to Adrian, or any motive to do anything other than help us solve a crime, and she had a clean record. However, I am very, very sorry that it misdirected our investigation. So, yes, it's enough for us. We're going to close the case."

His words sank in slowly. All of this. She had done all of this. Everything I lost, she took. I closed my eyes and saw my claws landing on her back, grabbing her, and my great orange and black wings beating the air around her and lifting her up with her head down and her arms and legs trailing limply. I opened my eyes and swallowed. Young was still talking. I had to stop letting myself think like this. It wasn't real, and it wasn't helping me. Sleep, I thought. I need sleep. I gave my head a tiny shake.

Young kept talking, but I wasn't listening anymore. I knew I should tell them about Adrian's money, but I couldn't do it. I could keep my good memories as long as I learned to forget about that damned account, and I intended to try. None of it mattered, anyway. It didn't tell me why Stephanie had done what she did, why Rhonda followed us, or why Adrian told me it wasn't over. I chuffed very softly. What were the words of a dead man, anyway? I knew what Young would call them. Delusions. I didn't need to hear that. Whatever the reasons, Adrian was gone.

Papers appeared in front of me, I signed them and said my thanks and goodbyes, and I left the room. I opened the front door to the station and stepped out into an army of cameras. Their shutters clicked and whirred. Microphones advanced at my face. Reporters fired questions at me.

"Tell us about Stephanie Willis, Mrs. Hanson. Did she kill your husband?"

"How was Ms. Willis connected to your husband? Did he have an affair with her, too?"

"Michele, where's your son? Is he going to be all right?"

"Are you still doing the Kona Ironman?"

"How has all of this affected your book sales?"

I shielded my face with my hand as I pushed through the crowd. I'd had my fill of vultures and their intrusions. This was my life, my wretched life. Or what was left of it. I made my way to the parking lot, dragging my throng with me. My parents had picked the Camry up for me last night from Waller, and I was grateful for it as I clicked the fob. Several reporters ran ahead to it, drawn by the flashing headlights.

A Hispanic-looking female reporter in a summer-weight tan suit blocked the driver's door, pen poised over her notebook. Print journalist. "Can you comment on the statement Rhonda Dale made this morning? Are you going to accept her olive branch?"

"Excuse me." I looked past her faceless form.

She didn't move.

My reaction took even me by surprise. My wings flapped on either side of me and I saw them—boney and black, dagger-tipped with a smattering of coarse black hair. I bared my fangs, more bat now than butterfly. "Get the hell out of my way, puta."

She took a step back, her hand to her throat. "What the hell's your problem?"

I raised my wings to their full span. "Really?" I hissed under my breath. "Really?"

She scurried away.

I tucked in my wings and retracted my fangs, then turned back to the group. "My family thanks you for your respect for our privacy at this time of tragedy and grieving." I got in the car. The reporters blocked my path. I blared the horn until they let me through.

I drove away from the station aimlessly. I had no job and nothing to do before it was time to train again the next day. Long bicycle, my brain inserted automatically. But I had totaled La Mariposa, and what was left of her was in police custody. Adrian had picked her out for me. Every component, every setting of that bike Adrian had customized himself. I could ride Sam's old bike, the one he rode ten inches ago in seventh grade, but it wouldn't match my body precisely enough to get me through the Ironman bike course. Body position and comfort mean everything in avoiding severe pain and even injury.

I turned right instead of left at the next corner. Ten minutes later, I pushed open the door of Southwest Cyclery on South Braeswood. Cold, dry air infused with stinging droplets of condensation hit me like a blizzard. I let the door swing shut behind me and inhaled the smell of rubber tires and lube oil. Bicycles hung from hooks on the wall and in the ceiling, and row after disorganized row displayed triathlon and bicycling accessories from ear plugs to seat covers. Adrian loved this place. I never really had until that moment. Something about the chaos that had repelled me before was calling to me.

A twenty-something man with sleeve tattoos on both arms greeted me.

"Is Pilar here?"

He twisted his face toward the back of the store and yelled her name. I winced. She emerged from the doorway to their bike repair shop. Pilar could have sprung from the same womb as the man. Both of them were tall and stooped with bright blue eyes that peeked out from under sun-bleached brown hair.

"I'm Pilar. How can I help you?"

I introduced myself and she shook my hand. "I'm going to Kona to do the Ironman in October. I totaled my bicycle yesterday."

Groans of sympathy came from both of them.

"I have a strong emotional attachment to it. My husband customized it for me, and he died recently. He said you helped him get the bike. His name was Adrian Hanson. I was hoping you'd remember it."

"Oh my God, I knew I recognized you. Mrs. Hanson! I loved Adrian. I just read about your wreck online one minute ago. You know—in the retraction that woman made where she said none of the stuff she blabbed about to the media was true." I blanched. "Here, let me show it to you. It's awesome. Completely vindicates Adrian, but I'm not surprised."

We went behind the counter and she typed a few keystrokes on the computer, then turned the monitor to me: *Dale Retracts Statement and Apologizes to Hanson Family.* I scanned down to the good stuff.

Dale said she was approached by Scarlett Thomas, the publicist for Juniper Media. Juniper, Michele Lopez Hanson's employer, published the Hansons' book, My Pace or Yours, *and also puts out* Multisport Magazine, *to which Adrian Hanson contributed a monthly column. "Scarlett showed me the picture of Adrian and me from his book launch, and she offered me $5000 if I'd send this story she had written to the media, with the picture. She told me it would be good publicity for the book and would help Adrian's widow and kids. And that it would help me get acting jobs, like in commercials, because she knew people.*

Last week Mrs. Hanson came to see me and I realized Scarlett was wrong. I'm not a bad person, and I admit I was interested in her husband, but I should never have followed him around, and I should have never taken money to tell lies. I'm glad the woman who took Mrs. Hanson's son and killed Adrian is dead. He was a great man." Neither Ms. Thomas nor representatives for Juniper Media could be reached for comment, and Mrs. Hanson declined to comment.

"Wow." Scarlett was an even bigger bitch than I'd thought. And that reporter had moved fast to print a diplomatic description of my comment about Rhonda, which was probably better than I deserved.

The young man spoke in a serious voice. "We loved Adrian. We never believed that stuff."

I cleared my throat. "Well, thank you. Now, about my bicycle—"

Pilar lifted a toe against the baseboard in front of the register and rocked forward in an Achilles stretch. "I remember your bicycle. He had it painted like a monarch butterfly."

"Yes." I tightened my lips to keep my voice from shaking. "La Mariposa. That's what we called it."

"I'm glad you and your son are okay."

"Thank you. Can you replace that bicycle? I want one exactly like it."

Pilar nodded, bouncing her hair. "I'll bet I can find one by this time tomorrow and have it in shipment within days."

"That would be wonderful. Adrian tweaked my bike, taking out spacers, cutting things down. I want to match the old one's settings exactly. And the paint job. The police have it now, but I could bring it in a few days. Could you do that?" I didn't have to tell two bicyclists how important this was.

"Absolutely."

I heaved a sigh. "Thank you. Thank you so much."

Pilar to the rescue. I was grateful, truly, I was. Yet this bike would only be a replica. How could an imitation ever be enough, really, once you'd had the real thing?

When I got home, Robert's car was parked out front. Great. I thought when he said he had Sam that he meant at his house. I needed privacy, alone time, thinking time. Well, I wasn't going to get it. I opened the door and headed in. Precious didn't greet me.

Robert's voice reverberated. "We're in the living room."

I set my purse on the island in the kitchen. "Okay." I went into the hallway bath and splashed cold water on my face. A gray-haired woman stared at me from the mirror. "You look like I feel," I told her. But I wasn't falling for the tricks of my overactive imagination.

I trudged into the living room. Precious was sitting in Robert's lap, purring as he scratched behind her ears. Traitor.

"Jeez, Mom, what happened to your hair?"

"What do you mean?"

Robert's brows rose to upside down V's, like insert marks. "Did you color it?"

My stomach knotted. "What color is it?"

Sam walked up to me and touched my hair. "Gray, or white, nearly."

I dropped down onto the ottoman and put my head between my legs as the room itself grayed out. Sam was at my side in half a second, patting my back. "I'm fine," I said. Only I wasn't. I thought overnight grays were an old wives' tale. I raised my head. "Thanks, Sam."

"I think you should get your money back." Robert sounded entertained.

"It's not color. I don't know what it is. I don't even know when it happened."

"That's freaky." Sam's voice held a lilt.

Robert scooted forward on the couch and his knee started to bounce. I wanted to scream and clamp it still with my hand. "Since you're going to be so busy for the next two months, I wanted to offer to let Sam stay with me. Kind of flip his living arrangement for a while."

Sam scowled. "Mom's fine. I have a car. We—"

I shook my head at him. "It's okay, Sam."

And shocking as it was to admit it to myself, it was. It was more than okay. This was the perfect solution to keep Sam safe from whatever it was that was still out there, whatever threatened me, and—I had to believe—anyone with me.

"You guys haven't spent any time together this summer. Sam hasn't exactly made himself available." I turned a serious gaze to Sam. "I think it's a good idea."

"Mom?"

"You only have two years of high school left. You'll regret it later if you don't spend more time with your father."

Sam slumped back on the couch, holding on to his elbows, one with each hand. "I do see Dad. I see him lots."

Robert beamed. "This is going to be great, Sam, I promise."

"Well, then, that's settled." I ignored the glares of my son.

Chapter Twenty-seven

Monday was a rest day. I got to Blake's clinic before eight. I didn't have an appointment. I only wanted to tell my story once.

The receptionist recognized me. "Michele, we've been worried about you. You disappeared on us. Then we saw the news, and I'm so sorry. Let me call Dr. Greene. We'll work you in."

She called her, but it was Blake who showed up. He smiled at me. "Michele, come on into my office."

I didn't want to, but all the resistance had gone out of me. His office was small, and diplomas hung on one of the walls. Texas State University chiropractic. Texas A&M bachelor of science. Pictures adorned another wall: Blake with clients, Blake in bicycle attire in a crowd of people in street clothes within a large crowd of other bicyclists in front of the courthouse on the square in La Grange, a spot I recognized instantly.

Blake saw me staring at the photo. "Me and my fan club. That's the start in La Grange of day two of the MS 150. I'm a hometown boy, so every relative I have comes out to say hello."

I nodded without replying. The MS 150 Houston-to-Austin ride for multiple sclerosis. Adrian and I did that together.

"You look like you could use a hug."

I didn't want a hug. "It's not as bad as it looks."

He hugged me anyway, then sat down at his desk and motioned at the chair in front of it. I sat with my left leg out straight. "You've had a rough week."

"Yes, I have."

"And no privacy. It must be hard, everyone knowing your business. I'm sorry. If there's anything I can do?"

I shook my head.

He put his elbows on the desk and clasped his hands. "What are your plans for Kona?"

"The same."

"You're sure?"

"I'm sure."

He frowned slightly, then lifted his eyebrows. "Let's go see Dr. Greene, then."

We left his office and walked with Dr. Greene down to the first exam room.

"How's your knee?"

I crossed my fingers in the hand they couldn't see. "About the same."

She probed my leg, knee to hip. "It feels like a rockslide from your hip down to your knee."

Blake stepped in. "Okay, the question is how do we get Michele ready to run a marathon on the tail end of a hundred-and-twelve-mile bike ride and two-point-four-mile swim, in—" he looked at the calendar on his phone, "yikes, in eight weeks."

I pressed my lips together hard. "I can do it. I only have to run this one race, then it doesn't matter if I ever run again. Whatever I have to do, I'll do it."

Blake crossed his arms. "Michele, if you want to finish this Ironman, you have to follow our plan from here on out. If you stick to the plan, it will be doable, but painful. Very painful."

I nodded. Pain was the only thing left that confirmed I was still alive.

***

An hour later, per my request, Brian met me at the rear entrance to Juniper. I was there per his. He held the door open and I ducked in. He followed me into what we called the "huddle room," right next to the emergency exit. He shut the door behind us.

I turned to him, but he wouldn't let me speak. "I'm batting first, Michele. That's not a request."

The old Michele might have fought him, but this Michele didn't care. I sat down in a black swivel chair and leaned my head back.

Brian lumbered back and forth across the room, punching the air in front of him with his index finger as he talked. "Juniper has canceled Scarlett's contract. Even when you ran out of here last week, she didn't admit a thing. I thought you'd lost it, honestly. It's not like you've had an easy time of it." He held up his hand so I wouldn't interrupt, but I wasn't going to anyway. "At that point, all I wanted was to make it okay for you to come back when you had calmed down. Everything's changed now, though. I didn't call that play she ran, and I didn't even find out about it until that newspaper article came out last weekend."

I shook my head.

"I know, Michele, I know now. But I didn't know then. Have you even listened to my messages from last week?"

I shook my head again. I had deleted them all.

"Well, that explains some things. When I woke up last Saturday morning and Evelyn handed me the paper, that's when I found out. That's when I realized the extent of this, this—" He stopped. He swallowed. "I'm sorry, Michele. About everything you've been through. It's been a tough season. I can't believe Juniper had anything to do with it, but we did, and at the end of the game, it's my team. I was blind to Scarlett." He dropped down hard into the chair across from me, and it oomphed in protest. "I don't care if we ever sell another goddamn copy of *My Pace*. I don't. Or if you write any columns. Or do the Ironman. Or come back to work with us, even though I would love if you did. I just want you to forgive me."

Just as I knew Adrian hadn't betrayed me, I knew the same of Brian. How to explain it to him, though, I didn't know. What I felt wasn't anger. I didn't have the energy for that, but I didn't have the energy to make him feel better, either.

"Brian, it's okay. We're good. I'm going to see this through with you and Juniper."

He nodded over and over, quickly, biting his lower lip. Then his eyes narrowed and he leaned toward me. "Michele, where's your locket?"

***

That evening while I was heating up dinner, a red blur out the side window caught my attention as Sam's 4Runner pulled into the driveway. My stomach clenched. I was barely managing to keep Sam and Annabelle at a distance. I didn't begrudge him visits—this was his home, too, after all. I just couldn't bear a confrontation. I was doing this to keep him safe, and I would protect him until my last breath. Maybe someday he would understand.

The door from the driveway opened with a bang and closed with a slam.

"Sam?"

He clomped down the hall, and when he entered the kitchen, I caught my breath. Whiskers had sprouted on his cheeks and he looked thicker, stronger. Angrier. Only two days had passed since I'd seen him last. But then, my hair had turned gray in an instant.

He smacked his keys down on top of the microwave and took a seat at a barstool. He picked up the papers in front of him before I could stop him and started reading.

"Those are mine. Give them to me."

After a few pages, he threw them back down on the breakfast bar and they spread out like a game of fifty-two-card pickup. He pointed at them. "What are these, Mom?"

"Things I need to do to get ready for Kona." I tried to gather them up, but he picked up a list and held it away from me.

He read aloud. "Stop newspaper. Cancel housekeeper. Give Precious to Sam. Empty refrigerator. Send Annabelle jewelry. Give clothes to Salvation Army." He shook the paper at me. "What is this about?"

"Someone has to take care of the cat while I'm gone." I snatched it from him and turned away.

He picked up a jar of pickles from the counter and threw it at the floor. It shattered. The sharp smell of vinegar filled the air. I whirled back around, staring at him. Neither of us looked at the broken jar, and I tried to pretend he hadn't done it.

"Don't you even care about Belle, Mom?"

"What?"

"Check out her Facebook status."

I scooped up the fan of papers and walked carefully through the pickles and glass to the office. He was just baiting me.

He raised the ante. "She hates New York, not that you'd know, and she wants to come home. Only she doesn't think you care enough to let her."

I stopped. He was so mad at me again, so fast, like he'd been after Annabelle first left, and leading up to our showdown in the car about him lying to the cops. Why couldn't he even try to understand? I retrieved my phone from my pocket and opened the Facebook app Annabelle'd loaded for me. Had I even opened it all summer? I went to Annabelle's profile page.

Her status was one word. "Alone."

Me, too, Belle. Me, too.

I looked back at my son. He had his hands behind his head and was leaning back with a stubborn look on his face.

"I'm coming with you to Kona."

Panic took flight like a winged creature in my chest. "Oh, no, you're not. You have school."

"It will be okay."

"Well, it's not okay with me. Your grades this year are what count for your college applications next fall."

"I can make up the work."

"Sam." I tried to regroup. "Thank you for offering. I'm going alone, though." Not that other people hadn't offered. My parents, Dr. Greene—even Blake, however inappropriate that was. I had politely declined them all.

I put the papers on my desk and came back to the kitchen, stepping over the pickle debris again. I scraped my uneaten barbecue sandwich into the trash. I walked over to Sam and put my hands on both of his shoulders. "I am proud of you. You are a wonderful son. I'm sorry you can't go with me." I kissed him on the cheek and my lips touched wetness.

I went to my bedroom, and a few minutes later I heard the door slam again. His engine revved, and then there was only the silence of the house and my fragile heartbeat, the heartbeat of a butterfly.

Chapter Twenty-eight

Nearly two months later, the morning before Kona, the town of Kailua-Kona was buzzing with tension and activity. I thought I'd be wound tight, but I wasn't. My seas were dead calm and my sails hung slack. I stayed to myself, mostly, trying to keep still enough that Adrian could find me. I had to believe he'd come.

I didn't have time to dwell on it, though. I'd been at work since before sunrise. By nine a.m., I was sitting at a mock desk in a borrowed office requisitioned by ESPN for a redo of our foiled shoot at Juniper the month before. Stephanie Willis had upped my news quotient again, not that I cared. Brian brokered a deal with ESPN and I'd agreed to the interview in return for a promise: they could film me all they wanted the day before and the day after the race, but I got the race day to myself, for my husband.

They sent the same producer I'd sort of met in Houston. The top of his bald head shone under the lights as he gave everyone their instructions. No surprise, but after he'd got an eyeful of me last time, he'd brought hair, makeup, and wardrobe people with him. The entire set smelled like Aqua Net. From my glossed lips and coiffed helmet of dyed-black-again hair to my aquamarine sweater set and strand of pearls, they had me looking like their vision of Michele, the widowed editor and author.

"Right now we just want day-in-the-life shots, like we got earlier today of you training." Pretending to be training, rather, in garb emblazoned with the logos of ESPN's Ironman sponsors, but I didn't quibble. "When we have enough, we'll hold up cue cards and you'll turn to face the camera and answer the questions."

"Like this?" I typed at the keyboard.

"Yes, good. Now, we're rolling, so I want you to act naturally, and don't talk to me anymore." I nodded. "In five, four, three, two, one, action."

My computer displayed nothing. I typed, *"I miss you, Adrian. Come back to me."* I reached for a paper on my desk and read it, then typed, *"I love you and I don't know how much more of this I can take."* I dialed my desk phone and told imaginary Sam I was sorry, and pretended Annabelle was on the line and told her I loved her more than ever. Probably doing it make-believe didn't count, but maybe they'd read my lips on TV. I listened to silence and ended with, "Buh-bye now." Buh-bye now? I never say that. The cameras were making me an idiot.

I saw motion out of the corner of my eye. The producer had sig-naled someone. The pouty male makeup artist walked to the camera and held up a cue card. "You lost your husband, training partner, and co-author, Kona qualifier Adrian Hanson, two months ago. How has this impacted your training?"

I had practiced this the day before. Thirty- to forty-five-second sound bites and done. I could do this. I took a deep breath through my nose and exhaled through my mouth, then started. "It's much harder without him. Adrian coached me, but it was more than that. He made it fun, and that made it easier. It was like date time for us. But he's still with me." Or he was, I thought. "His words are in my head, and in our book, and I have his memory to carry with me. He never even knew I'd gotten into Kona. I'd saved that as an anniversary surprise for him, and to be truthful, waiting to tell him allowed me to make sure I could really do it, that my head was in it and my body would hold up. Since he died, I've stuck to this because of him, and for him, through tragedy, loss, and injury. I wouldn't be going for Kona without him."

I left out a few things, like the part about Adrian joining me for workouts after his death, and his desertion after Stephanie died. That his missing savings account tormented me during the long hours I trained with nothing to distract me. That I couldn't sleep at night because I was worried about dangers he should have explained to me so I could protect our kids.

Sometimes the real story isn't the story, I thought. Sometimes the real story is just no one else's damn business.

The pink-haired stylist's turn. She held up her cue card. "You have a customized bicycle that will make it easy to pick you out during the bicycle leg of the race. Tell us about it."

"Adrian called me his little butterfly. He customized a Trek Pilot to fit my rather undersized frame," I smiled, "and had it painted orange and black like a monarch butterfly and had 'La Mariposa' stenciled on the center post—that's Spanish for butterfly. My papa's originally from Mexico, and he nicknamed me Itzpa after an Aztec butterfly goddess years ago. Adrian told me that on that bike, I really could fly. A month ago, my husband's killer tried to run me down while I was on La Mariposa, and it was totaled. I'm riding an exact replica on Kona, thanks to Pilar at Southwest Cyclery in Houston."

The makeup artist held up another card. I read the words, but they weren't ones we had practiced. "Adrian gave you another butterfly gift. Tell us about the locket you'll be wearing at the race." What kind of sick joke was this? I'd told them earlier that I lost the locket in the wreck.

Brian walked toward me from off-camera. He'd come to Kona to handle the book promotions and media until he could find a replacement for Scarlett. Good, he would explain it to them again. "Michele, a replica of your bicycle might work, but not for your locket."

I bobbed my head. My hands were suddenly cold. "Exactly."

"I couldn't stand it that you lost it. I called the Waller police and HPD. Neither of them had it in evidence. I searched the crash site for it. I walked that ground over and over. I went back and used a metal detector. I couldn't find it. It was sudden-death overtime."

Movement from stage left caught my eye again as a police officer came and stood beside Brian. He looked so familiar. When he addressed the camera and said, "I'm Officer Dodge, from Waller, Texas," I knew his voice instantly. What in the hell was he doing on Kona? Had ESPN brought him here? Or Brian? A rush of emotion and memory swept over me like a tsunami. Terror. Hope. Joy. Sam. "Your boss called me originally to check evidence for your necklace. He called me again and asked if I could think of any other places to look."

My eyes left Dodge for a moment to take in Brian's face again. His cheeks were bright red, like a cherry on top of the blueberry ice cream of his damn Texans jacket. I wanted to run from the set so I could cry in private, cry for having ever doubted Brian, for all the times I shut him out in the last two months.

Dodge continued. "So I remembered our long ride in my squad car, and I looked for it there. I couldn't find it. Brian asked me if he could look. Darned if he didn't take the seats out of the car. I told him this must be one hell of a necklace, and he said yes, but it was more that Michele was one hell of a woman."

That was too much. My lips trembled, my eyes flooded, and a wretched sob escaped from my throat.

Brian put his hand in his pocket and lifted my locket from it. He held it toward me. "God knows how, but it ended up caught in the bottom of the front seat and I found it, a three-point shot at the buzzer. It's in perfect condition, without a scratch."

I clasped my hand around the cold butterfly. I turned my hand over and stared at it, but I couldn't see anything through my tears. "Dios mío."

Dodge put his hands in his pockets and lifted his shoulders. "I wouldn't have believed it could have been in there if I hadn't watched him disassemble my whole car in front of me and pull it out of the bottom of that seat."

As the butterfly sat in my hand, it grew warmer. I pressed it to my face and could almost imagine the little monarch's heart had started to beat.

Brian clasped my upper arm. "The chain was broken, but I had it repaired."

I dangled the butterfly against my chest and pulled the two ends of the chain to meet in the back. By feel, I fastened the clasp. The warmth of the butterfly spread across my chest. I had a piece of Adrian back. I stood up and embraced Brian, then Dodge, then again Brian for much longer.

"Thank you," was all I could manage, but I patted him to make up for it.

The ESPN staff clapped. I'd forgotten they were there.

Chapter Twenty-nine

After the sobfest of my interview, I had to spend the rest of the morning doing other press and signing books before I could escape back to my room. I wanted a nap, but I had a long way to go before I could rest, including the need to fuel and hydrate in preparation for the race, and to send Brian one last blog post before I went to sleep. If I slept at all.

The room was spartan except for La Mariposa the Second leaning against the wall outside the bathroom. Maybe that wasn't fair. The space was spare, but it was tasteful. The white wicker furniture and pale yellow cushions were brand new. A pillowy white comforter covered a sturdy mattress. Maybe if Adrian were there I would have had more enthusiasm.

A few years ago at one of my first triathlons, Adrian gave me his take on pre-race hotel rooms. "Some coaches warn their athletes against sex the night before a race. The theory is that it saps your energy."

"Oh, really?" I said. "What does my coach advise?"

"Your coach thinks that for every orgasm you have, you'll shave a minute off your personal-best time."

"Well, don't just stand there." I'd pulled my short silk nightdress up and over my head. "You've got a lot of work to do."

I shut the door on the room and my memories with a click.

I ate a seafood salad lunch at Splasher's Grill, which Adrian would have enjoyed, then walked back toward my hotel. My knee felt tight. Maybe the walk would warm it up before I had to go set up my transition area and run through a light workout on the course.

As I stepped outside, I noticed the sign on the coffee shop across the street. "Serving only the freshest homegrown Kona." Another thing Adrian would have liked. And I heard a woman's voice. "That's her."

I glanced across the street and saw multi-time world champion Ironman Mirinda Carfrae. Wow, I thought. She's amazing. And almost as short as me.

A door bell jingled and a store I hadn't noticed before caught my attention. A small sign swung from the awning: The Flying Flower. I stopped in the shade of the awning to look at the time on my Garmin and the woman's voice caught up with me again. "She's cute, but not gorgeous like he was. I read on People.com today that her publicist used to buy flowers and tell her they were from him."

A second woman answered. "Poor thing. People say she looks like that Mexican actress, but I don't see it . . . did I ever tell you about the shiteous movie I watched that she was in? *Señorita Justice.* Don't waste your time."

I swallowed. They weren't talking about Mirinda. They were talking about me and Eva Longoria. I had to get away from their eyes. I pushed backwards against the door of The Flying Flower and it swung open. I stumbled in and pushed it closed. I stood stock still, straining to hear them, but in the sanctuary of the store I couldn't make them out anymore. Good. The veil over my other senses lifted as I turned around to look at the shop. I inhaled vanilla and coconut. Cool air licked at my sleeveless arms and I shivered, but not from the cold.

The tiny space was filled with butterflies. Giant suspended gauze monarchs. Blue butterfly tea sets. Yellow butterfly aprons. Butterflies of every color and type danced through delicate paintings and vibrant photographs. I walked into their midst and turned slowly in a full circle.

"Let me know if I can help you," I heard. The voice sounded creaky and aged and like it had come from the direction of the counter, but I didn't see anyone. I searched the room for a silvery butterfly with blue-rimmed wings that matched the voice, then I caught myself. I shook my head. I couldn't allow my imagination to start jacking with me. I only had to get through two more days, and then it wouldn't matter what my crazy head told me anymore.

Gray waves popped up behind a counter. See, Michele, I thought. Human, not butterfly.

"Your shop is amazing."

"Thank you." The head rose farther into the air, revealing lapis lazuli eyes and impossibly white skin with so few wrinkles that the hair made no sense. But then neither did mine. "Ah, dearie, are you here to do the big race?"

"I am, but how did you know?"

"Because you look hungry."

A laugh shot out of me from I don't know where. "Yes, I guess so."

"You like butterflies?"

"My husband did."

She lowered her chin, looking up at me from the deep of her eyes. "My partner, Johnna, did, too. She was a lepidopterist. A scientist. I just think they're pretty."

I watched, fascinated, as golden strands of light made their way from her chest to the floor and over to me. They shone up my leg and my stomach until they reached my chest, then the slack went out and I felt a tiny tug and heard a pop. I stepped closer to her. As soon as I did, I saw what I was doing. Again. Stop it, Michele. Get out of your head. "She studied them here?"

"The monarchs here were her obsession."

"I didn't even know monarchs migrated this far."

"The ones here now don't migrate at all. They live and die here. They didn't always live in the Hawaiian Islands, though. They came in the mid 1800s, when milkwood was introduced. Johnna believed that some of the monarchs on Kona descended from a strain of monarchs who had longer wings with narrow tips, which enabled them to fly farther than regular monarchs." She looked fragile for a moment, her eyes cloudy. She fluffed her silver hair. "Not everyone agrees with her, but it's a beautiful mystery, don't you think?"

I couldn't speak. I just nodded slowly as orange and black flying flowers filled the sky in my mind. They swooped and dipped, their formation fluid against the ocean below them. Their current eddied then swirled downward, and they landed on a tiny patch of green.

When they settled, I found my words. "Wouldn't the butterflies with the longer wings have moved on?"

"You mean why did they stay?"

"Yes," I said, even though I suspected I had asked something else.

"Maybe Kona was just a better place than the one they left behind."

"Yes." My words slipped out in a whisper.

"I'm going to show you something special. Come with me." She turned and opened a hidden door covered in monarch paper. The pattern lined up perfectly with the paper on the wall around it. I hurried after her. As I stepped through the door, I saw that it entered into a back room larger than the shop in front. Flowers were everywhere, and flashes of color flitted around.

"It's my own butterfly farm. But that's not really what I wanted to show you. Here." She beckoned me with her long fingers. She pointed into the foliage. "See the white one?"

"Yes. What is it?"

"My monarch. Well, it's not really mine. Johnna called them Kona Whites. I don't know if that's really their name. Johnna said the Kona Whites reminded her of me. She called me her white-winged butterfly." The woman held her finger out, and the white butterfly lit upon it.

I palmed my locket. "My husband called me Butterfly, but he got it from my papa, who nicknamed me Itzpa, his little clawed butterfly, when I was very young."

She turned her finger back and forth, admiring the winged beauty. "Ah, Itzpapalotl, warrior. You're a fighter, then."

I lowered the locket. I remembered the fights that had earned me the nickname, and my rage toward Rhonda and fight against Stephanie. "I used to be."

She nodded, but her eyes never left the butterfly. "Well, if we learn nothing else from the butterflies, I guess it's that the seasons change and things live and things die." She walked back to the door to her shop, gesturing me before her. "Good luck in your race tomorrow,

Little Itzpa." She flicked her finger and the Kona White flew away before she opened the door.

That afternoon at my transition area I walked through my race prep checklist one last time before I called it a wrap. I had planned my race using everything Adrian ever taught me, and I knew that to finish the next day, I had to race my plan. Preparation is everything, and it would be too late to realize on the course that I needed a tire tube or some moleskin. Another pack of energy gel. Sunscreen. All of it was in place, though, and I'd shaken my jitters off on the course with a quick swim, bicycle, and jog.

I walked down Ali'i Drive, my mouth moving as I affirmed and visualized, another part of Adrian's race prep. I watched myself swim in my mind's eye. My body glided through the water until a fin rose from my back and a strong dolphin flipper replaced my feet. "I am the dolphin," I whispered. "I am the dolphin." Maybe my imagination was good for something. Before I moved mentally to the bicycle leg, I found myself standing in front of a blue clapboard church, right on the beach. The sunset aimed its full glory through an etched-glass window, and like the golden threads I'd conjured earlier, pulled on me. I walked into the back of the church. There was already a full house of athletes inside, and the sanctuary smelled like the inside of a yellow school bus.

At the front, a priest was speaking. I'd stumbled upon a Catholic church. Wouldn't my abuela be happy, God rest her soul?

"Tomorrow," he said, "even the strongest of you may need an angel. You will be putting your body and mind through an incredible test. Believe in your angel, and it will come to you when you need it most."

I want to, Father, I thought. I want to believe so much. I knew how badly I needed help, and about all the things that would make Kona so difficult for me. An Ironman is an endurance test, and the conditions on Kona are unique and punishing. The water is too warm, even for me. I would have to bicycle through fifty-five-mile-per-hour crosswinds, and the forecast for the afternoon marathon, to be run on my bum knee, was ninety-two degrees.

Yes, I could use an angel, only mine was nowhere to be found.

When the service was over, I walked out of the church and down toward the starting line, where the Texas triathletes had organized a memorial for Adrian. Hundreds of people were gathered there. Hundreds. I fought back a crippling onslaught of emotion. Where was the practical and compartmentalized woman I used to be when I needed her?

"Michele?" I turned toward the male voice. It was James Harvey, an Austin triathlete Adrian had known for many more years than he had known me.

"Hi, James."

"We're ready to start the memorial. How about you?"

Never. "As I'll ever be."

James lifted a bullhorn to his mouth and his deep voice rumbled over the beach. I slipped away a safe distance from all the eyes that had shifted his way. "Thanks for coming, everyone. We are here to honor our friend and fellow triathlete, Adrian Hanson. You all knew Adrian. His words painted the picture of our sport. There's his beautiful wife and co-author, Michele Lopez Hanson, now."

James waved at me, and hundreds of heads turned. I saw cameras swing my way, including ESPN. Fine. It wasn't race day yet, but apparently I hadn't moved far enough away. I waved back, and I fought the urge to turn and not stop running until I was in my hotel room in bed.

"We could spend all night here if I passed the microphone around telling stories, but Adrian would not approve of us missing our beauty sleep." The crowd tittered. "Volunteers are passing around lighters and Sharpies. Here's what we want you to do. Take a Sharpie and write a message to Adrian, like his name, or 'In memory of Adrian.' Do it some place that won't conflict with body-marking tomorrow, but make it show. Then pass it along to your neighbor. When we're all done with the Sharpies, we'll flick our Bics."

The crowd hummed as people wrote on their arms and legs. I wrote "For Adrian" on the side of both my shins. The lump in my throat was so big it nearly choked me. I swallowed hard, and it came loose.

James spoke into the bullhorn again. "You guys, please spread the word to everybody that couldn't be here tonight. I'd love to see Adrian plastered on every leg in Kona tomorrow, okay?"

The crowd cheered. A teeming mass of mostly-strangers engulfed me. The skyline shifted, and I realized I had vertigo. I wanted to hold onto the person next to me to steady myself. I wanted Adrian there, seeing me sway and catching me before I knew I needed him.

"Light 'em up, hold 'em high, and let's observe one minute of silence while we remember our friend Adrian Hanson. Adrian, buddy, I was going to kick your ass tomorrow. I'll have to do it when I see you on the other side."

Hundreds of lighters snapped and lit around me. I held my glowing hand aloft. I faltered and swayed. I felt the eyes of the man standing next to me. He leaned toward me. "Michele?"

I dipped my head in answer.

The stranger reached down and grasped my hand. His touch was electric, and a tiny gasp escaped before I could hold it in. The vertigo grew worse and I struggled to stay upright. The woman next to me put her arm around my waist, taking some of my weight on her. I concentrated on the feeling of my feet against solid ground and my body like a tree, rooted but able to sway without falling. The vertigo started to recede, but the minute stretched on a very long time.

James spoke into his bullhorn again. "Amen."

"Amen," the crowd responded.

I released the hand of the man beside me, and the woman withdrew her arm from my waist as James wrapped up.

"Michele is here to race, keeping up the family tradition for her husband. Y'all encourage her out there tomorrow. Go get some rest, and I'll see you here tomorrow bright and early."

I turned to thank my angels, but they were gone.

Chapter Thirty

I treaded blue water off of Kailua Pier early the next morning with over two thousand other racers, but more alone than ever. Now I only had to swim 2.4 miles, bicycle 112, and run 26.2. All in all, fourteen hours to go, and it's over, I told myself. Fourteen was my target time, based on my training performance. Worst case would be just under seventeen at midnight, when they cut the race off. Either way, less than a day and it would be over.

Spectators and journalists lined the beach all the way up to the street. The entire span of water from the beach to the start was a bobbing rainbow mass of rubber-encased heads, all jostling for the perfect starting position. I jostled my way toward the back outside edge of the pack. Everyone would be after a personal-best time today. They were here to compete, and the swim could get rough. I moved farther to the side.

"Be the dolphin, Michele, be the dolphin," I chanted, my teeth chattering with terror, but as fear engulfed me, the vision of the dolphin faded.

"Adrian? Adrian!"

My mind screamed out his name, looking for him in every face. I'd always counted on him to get me through that part. Even if he was twenty yards away, I could lock eyes with him, and it helped steady me. All I had of him now was his locket tucked into my tri-suit.

When the horn sounded and the mad start began, Adrian wasn't there, but Kona was on. I dropped my head into the water and ordered my body into motion. My dolphin body, I told myself. My sleek, strong dolphin body. Fear still gripped me and my breath came in useless gasps.

Slow down, I told myself. Get into your rhythm. Reach kick pull kick reach kick pull kick.

Whack. Another swimmer kicked me in the face and my goggles came off my head. I stopped short and in the chop I sucked in a lungful of water. Arms slammed into me. More feet kicked me in the shoulders, in the chest. I couldn't breathe. I couldn't think. I couldn't see. I had to find my goggles and move out of the way or this would be over before it had started, with me drowning before the first buoy.

A woman stopped. "Are you okay?"

"I lost my goggles."

"I'll help you."

Her green eyes pulled me in, and some of my tension slipped away. "Do I know you?"

"Maybe." She nodded twice, then disappeared under the water for three seconds. She popped up again in front me. "Here you go." She handed me the orange goggles.

"Thank you."

We both dropped our heads and swam again. I lost sight of her in seconds. I hadn't even gotten her name, and she'd given up time and energy to help me, but I couldn't dwell on it. I had to refocus, find my center, re-vision myself back into the race. I tried not to think of the immensity of the ocean around me, the crushing volume of that water, the things alive below me, my insignificance, but I couldn't put the thoughts back in their boxes. Hundreds of us were bunched together and it was claustrophobic. After a few minutes or a few seconds—I wasn't sure—I started huffing my breaths again. I was close to hyper-ventilating. I rolled over on my back and gasped for air.

Dolphins don't panic, Michele. Dolphins love to swim in pods.

"Chinga la bunch of dolphins," I shouted at the sky. It helped. I kicked my way to the outside of the thrashing horde, using my arms to steer, a dolphin on its back. When I was clear of the traffic, I rolled back over and swam freestyle. Better. Then, just as my heart rate and respiration slowed to a maintainable level, an arm karate-chopped my neck and the arm's owner passed under me, shoving my body up out of the water.

Chinga la bunch of him, I thought. I kicked with strength I didn't know I had and landed on his back. I punched him once, as hard as I could, in the kidneys. Then I sagged off him back into the water in a defensive posture, fists up like a lunatic. He didn't even break stroke. I snorted and dropped back into the water. What, did he think he was going to win? Fat chance, buddy. I swam with my middle finger extended in his direction for a couple of strokes, and I felt better.

I was looser now, swimming better. Be the dolphin, Michele. I reached long, pulled hard, and exhaled completely. I kicked shallow and tight, saving my legs for the bike and run. What I lack in upper-body power I make up for in natural buoyancy through the tush, and Adrian taught me to use my curves to my advantage. Efficiency. It was all about efficiency. Now my rhythm came easily, and every few seconds the following sea gave me a gentle push.

"Look at me, Adrian," I said to him, wherever he was. *"You can hide $200,000 from me, but that doesn't stop me from doing this. Doing this* without *you."* Instead of sadness, exhilaration tingled through me. *"Doing this for you."*

I made my turn at the halfway point and headed back toward the start. On the ocean floor, scuba divers were looking up at us. One of them held a sign: "Adrian Hanson 1969–2014." I stopped swimming and scissor-kicked myself above the water to sight down the shoreline, and I made a miraculous discovery—I wasn't last. Not even close.

The swimmers were spread out far and wide now. The swim leg winners were probably nearly back to transition, but I was ahead of at least ten or fifteen percent of the pack. Even swimming against the current now, I felt strong and almost giddy.

You're not just a dolphin, you're a rock star, I told myself. A part of me knew my euphoria was just runner's high, but I didn't care. Endorphins were dancing inside me, and it was wonderful. Before the day was over, the chemistry would change and exhaustion would set in, but it wasn't there yet, and I was the dolphin. I was going to be the damn dolphin all the way back, the whole way to the beach.

Mentally, I consulted my race plan: When the euphoria hits, back off. It's a trick. No premature celebrating. Pace yourself. Be efficient. Finish smart. I refocused on rhythm and counted beats to get myself under control, to race my plan.

Reach kick pull kick reach kick pull kick. Reach long, pull hard, kick light, exhale full. I repeated my instructions over and over, not letting anything else into my brain, until my fingers hit sandy bottom beneath me.

I had done it.

I stood up and fell face first, laughing, and then tried again. I had just finished the Kona swim, in the world championships, even if I was only a lottery racer. Adrenaline rocketed through me as I exited the water and ran to the transition area to find my bicycle.

"Mom! Go, Mom!" There were probably four hundred mothers in that race, yet I tracked my boy's voice. "Way to go, Mom!" the voice shouted again, and my eyes caught sight of him. Sam, my sixteen-year-old son, Sam, who was supposed to be back in Houston at his father's house, who I had told not to come. He ran along the mesh fencing beside me and slapped me a high five. I was too confused to be angry, too moved to ask questions. "I love you, Mom!"

"I love you, too, Sam Jackson!"

"What about me?"

I looked behind Sam and saw Annabelle's hair before I saw her face. Her wild curls blew in the wind, as big as she was. I couldn't let myself cry. "I love you, Belle Hanson!" I held up my palm and she ducked in front of Sam to smack it.

Dios mío, protect my children while I race, because that's what I'm here to do, I thought, and I ran for La Mariposa the Second. I had to keep my grip. Seconds saved here by skipping steps could mean disaster later on the course if I didn't have the gear I needed. Preparation would keep me safe. First I rinsed seawater from my body and slathered on Hoo Ha Ride Glide without shame. Then I recited my list and touched each item in the bento bag on my top post, tucking the smaller ones into the pockets at the small of my back. Water bottles,

Nuun tablets, Gus, Quest Bars, sunscreen. I put my precut moleskin patches on my ankles where my shoes rubbed. I opened my saddlebag and finished my list: extra tubes, one tire and CO_2 cartridges. Check, all. I ran the hundred yards with my bicycle, ankles wobbling in my bike shoes, to the mounting zone.

Two wired teenagers had run ahead of me and screamed my name. I snapped the chinstrap to my helmet, shoved on my sunglasses, and swung my leg over.

"Go, Michele!"

"You can do it, Mom!"

I pumped my fist in the air. Despite my vow not to cry, the tears fell anyway. When would I finally be cried out? I had leaked more water from my eyes in the past three months than most people do in a lifetime. I wiped them away roughly. I had to be able to see the road. Concentrate, Michele. It's time to fly. You'll be on this bicycle for seven hours. Be the butterfly.

I clipped my right cleat in, but a thought stopped me cold. Adrian had told me it wasn't over, and I'd held the kids away from me to keep them safe. Now, here, on Kona, they were on their own. I looked into the crowd. So many people. So many, many people.

I yelled in their direction. "Who brought you here?"

Annabelle beamed. "Nobody. We brought each other."

What idiots raised these kids to be so dang self-reliant and independent? "Be careful, you guys. I'm serious."

Sam laughed. "Don't worry, Mom. We won't talk to strangers."

"Promise me, you guys. I can't leave until you promise me."

Two nods, looking at each other, then me. Annabelle acted as spokesperson. "We promise."

That would have to do. I swallowed, and then reset my Garmin. My swim time, including transition onto the bike course, took less than seventy-eight minutes. That meant I swam the course in about seventy-six minutes, including having a panic attack and a fistfight. I'd never swum that distance in a pool faster than eighty.

If I could swim like that, then I could do the rest of this.

I looked back at the two people I loved most in the world one last time, tucked their images into my heart under my locket, and began to pedal.

Chapter Thirty-one

How quickly things changed. The bicycle course cut through a lava field, which was pretty to look at in an austere way, but it was a giant grill and I was a slab of ribs. I tried to visualize past it for Adrian's sake, but I failed. Every cold image I conjured ended up melted, then boiled, steamed, and burned into a black residue.

"You're missing a really sucky time, Adrian," I said aloud, but the wind stole the sound away.

Meanwhile, the leaders were starting to whizz past me in the other direction. They'd finish the marathon before I made it off my bike. I would be lucky to finish out of the bottom ten percent. I passed a young female rider in head-to-toe lime green as she loaded her bicycle into a SAG wagon. At least I'd beat her.

On my right, a rider was bent over his back wheel, changing a flat. He couldn't have been any older than Annabelle. I was so tempted to stop, but I didn't know how I'd get going again if I did. Besides, he was supposed to flag for help if he needed it, and he hadn't. I rode on, feeling like a jerk.

I kept going. Even down in the aerobars, I was far from flying. It was more like crawling. Crawling across glass. The bumps strained my neck and back with no respite, and because of the headwinds—which were gusting up to forty mph, I'd overheard as I passed a rest stop—I stayed flattened in position from the start. I'd lose most of my forward momentum if I sat up, and the tradeoff of less neck strain in favor of slower speed wasn't worth it, so I forced myself to ride through the pain. I lifted an arm, shook it, and laid it carefully back into the aerobars. I repeated with the other arm, then very, very carefully I rolled my neck. My bicycle had a tendency to follow my eyes, especially when I used the aerobars, and I couldn't afford a wipeout.

But thanks to Stephanie Willis and the conditioning time I'd lost on the *real* La Mariposa because of her, my neck couldn't take much more.

Of course, losing La Mariposa and my neck strength paled in comparison to what she'd really cost me.

I fought the downward spiral those thoughts could start, but I didn't have the willpower and I spun helplessly around Adrian's warning and his missing money. I had an incredibly bad vibe about Sam and Annabelle being there, being alone back in town, and it came back in a rush. I wished they'd stayed far away from me and Kona.

Over the past month, I'd tried to block that stuff out, tried to block everything out. I'd kept my stress level so low I almost didn't have a pulse. I thought I'd learned how not to feel. I'd licked this, hadn't I? Because it just didn't matter as long as I kept the kids safe. Which I couldn't do if they followed me around like little lambs.

"Stop, just stop." I was muttering aloud, a crazy woman on a bicycle on a tiny island in a giant sea. I forced myself to focus on my body position and on easing the strain on my neck without sitting up.

Yet that didn't help and my torturous thoughts didn't stop. My emotions returned in a landslide, raw and ugly. "What did you do with that money, Adrian?" I screamed, not caring if anyone heard me. I sat up and the wind slammed into my chest, slowing me down so much it felt like I was going backwards. "Do you have a baby mama out there? Did you pay someone to throw a race? Did you order a hit? Was someone blackmailing you? What did you do, Adrian? Who's coming for me?"

I collapsed back into my bars. "Chingate, Adrian," I whispered. "Chingate."

"On your left." A woman at least twenty-five years older than me went past.

I kept going.

"On your left." This time it was a man about my age, carrying far more flesh than was healthy.

I kept pedaling. The rhythm eventually soothed the worst of my rage and replaced it with a deep loneliness, a black emptiness. On the swim, adrenaline and endorphins had sustained me. The accomplishment, and seeing my kids, had pushed me through transition. Out there, alone, hurting, and exhausted, though, there was nothing. Crowds were few and far between. Riders spread out to prevent drafting. It was just me in poor company for seven hours. How different it would have been if Adrian had kept his promise and come with me.

My balance was off, and I felt a little dizzy. I realized I hadn't run through my course checklist in a while. I looked at my Garmin. It was far past time to hydrate and eat a Quest Bar. I sat up and pulled a chocolate chip cookie bar from my bento bag and ripped it open. It had melted. I squeezed the wrapper and it oozed into my mouth. I followed it up with Nuun, counting my sips to make sure I didn't short myself on any pulls. I added five since I was late. I glanced down as I stuffed the wrapper back into the bento and saw that white salt had surfaced through the brown fabric on my thighs. That meant I was underhydrated. Way to go, Michele. You're too late. Well, chingalo.

"Did you hear me, Adrian? I said chingalo. I don't care if I finish. I don't care if I live through today. I don't care if I never go back to Houston. Chingala."

I came up on the long climb to the turnaround. I was nearly halfway, but this was much more than just another hill. On my way up, the infamous crosswinds swept across the road and nearly took me down. I lifted out of the aerobars one hand at a time and sat up again for better stability. After the turn, I'd have a tailwind instead of a headwind, I told myself. I could make up speed on the downhill.

Minutes later, however, I discovered an ugly truth: there were no tailwinds. How could the wind on that damn island blow in every direction at once? My speed fell dangerously low and I wobbled along. My knee started hurting. I started up another hill.

Suddenly I heard a loud crack, and my legs spun the pedals crazy fast, all tension gone. I weaved into the road, into the paths of other riders.

A man screamed in a high-pitched voice as he rode at me. "Watch out, lady!" Not a man. The young boy from earlier, the one changing a flat.

"I'm sorry!"

I pulled over to the side of the road. Oh, please, not my chain, I thought, but I knew it was. I looked back over my shoulder, and I saw the coil of traitorous links in the road. It raised its head like a cobra and hissed. Get a grip, Michele, I told myself in my mom voice. This is not the time for your make-believe games. Riders were dodging the chain, cursing. I darted into the road and retrieved it before someone punctured a tire. I dismounted and stood beside La Mariposa the Second.

So this was it. Kona, for Adrian, for me, would end with a broken chain. I didn't have enough fluid left in my dehydrated body to cry, so I backed off the road and sank cross-legged to the ground. The lava fields behind me broiled my back, but I was past caring. Let them fry me like a roasting chicken. It just didn't matter anymore.

A rider pulled to a stop beside me. I didn't look up.

"Hi there. What's the problem?" A woman's voice. Calm. Friendly.

"Broken chain. No spare. I'm done."

"Why don't you use mine? We're both on Trek Pilots, three rings, ten-speed, so it should fit."

She had a spare? The odds against it were incredible. No one carries a spare chain. They're too heavy to lug a hundred and twelve miles, and, besides, chains rarely break. I looked up—and into the green eyes I saw on the swim.

"Did we meet in the water?"

"Maybe."

"I think you're my angel, then. The priest told us to believe in our angels." I stopped. I wasn't making sense even to myself.

"Maybe so."

I stood and brushed off my shorts. "Nobody carries an extra chain."

"I do. And the tool, too." She slipped off her seat but remained poised over her bicycle with both feet on the ground. The leg facing me had "RIP AH" written on it in black Sharpie. She twisted around and unzipped the bag behind her seat, then pulled out a chain and the little tool. I had a clear view of the bag, and it had nothing else in it. No tire, no tubes, no CO_2 cartridges. Just a chain, a tool, and a tiny can of chain lube, which she handed to me. She zipped her bag closed. "Do you need help changing it?"

"No, I can do it. But how can I repay you? You've saved me twice."

She pointed at the stenciling on my monarch bicycle. "Fly strong, be safe. See you on the course." She clipped in and pushed off.

"Thank you," I called after her. I saw the bib number on her back: 2200. I needed to remember it so I could thank her after the race.

Adrian had taught me to change my chain, but I'd never had to do it without him. It should have taken five minutes. It took fifteen, fifteen of inhaling the smell of Papa's gun oil, fifteen minutes of smearing it all over my hands and arms. The chain fit, though, and when I started to pedal, it stayed on. "Thank you." I pointed upward.

I rode on. I had fifty miles left to go across hot lava fields before I would even get to start the run.

Fifty miles with no Adrian.

Forty-nine miles. Picturing a page of bank accounts with one missing.

Forty-eight miles. Riding in my smallest ring at a pace that would have embarrassed me back in Texas.

Forty-seven miles. My knee screeching in pain and me dreading what that meant for my run.

Forty-six miles. Looking over my shoulder for the doom foretold by Adrian and worrying about my kids.

The odometer kept racking the miles up as I counted them down. Somehow I managed to overcome the noise in my head and pedal another three hours.

114.4 miles down. 26.2 to go.

Chapter Thirty-two

The cheering started as soon as I reached the transition area.

"Go, Michele!" I tracked toward the sound of her voice and spotted her. Annabelle's blonde hair made her easy to find.

Sam yelled so loud his voice cracked. "Way to go, Mom!"

It wasn't just them. They had convened a whole pep squad for me. Well, they'd had nearly eight hours to work on it. Didn't that mean they'd talked to strangers, though? I didn't like that at all. But they were sweet, and the little group cheered me on like a winner. They even held up posters in Annabelle's handwriting.

"Racing for two," one read.

"Michele Lopez Hanson is My Hero."

"Rock it, Mrs. Hanson."

"You've got this, Michele."

I lifted my thumb, barely. I tried to smile. Then I stopped my bike, and down I went like a novice, ingloriously, humiliatingly, and painfully. I had forgotten to clip out of my pedals.

"Mom, are you okay?" Sam strained against the fence, leaning toward me.

My mind, numb before, jerked sharply back into focus. I made an okay sign with my fingers, and the crowd cheered again.

Annabelle grinned at me. "You're the tenth person to do that since we came back here to wait for you."

I clipped out the other foot and stood myself and the bicycle up. I hobbled it to my transition area and carefully hung her on the rack. She had done her best, and we'd made it within the time limit. I took a water bottle out of its holster and squirted off the road debris from my little tumble. I tried to dry-swallow two Aleve, then gave up and squirted the last sip of Nuun into my mouth to chase them down.

Checklist time. Moleskin on toes, socks, shoes tied but loosened to make room for more swelling in my feet. Body Glide on my inner arms.

More sunscreen. My vented white cap. I was forgetting something. I reached up out of habit to touch my locket, and realized that it was the last item on the list. Locket tucked into the top of my tri-suit. Check. I doused myself with my last bottle of water, then turned to begin the painful plod out of the transition area on quads that felt like burning bricks and a knee that made every other step torturous.

The first part of the course ran in front of the line of spectators. The crowd size peaked to greet the top finishers, and most of the twenty-five thousand were still there. When I returned, all but a few would be gone. They cheered me out of transition and onto the course now. Sam and Annabelle wove between people, yelling all the way.

"You can do it, Mom."

"Michele, do you see all the signs for you and Adrian? They're everywhere!"

"You're almost done, Mom." If five hours of running in ninety-plus weather counted for almost, I thought. Who was I kidding? Five was overly optimistic at this point.

Annabelle flapped her hand at me. "Did you see our shirts?"

I mustered the energy to turn and look at them. Their hand-lettered white t-shirts said "IronSon" and "IronDaughter" on them. I smiled as big as I could. "Have you been okay? Has anyone bothered you?"

"We're fine," Annabelle said. "You can do this!"

I pointed my eyes ten feet in front of me on the road and trotted out of town. Now my real test began, starting with the biggest hill on the course, right out of Kailua-Kona. My biked-out legs screamed in protest, and I was reminded how much uphill hurt my bum knee. I leaned forward and locked my knees out gently for a few extra inches in each stride. I missed my Shuffle so much.

Soon after I crested the hill, I came to the first aid station. Volunteers thrust cups at me and shouted encouragement. I slowed my trot and doused myself with water. I gulped red stuff. I left with half a banana in my mouth and a quarter of an orange in my hand.

The run route was flat, mostly, but the heat made up for the lack of hills. The temperature in Kona has killed many dreams, but I wasn't there to quit. The consolation for a back-of-the-pack racer like me was that I would get to do part of my run after the sun set. I had hours to go before that relief came, though. I let my mind go slack, trying for a sort of hypnosis that I could sometimes reach on long runs. If I could get there, I could escape the storm clouds in my head. I waited for Adrian or the nothingness to come, but neither did.

Instead, memories came. I replayed my first marathon, when Adrian insisted on running with me to cheer me on. The disparity in our abilities irked me. He started running backwards, talking to me and making me so mad I wanted to punch him. I stopped in the middle of race traffic and let him have it. "Gloater," I accused him. "You're fast and in great shape, I get it. Stop rubbing it in my face." Twenty minutes later, I'd calmed down enough to continue.

Afterwards, I told him that I beat my goal time.

"No you didn't, Michele."

"Yes, I did, if you subtract the twenty minutes we were stopped."

"You can't subtract the twenty minutes. It's total cumulative time."

I didn't budge.

"You're impossible." He shook his head.

I leaned my tired, sweaty body against his. "You'll never leave me." A statement, not a question.

He kissed my hair. "Never."

But he had.

"But you did." I tried to yell it, but it sounded puny in my ears. "You promised you'd never leave me, but you did. Then you promised you'd be here with me, but you're not." I knew it wasn't his fault he got murdered. I knew I had to remember the good times. I couldn't let myself do this. I had to stay mentally tough. This wasn't real. It was just my mind playing tricks on me, and I had to fight it off. Yet my rational mind gave way to a sort of delirium as the heat fried my brain like a state fair Twinkie.

I tried to figure out how far I had to go. If I knew how far, then I could estimate my steps and divide them by two and know how many more my knee had to endure. I'd been racing since seven a.m. I checked my Garmin, but for some reason I couldn't make sense of it. The stopwatch read one hour and twenty-nine minutes. But that couldn't be right. It didn't look like breakfast time out there. It looked like the Sahara desert.

"What do you think, Adrian? How much longer do I have to keep going?"

My footsteps vibrated with a deep sound inside my head, like mallets hitting a bass drum. I liked bass drums but I liked bass guitars better. I loved the bassline in "Can I Walk With You?" I wanted to walk. Adrian wouldn't let me walk. Adrian wasn't here. Why wasn't he here? Would I catch up to him soon, or had he already finished? When we finished we could take a shower. A shower would feel good. Cold would be good. I usually like hot better than cold, but not today. Today my knee hurt. The knee bone's connected to the leg bone. I had to keep running on my legs.

Another aid station. I stopped and poured cup after cup of water on my head and drank three cups of the red stuff.

"Has Adrian Hanson come through here yet?" I asked a volunteer.

"Have a great race." She smiled. "You can do it!"

Huh. He really should have finished the whole race around the same time I finished the bicycle leg. Maybe he hadn't been back through yet. If he'd had a problem, he could still be out here. We would pass each other, and he would hold out his hand and I'd let mine hit his as he went past me in the other direction at twice my speed. I needed to do that now. *"Adrian?"* He was probably around the next turn.

"Adrian, I need you." I wasn't sure if he could hear me, but I had to keep trying. I tried and tried and tried, but nothing. I started to cry, but it was just noise with no tears. *"Where are you? Why aren't you here?"* I shivered. When had it gotten cold out here?

Then I remembered. Adrian was dead. He wasn't here. God was, though, fearsome and mighty, but surely He didn't expect me to keep going without Adrian? The best of my life had passed me by. If I kept going, it would hurt this much forever. I didn't want to keep going.

"No, it's not fair. You can't make me."

I stopped running and limped a few steps off the road. I stared out to sea, over the high tumble of jagged lava rocks. The wind blew hard and hot in my face. Grill. I was standing beside the world's biggest grill. Good, because I was still freezing to death.

"You can't make me," I repeated. Did He not hear me? I was done. No one could make me change my mind. No one needed me anymore. Sam had Robert. Annabelle had Diane and that boyfriend. Jay. Jay rhymed with betray and Adrian had betrayed me. He had. He wasn't so perfect after all, with his tricks and secrets. And worst of all, he'd left me. He'd left me to spend the rest of my life alone, and I'd decided I didn't want to do that, and so I wasn't going to.

"You can't make me."

The scream of a siren rose above the howl of the wind. It hurt my ears. I couldn't see it, but it was getting louder, so, so loud. I put my hands over my ears. The road between the sound and me turned against a big outcropping of the rock. I tried to see around the corner, but how could I? There was a big rock in the way. I stared in the direction of the sound, but I didn't see anything but that rock. And a white butterfly.

White butterfly. Was that the kind I saw in that store in town? White butterfly, white skin. I walked into the road, following it. The white butterfly had long wings like me, and claws. I wanted to touch it, but it was getting harder to see. The sky had turned off the light, and it was swallowing the butterfly. There it was, just a little farther around the corner of the rock. I stepped toward it as the noise screamed in my ears. "Hush. Stop that," I whispered. The noise grew so loud that I forgot all about the white butterfly. My throbbing knee buckled, and I caught myself on the ground with my hands. "I'm going to get hit by an ambulance. Good. Then I can stop." I crouched, pressing my fists hard into my ears. Flashing red beams of light swept over me. I shut my eyes to block it out. Then there was a new sound on top of the siren. BWAHNK BWAHHHHHHHNK BWAHNK. It sounded like the horn on the 4Runner, Adrian's car before, but Sam's now. Sam. Sam was waiting in Kailua-Kona with Annabelle. I couldn't let this happen.

And then over the siren, a woman's voice screamed, "Jump, Michele! Jump now!"

I jumped to my feet and to the right, jumped away from the noise. I fell to the ground on the side of the road. A squeal. A whoosh of air. I screamed louder than all of the noises. I crushed my face into the dirt and tugged my hair with both hands. I yowled in pain and grabbed my locket from inside my tri-suit and flung it away from me.

A man's voice shouted, closer to me than the sirens, "What the hell, lady? Are you trying to get yourself killed?"

I looked up into the red lights. I came up on my hands and knees.

"Are you okay?"

I shooed the talking man away with my hand.

The woman's voice again. "She's fine. She fell, and I'm helping her."

"You're sure? I can call for transport. We've got to go though." He jerked his thumb back at the ambulance. "Severe dehydration, cardiac arrest."

I bobbed my head along with the siren, RAH-EEER RAH- EEER.

"We're sure."

I heard a door slam, and the lights flew past me and the sound faded into the distance. After a few minutes, I stood up. It hurt, it hurt so much. I brushed the gravel and sand off my body. I didn't get to stop after all. I wanted to, but I had to keep going, and that was all there was to it. I didn't get a choice.

I did a double take. Green eyes that I could see even without the sun. "It's you."

"Hello, Michele. It's me."

"Thanks for helping me again."

She dipped her head in a nod. "What's the matter?"

"I can't find my husband."

The green eyes stared back into mine. "I think you need something to drink." She had a water bottle in her hand, and she extended it to me.

I drank.

"Go slow."

When it was empty, I handed it back to her.

"Now eat this." She ripped open a chocolate Gu.

I did as I was told. I was already feeling better. I sighed. I had a long way to go to get back to Sam and Annabelle. The wind blew a little cooler now, though, and the sun was gone. That was good.

She pointed at my chest. "You dropped something."

I nodded, slowly. What had I dropped? My butterfly. My butterfly had flown away. The urge to find it overpowered everything, even my pain.

"Where are you, butterfly?" I looked around me, in the air, on the ground. No butterfly, but I caught sight of the woman's leg. "I <3 MLH." That was odd. I'd ask her about it when I found my butterfly. I crouched down, close to the ground, and my eyes followed its flight path from minutes before, straight to my left. I got up and walked in that direction, zigzagging over the rocks as they fell away from the road.

"There you are." My legs trembled as I climbed down. I had to use both hands to help with my descent. There it was. I scooped the butterfly into my hand. "I'll have to carry you, but I'll be very careful."

I scrambled back to the road, using only my right hand for balance, every muscle in my legs screaming in protest.

I held it aloft to show my friend. "I found it."

No answer. I looked all around me. The woman was gone. Well, I had my locket. "I think I can do this now." I put the chain over my neck but it fell to the ground. I picked it back up. Well, I would just have to carry it.

So I did, and I ran. It hurt. But I kept going. Full dark fell. I came to the turnaround, and the next aid station. A man handed me a lightstick, and I stuck it down the front of my top to keep one hand free for food and liquid, one hand for my locket.

The volunteer talked to me while I drank red stuff. "Did you see a runner down? Somewhere between here and the last aid station?"

"No." I stuffed an orange into my mouth, then another and another, and chased them with more red stuff. I felt better than I had since the swim. "Is someone in trouble?"

"We thought so. The SAG wagon couldn't find anyone, though. Keep an eye out. Stay hydrated."

"I will."

And I ran again, my lightstick in one hand and my butterfly in the other. Time ticked by, miles passed, and I ran. I ran until I found the road ahead of me dotted with fireflies bouncing along toward the brighter light of Kailua-Kona. I followed them. A song started in my head and I smiled. "Can I Walk With You?" Who needs a Shuffle? I let it play. It made me think of Adrian, and I missed him, missed him to the center of my being, and I always would. I hated that we hadn't had Kona together.

Well after nine p.m., I stumbled into town, making my way back down Ali'i Drive the way I'd left over five hours before. I had done it. "There you go, honey," I whispered. "I'm sorry I couldn't give you a better time, but you're crossing the finish line with me." I reached up for my locket. It wasn't there. For a moment I couldn't breathe, then I remembered it was in my numb left hand.

"Are you there, my love?" I checked one more time, but I knew he was gone. It was just me out there, running alone, with nobody in the world aware that at that moment I was about to become an Ironman, that I would complete Adrian's Kona dream. Nobody except for me.

Me and my kids.

Sam and Annabelle fell in on either side of me when I had a quarter mile to go. Despite my fears, nothing bad had happened to them in Kailua-Kona. I swung my head back and forth to look at them under the streetlights. They were somber. Sam had tears on his cheeks. I wanted to wipe them away forever, to tuck him and Annabelle into my heart where they'd be safe and never scared.

Only I could barely take care of me. I hurt. My thighs, front and back, were cramping. My damn left leg from knee to hip screamed in agony. My right foot felt like a bloody stump. I was weak and dizzy, and I wanted to throw up. I had nothing left.

No, I thought, not nothing. I dug for the last of my strength, that part I hid from even myself, the part I saved just for them. "Let's finish like Adrian." I found a smile for them, a real smile. I stuffed my locket and chain into my top one more time. I grabbed their hands, and we ran across the finish line together.

Chapter Thirty-three

"Holy Mary Mother of God" was the first thing I said when I woke up the next day, hurting everywhere.

Annabelle lay beside me in bed. "Shhh."

Sam was sleeping on his back on the couch with his legs bent over the arm. "Sam, I need your help."

He didn't answer, so I threw a pillow at him. Pain shot through my neck and shoulders. We both groaned.

I looked at the time on my Garmin. Eight o'clock. "Sam, I have a book signing and we're going to be late. Get up and help me."

Annabelle rose on her elbows. "Come on, Michele." She slipped out of bed and came around to my side.

"Can you pull me to my feet, then let me lean on you to walk to the bathroom?"

She grabbed my hands in both of hers and pulled. I screamed softly.

"Mo-om, keep it down."

"He's no help," I muttered.

"Tell me about it. If it had been up to him, we wouldn't be here. When we made our connection in Los Angeles, the gate agent had to call for him on the intercom because he was in a bookstore reading a gaming magazine."

This got Sam up, and he hollered at Annabelle. "I was on my way."

Annabelle and I looked at each other, and she shook her head. We shared a smile.

An hour later the kids flanked me and the enormous and completely inappropriate arrangement of lilies sent by my parents as I signed book after book. My right hand was about the only thing that didn't hurt. Brian hovered behind us, the happiest mother hen on the island. He'd been in cahoots with the kids on their travel plans all along. Both of them had sworn blood oaths to their other parents that I'd asked them to come, and then they'd bought tickets on miles. Brian met them at the airport in Kailua-Kona, and they stayed with him the night before the race. The man was just full of good surprises.

He handed me a cup of coffee and said, "I hope we brought enough books. It seems like everyone on this island wants a copy and a photo with the champ."

My hand closed around the words "Kona Coffee Café" on the cup sleeve, and a sadness ripped through my core. Adrian. Well, he wasn't here. I pushed the feeling away.

"I'm happy for you, Brian." And I really was. I doubted I'd ever make a cent off *My Pace or Yours*, but if it injected money into Juniper, then it was the start of something great, and was the least I could do for him.

I looked up into a camera lens. ESPN. The producer walked up to me.

"Do you mind if we interview your kids?" he asked. "We talked to them yesterday. Brian said you'd be okay with it, and they really wanted to do it."

"I'll bet they loved that. Sure, go ahead. It looks like I'll be busy for a while here." I gestured at the line.

"Thanks, Mom."

The producer motioned to the cameraman and they walked a short distance away with Sam and Annabelle. As I signed, I kept one eye on the kids. Annabelle grew shy in front of the cameras and Sam puffed up. I laughed. "Those are my kids," I explained to the woman whose book I was signing.

"The girl looks a lot like you."

I didn't bother to explain that the fair-skinned, fair-haired beauty wasn't my blood relation. I looked at Annabelle. "Why, thank you." Then I froze.

A man had pulled Sam and Annabelle aside. He looked familiar but I couldn't place him. He had plastic cups in his hands, and he gave them to my kids. Alarm bells went off in my head. "Brian, is he with us?"

Brian looked. "Never seen him before."

The ESPN producer had come back to my table. "Is he one of yours?" I kept pointing.

He shook his head. "Nope."

The man put one hand on the Sam's shoulder, and another on Annabelle's, and he guided them out of the tent. "You're not safe. It's not over," Adrian had told me. My instincts shrieked in warning. This was it. I knew it was going down on Kona. I'd felt it out on the course.

I jumped to my feet and shouted, "Stop."

The trio kept moving. I bolted from behind the table, nearly crashing to the ground as my left knee took my weight. The chair fell over in the grass and my table teetered. A gasp rose from the crowd.

"I said STOP!" I was screaming as I bore down on the man leading my kids away.

Three sets of startled eyes fixed on me.

"Mom, what is it?"

I winced and shifted all my weight off my knee. "Him," I gasped, through the pain. "Get away from him."

Annabelle clutched her cup in both hands. "It's okay, Michele. We know him. From yesterday."

"Now. Please."

The kids stared at me, but they stepped toward me. The man did, too.

"Stay away from us." I tensed, ready to pounce.

His head drooped. "Michele, I'm so sorry."

Hackles rose on my neck. Images flashed through my mind. Bad images. This man, talking to Adrian, a woman in pink behind them. A glass window and a Taurus driving by outside. Pressed Dockers and anxiety.

I threw my arms around my kids and pulled them to me. I felt them squirm. Annabelle whispered, "Michele, people are watching. There are cameras."

I narrowed my eyes to slits. "Do I know you?"

His breath gushed out. "Oh, shit, you don't recognize me. I'm Connor Dunn. We met at your book launch. I was a friend of Adrian's."

Connor Dunn. The one who sent me the nice letter after Adrian died. The one whose calls I hadn't returned, who corralled Adrian for a tête-à-tête the night before he died, who Adrian lied about.

"I remember you. I don't want you near my kids."

"Didn't you read my letters?"

"One right after Adrian died."

He shook his head. "I called you. When I couldn't get hold of you after what happened to you and Sam, I sent you a letter, explaining. Look, I hate to do this here, but what I said was—"

I hissed at him. "Not another word."

"It's about Stephanie, Mom. He used to be married to her."

The blood drained from my face, drop by drop, leaving a trail of icy cold behind. I started to buckle, but the kids held me up.

Annabelle put an arm around me and started patting. "You should let him tell you, Michele. He told us yesterday. We thought you already knew."

A little voice inside me whispered, "It's about the money. It's about what Adrian did with the money." I looked up at Connor. He didn't have horns or a forked tail. I didn't know what to think, what to do.

Sam made a rolling motion with his hand at Connor. "Go on." Cheeky kid.

Connor closed his eyes on an inhale and opened them on an exhale. "Stephanie was not well."

I snorted. "Not well is an understatement."

"Yes, I'm sorry, you're right. She had developed paranoid schizophrenia. She self-medicated with alcohol and refused the treatments that could have helped her. I met my wife, Angela, when I was separated from Stephanie." He indicated a tall, thin woman who had appeared from nowhere. A woman who looked like an Ironman—and then I remembered. Yes, he'd told us she qualified when we met in August. "Stephanie blamed Angela for our divorce until she broke into my house one day and read a wedding card your husband sent me. He had congratulated me on marrying Angela and said he hoped my second time around was a personal best. Stephanie took back her maiden name and became obsessed with Adrian, that he had—in her words—pimped Angela to me and wrecked our home."

I put my hand over my mouth and talked through my fingers. "Why didn't you tell Adrian about it?"

"I did, at your book launch."

I pressed my forearm against my stomach.

"I thought she would harass him, but I never dreamed she could hurt anyone. The police said the person who hit Adrian drove a truck, so it never crossed my mind it could have been her. I didn't learn what she'd done until she came after you and Sam. You didn't return my calls, so I wrote to you. I guess you never got it."

There was a tall stack of mail on my counter back in Houston, so maybe I had. I exhaled hard, then with Annabelle's arm still around me, I leaned close and whispered very softly in his ear. "Do you know if she blackmailed Adrian?"

He stayed close and whispered back. "What? No, I don't know anything about blackmail."

"Nothing about any money or payoffs?"

"No. Nothing."

I took a deep, shuddering breath.

Sam's eyebrows drew to a peak together. "What was that about?"

I licked my lips and avoided Sam's eyes.

"See? We told you he was all right," Annabelle said. She patted me again and squeezed.

I nodded slowly. I wasn't sure if I felt better or worse. Adrian died because he was a joyful, open person. Because he shared that with a friend, because of his words. Because dark hates beauty and light and will snuff them out if it can.

This man, though, this man wasn't the dark. My gut told me to trust him.

"Maybe we could start over. How about you introduce me to your wife?"

***

My last blog post was in, the book signing and filming was over, and I didn't ever have to train again, except for fun. The feeling was bittersweet, but I was determined to enjoy it. Annabelle, Sam, and I decided to spread Adrian's ashes out on the course. We drove a rented PT Cruiser along the race route searching for the perfect spot.

I smacked my hand on the steering wheel. "Hey. I need one of you to look something up for me on the race site."

Annabelle rode beside me in the front passenger seat. She had her phone in her hand. "Ready."

"Okay, go to the place where you can find racers by their bib numbers. I want you to look someone up by her number. She helped me on the swim and bike legs."

Annabelle's finger danced on the touch screen. The rental boxcar rolled along silently, and I admired the view of the lava fields from the comfort of the air-conditioned car. "What's the number?"

"Twenty-two hundred."

Seconds later, she shook her head. "It says that's an invalid number."

"Check your typing. Twenty-two hundred. Two two zero zero."

"I typed it right. Invalid number."

I knew that was the number my race angel had worn. I pictured her as I remembered her from the bicycle course: green eyes, RIP Adrian on her leg, 2200 on her back.

Annabelle bounced in the seat and pointed out the window. "Here. This is where we should scatter Dad's ashes."

I pulled to the side of the road, rocks and a blind turn on our left and a field of lava on our right. Blue water sparkled in the distance past the lava field. I didn't remember it, and I had run past it twice. The run already seemed unreal. I reached up and touched my warm butterfly locket hanging from the chain I borrowed from Annabelle.

Sam leaned over the front seat. "Here? In the lava field?"

"No." She pointed. "In the water. Dad would want to be away from the pack, somewhere only really amazing people would ever go. People like us." She grinned. "And it's beautiful out there."

She was right. The sea sparkled like a disco ball, and I could see Adrian dancing from rock to rock, a giant kid, then turning to me and holding out both hands.

I switched off the ignition and grabbed the urn. I got out and hiked ahead of the kids with my muscles complaining the whole way. When I finally reached the water's edge, I flattened my palm against the dry sand. It was a mix of colors, among them the black, red, and purple lava residue. Warmth spread from my hand up my arm.

"I love you, Adrian."

The kids came up on my left and I looked up at them. "Do you want to take turns?"

They looked at each other, then shook their heads.

I uncapped the urn, slid off my flip-flops, and waded over the sandy bottom until the water lapped my thighs but didn't wet the hem of my shorts. I looked back at the kids. They had moved to the water's edge. Annabelle grabbed Sam's hand, and they stood there holding on to each other. I took a deep breath and turned back to the sea.

"Adrian, I hope you'll always have a following sea and a tail wind, and that the temperature is never over seventy-five. You'll always be my personal best. I'll see you at the finish line, my love."

I scattered his ashes around me, watching them clump and mix with the water, then surge back and forth in a choppy path out to sea. I waded back to the kids with dry eyes.

"We have something for you." Sam held up a package.

"Ah, you guys are so sweet. You didn't have to."

Annabelle shook her head. "It's not from us."

"Then who?"

"Dad got you something, and he told us about it and hid it and a bunch of papers in Sam's closet because he knew you'd never go in there. Then he was gone, and at first we forgot."

Sam stepped closer to me. "And when we remembered, we decided it had to be for a special occasion, because it's something big. So we decided to do it after you got back from Kona." He looked at Annabelle.

She held her whipping hair away from her face in a one-handed ponytail. "Except we got worried you wouldn't, because there was nothing on your calendar."

"What?"

"You know, Mom. You and Adrian always used to have a race, and after 'Race Day' it would say, 'Rest Week,' and then 'Week One Kentucky Half Ironman Prep.' And it would be one race after another." He shook his head. "But not this time."

"So we came." Annabelle kicked the sand.

"Here you go, Mom." Sam handed me the package.

When I touched the bright yellow paper, the sand and the sea and the black lava spun around me, and I stumbled. Sam grabbed my arm and guided me inland a few yards. I sat down on the sand and opened Adrian's gift. Inside the wrapping was a framed picture of a smiling Adrian standing in a grove of oaks beside a pond. There was a sealed envelope tucked into the corner of the frame, outside the glass. I ripped it open. It held a deed, title insurance, and a letter. A letter from Adrian to me. The words covered the whole page in his narrow, messy script. I squinted in the sun to read it.

> *Michele:*
>
> *I am sitting here looking at pictures of you. It overwhelms me how much I love you. Thank you. Thank you for wanting us to be together, loving me, having patience with me when I do stupid things, and knowing in your heart who I am and wanting me despite my (many) flaws.*
>
> *Speaking of my flaws, I did something. We dream of building a house together in the middle of Texas bicycling and running heaven. Well,*

I bought the land. Let's go build the house. Think of it as a $200,000 investment in our retirement account, in my own special way.

Happy anniversary.

Adrian

I sat holding the letter, written in his hand, the words ringing out in his voice as if he stood right there talking to me now, and happy and sad exploded like Roman candles in my chest at the same time. Oh, this was my Adrian. I couldn't believe I'd doubted him, that I ever let anything take away what I knew was real, even for a second. And the tears started again, but these were good tears, the kind that washed away bad feelings and worse thoughts and left nodding tulips blooming in their place.

"It's land, Mom. That little town where you guys had your wedding."

Yes, this was my Adrian.

A white butterfly with long tapered wings flew in front of me. I tried to touch it, but it flew off toward the ocean and the trail of Adrian's ashes, then disappeared from sight.

"Are you ready?" Annabelle held out a hand.

I reached up to take it, clutching my treasure tight in the other hand, and felt myself slip back into place.

The End

Now that you have finished *Going for Kona*, won't you please consider writing an honest review and leaving it on Amazon and/or Goodreads, or any other online sales channel of your preference? Reviews are the best way readers discover great new books. The author would truly appreciate it.

Acknowledgements

Thanks to my husband Eric for sending me into a snit one fine November day in 2009. Because of that, and because of all the miles we have logged together on feet, wheels, and water, *Going for Kona* was born. Eric gets an extra helping of thanks for plotting, critiquing, editing, listening, holding, encouraging, supporting, browbeating, and playing miscellaneous other roles, some of which aren't appropriate for publication.

To each and every blessed one of you who have read, reviewed, rated, and emailed/Facebooked/Tweeted/commented about the *Katie & Annalise* books, I appreciate you more than I can say. It is the readers who move mountains for me, and for other authors, and I humbly ask for the honor of your honest reviews and recommendations.

Blessings and hugs to my cousin Michele who saved this book without even knowing it by inspiring the fictional Michele.

Editing credits go to the eagle-eyed Meghan Pinson, who may or may not share some traits with Michele. The beta readers who enthusiastically devote their time—gratis—to help us rid my books of flaws blow me away. The love this time goes to Stephanie, Ginger, Ridgeley, Nancy, Terry, Melissa, Lisa, Jo, Rhonda, Rebecca, and Debbie. They are rivaled only by the equally-appreciated critique circle partners (Gay, Melissa, Patty, David, Enos, Bill, and Kyle) who worked through this book with me.

Kisses to princess of the universe Heidi Dorey for fantastic cover art. Thanks for evolving with us as we evolve with the world of publishing.

Finally, my eternal gratitude to Eric and our kids for teaching me the ways of blended household love.

About the Author

Pamela Fagan Hutchins holds nothing back and writes award-winning and bestselling romantic mysteries and hilarious nonfiction, from Texas, where she lives with her husband Eric and their blended family of too many pets and the youngest few of their five offspring. She is the author of many books, including *Saving Grace*, *Leaving Annalise*, *Finding Harmony*, *Going for Kona*, *How To Screw Up Your Kids*, *Hot Flashes and Half Ironmans*, and *What Kind of Loser Indie Publishes?* to name just a few. In 2014, just two years after publication of her first book, the *Houston Press* named her as one of the Top 10 Houston Authors.

Pamela spends her non-writing time as President of the Houston Writers Guild, a workplace investigator, employment attorney, and human resources professional, and she is the co-founder of a human resources consulting company. You can often find her hiking, running, bicycling, and enjoying the great outdoors.

You can buy Pamela's books at most online retailers and "brick and mortar" stores. You can also order them directly from SkipJack Publishing: http://SkipJackPublishing.com. If your bookstore or library doesn't carry a book you want, by Pamela or any other author, ask them to order it for you.

You can connect with Pamela all over creation, and should:

Website http://pamelahutchins.com

Email pamela@pamelahutchins.com

New releases newsletter http://eepurl.com/iITR

Facebook http://facebook.com/pamela.fagan.hutchins.author

Twitter http://twitter.com/pameloth

Goodreads http://goodreads.com/pamelafaganhutchins

Amazon http://amazon.com/author/pamelafaganhutchins

Linkedin http://linkedin.com/in/pamelahutchins

If you'd like Pamela to speak to your book club, women's club, or writers group, shoot her an email. She's very likely to say yes.

Books by the Author

Fiction from SkipJack Publishing:
Saving Grace (Katie & Annalise #1)
Leaving Annalise (Katie & Annalise #2)
Finding Harmony (Katie & Annalise #3)
The Jumbie House (Katie & Annalise Outtake)
Going for Kona (Michele, #1)
Heaven to Betsy (Emily, #1), coming mid-2015
Earth to Emily (Emily, #2), coming mid-2015
Hell to Pay (Emily, #3), coming mid-2015

Nonfiction from SkipJack Publishing:
*The Clark Kent Chronicles: A Mother's Tale Of Life
With Her ADHD/Asperger's Son*
*Hot Flashes and Half Ironmans: Middle-Aged Endurance
Athletics Meets the Hormonally Challenged*
How to Screw Up Your Kids: Blended Families, Blendered Style
How to Screw Up Your Marriage: Do-Over Tips for First-Time Failures
Puppalicious and Beyond: Life Outside The Center Of The Universe
What Kind of Loser Indie Publishes, and How Can I Be One, Too?

Other Books By the Author:
Eve's Requiem (anthology), Spider Road Press
OMG - That Woman! (anthology), Aakenbaaken & Kent
Ghosts (anthology), Aakenbaaken & Kent
Easy to Love, But Hard to Raise (2012) and *Easy to Love, But Hard to
Teach* (coming soon) (anthologies), DRT Press, edited by Kay Marner &
Adrienne Ehlert Bashista

Audiobook versions of the author's books are available on
Audible, iTunes, and Amazon.

Contributors

Humble thanks to the following for offering their support of *Going for Kona*:

Janice D'Agostinio
Sandra DiGiovanni
Linda Isbell Gurasich
Sonja Larsen Hanselman
Jules Holden
Lisa Tidmore Henthorn
Dina LaFollette-Gilmore
Jim Matej
Kyle Russell
Stephanie Hayes Swindell
Elizabeth White-Olsen
Gay Yellen